Staged Evidence

A PEN & DAGGER NOVEL

STAGED EVIDENCE

TRACI HUNTER ABRAMSON

THORNDIKE PRESS
A part of Gale, a Cengage Company

GALE
A Cengage Company

GALE
A Cengage Company

Thorndike Press, a part of Gale, a Cengage Company.

Thorndike Press® Large Print Clean Reads.
The text of this Large Print edition is unabridged.
Other aspects of the book may vary from the original edition.
Set in 16 pt. Plantin.

LIBRARY OF CONGRESS CIP DATA ON FILE.
CATALOGUING IN PUBLICATION FOR THIS BOOK
IS AVAILABLE FROM THE LIBRARY OF CONGRESS.

ISBN-13: 978-1-4205-3672-0 (hardcover alk. paper)

Published in 2026 by arrangement with Shadow Mountain.

Print Number: 1 Print Year: 2026
Printed in Mexico

For Daniel Quilter
Thank you for helping me find the twists
and turns in this story.

Chapter 1

Tessa shifted the overly full hanging bag in her arms as she hurried through the brisk October night and climbed the three steps that led to the entrance of the Manhattan skyscraper. With no doorman on duty right now, she pulled the door open, using her foot to keep it from closing before she could use her elbow to open it the rest of the way.

Peeking over the top of the clothing she carried, she approached the welcome desk.

The man behind the desk stood and straightened his suit jacket. "Can I help you?"

"Yes. I have a delivery for *Last Night,*" Tessa said, referring to the new hit television show starring Ian Sawyer, who had become a good friend of her sister's. "I'm Tessa Seidel. I should be on the list."

The night guard typed her name into his computer. "I don't see your name here."

"Try Greta Meyer. I'm her assistant."

He typed something again. "Yep. It says, 'Greta Meyer or representative.' Your name is in the notes." He handed her a clipboard. "Sign in here please, and I'll need to see your ID."

Tessa balanced the clothing bag on the counter and fished her driver's license out of her phone case. She passed it to the guard and checked the time on her phone to jot it next to her name. Ten twenty at night. She should be home by now, but no, her boss had insisted the clothing being used for tomorrow's taping needed to be in the studio tonight.

Usually, Tessa loved her job as the assistant to one of the top talent agents in the country. Tessa had the opportunity to work with the various models and actors Greta represented as well as a number of designers who often provided free clothing to famous people who would then endorse their labels. Tessa and her sister, Kimber, had both benefited from that particular arrangement more than once when they had accompanied Greta to various events.

After the guard handed her driver's license back, Tessa made her way to the elevators and used her elbow to press the Up button.

She still couldn't believe Kimber had left her job at the CIA to pursue writing, but here they were, both living in Manhattan. At least, most of the time, they both lived in Manhattan. At the moment, Kimber was staying at Ian Sawyer's beach house in the Hamptons for some sort of writers' retreat with Ian's wife.

A little pang of envy surfaced. Tessa had been to the house several times over the summer. If she'd been able to get work off, she would have gone with Kimber just so she could sit out and enjoy the view. Of course, that was assuming her sister would let a nonwriter crash her retreat.

Tessa had to give Kimber credit. When she committed to something, she was all in. And no doubt, Tessa's former-CIA sister would kill her if she knew Tessa was out at this time of night without a ride already planned. Despite both of them studying martial arts growing up, they preferred avoiding situations where those skills might be needed. Maybe she'd request an Uber once she dropped off the clothes upstairs.

Under normal circumstances, she would have taken Greta up on her offer to let her use her car and driver tonight, but Tessa hadn't had the heart. Greta's driver had scored tickets to the season opener for the Knicks game, and he'd been so looking forward to it. Tessa wasn't about to be the reason he couldn't go.

The elevator opened, and she stepped inside. Shifting the clothing bag in her arms again, she used her knuckle to press the button for the sixteenth floor.

With it well after normal working hours, she rose all the way to the correct floor without a single stop. She supposed that was one advantage of working late.

The doors slid open, and voices carried to her.

"You can't be on this floor without authorization," a woman said, her voice insistent.

"I just have a few things to check on," a man countered. "It won't take me more than another hour."

"I don't care. You weren't on the schedule, and I'm not going to wait around for you to finish."

"You don't have to wait on me. I already cleared this with Bob."

Tessa hadn't expected anyone to be in the studio beyond maybe a security guard. Not interested in walking into the middle of an argument, she turned away from where she'd heard the voices and headed down the hall toward the room where the costumes were kept. She tried to turn the knob. Locked. So much for the wardrobe manager waiting to take this delivery.

And this was why Tessa had wanted to wait until morning to deal with this. She blew out a frustrated breath and considered her options. She couldn't leave several thousand dollars' worth of apparel hanging off a doorknob, but she needed somewhere she could secure it all. The last thing she wanted was to haul the clothes home and then bring them back early in the morning.

Tessa called Greta. It went straight to voicemail. Of course. Greta probably had it on silent since she was supposed to be attending a musical on Broadway tonight.

Maybe the people she'd heard earlier could help her. She headed back toward the elevator as a dark-haired man in his late thirties walked into it.

Still a good twenty yards away, Tessa called out. "Hey!" She quickened her step, but the doors slid closed before she could reach the elevator. "Great," she muttered.

Returning the way she'd come, she tried the various dressing-room doors as she passed them. And even though the locks were coded rather than keyed, no one had bothered to give her the code for wardrobe.

She reached Ian's dressing room.

Not sure if he would still be awake, she texted him. *So sorry to bother you, but I need to secure some costumes on set, and ward-*

robe is locked. Any chance you can give me the code to leave everything in your dressing room? She hit the Send button and hoped for the best.

A few seconds passed before her phone rang. Ian.

"Hey, Ian. Thanks so much for calling," Tessa said. "Would it be okay if I put these clothes in your dressing room?"

"Absolutely. The code is 4279. Just hang them up on the rack behind the door. I'll let wardrobe know where they are when I get on set in the morning."

"You're a lifesaver."

"Happy to help," Ian said. "I'd better get to sleep, but if you see Kimber before I do, give her my best."

"I will." Tessa ended the call and adjusted the garment bag so it was draped over her shoulder. She punched in the code, opened the door, and hung the clothes on the rack.

As soon as she locked the dressing room, she headed toward the elevator.

A woman screamed, and Tessa froze. Was someone shooting a scene tonight, and she'd simply missed it?

Creeped out by the possibility that the argument from earlier had turned ugly, Tessa pulled her cell phone from her purse, prepared to call for help in case the scream had been real.

She passed the elevator and headed toward the open door three offices down. Too bad those people had been arguing, or she likely would have walked past that office a few minutes ago when she'd been looking for a place to store the clothes.

She reached the open doorway and peeked inside. A woman lay on the floor, fresh blood visible in her blonde hair, her body at an awkward angle. Tessa gasped, and her heartbeat quickened.

Her phone still in hand, she rushed to the woman's side. The carpet squished beneath her foot, and Tessa prayed it wasn't blood that had soaked it.

She leaned down and put her hand on the woman's shoulder. She jostled it slightly. "Ma'am? Can you hear me?" No response. Tessa pressed her fingers to the woman's throat the way she'd seen actors do on TV. Nothing. She slid her fingers over, pressing against where she hoped to find some sign that the woman was still alive. Still nothing. She really should have paid more attention to her PE teacher during health class.

She straightened and unlocked her phone.

Footsteps approached.

Tessa whirled. She was halfway through dialing 911 when a man in his thirties rushed into the room.

She startled, and a scream tore from her.

"You!" The broad-shouldered man grabbed her arm, knocking Tessa's phone to the floor. He pulled her toward the office door.

"Let go of me!" Tessa shouted.

He didn't stop, and he didn't let go.

Tessa dug in her heels and shouted, "No!" She wasn't about to be this man's next victim.

The man jerked her arm harder and leaned toward the door.

The instincts honed during Tessa's years of martial-arts classes kicked in, and she grabbed the man's thumb, twisting it until his hold loosened. Then she planted her foot behind his leg and used her other hand to shove him.

He tried to take a step back, but he tripped over Tessa's foot, finally releasing her.

The moment she was free, she sprinted past the elevator to the stairs.

Footsteps pounded behind her, and she raced through the stairwell door, pulling it closed behind her. A quick glance through the stairwell window revealed the trail of blood on the hallway carpet.

Tessa kicked her shoes off and picked

them up before turning toward the stairs. Up or down? Down would get her out of the building faster, but that was what her pursuer would expect.

She raced upward.

She made it just past the bend in the stairs when the stairwell door opened again.

She froze. If the man couldn't hear her, maybe he'd go down instead of up.

He didn't do either. He just stayed where he was.

He spoke after a few seconds. "Hey, we've got a problem. I need you up on the sixteenth floor." He paused. "And watch the stairwells. We're looking for a woman, mid- to late twenties, brown hair, wearing a red jacket."

Tessa barely dared breathe. The murderer had a partner, and it was just a matter of time before one of them found her.

She needed to think like her sister. What would Kimber do?

If Tessa kept climbing the stairs, the man she'd fought with would hear her. She looked down at her bare feet. Or maybe not.

Moving slowly, she took a cautious step onto the next stair. When that movement didn't result in a response from the man, who had yet to close the stairwell door, Tessa took another step. One by one, she ascended eight more steps until she reached the next floor. Suspecting that the sound of the door opening would echo to the floor below, she continued upward, now moving a little faster.

At the eighteenth floor, she opened the door and stepped out into a sterile hallway lined with offices.

Wanting nothing more than to escape, she hit the Down button for the elevator, then remembering the man's comment about her jacket, she took it off and left it on the floor.

When the elevator arrived and the doors opened, she held her breath, praying it would be empty. It was. That simple fact brought tears to her eyes.

She stepped inside and hit the button for the lobby. Again, she uttered a prayer, this one spoken out loud. "Please don't stop on the sixteenth floor."

The elevator went into motion. Her heartbeat quickened as it moved downward. When it continued past the studio's floor, she dropped her shoes onto the floor and grabbed on to the elevator railing to steady herself. Then she stepped into her shoes — no need to draw attention to herself.

The doors opened when she reached the ground level, and she braced for a potential confrontation. To her surprise, the guard desk was empty.

Not about to wait for the man upstairs and his partner to find her, she hurried toward the doors. She'd barely stepped outside when she turned and saw the man who had grabbed her, her phone in his hand. Her heart sank. Her driver's license was in her phone case. This man knew where she lived.

Terrified, she hurried toward the subway. The brisk October breeze chilled her bare arms, but she wasn't going to think about that now. At the moment, she needed to get away from those men, and she needed to find help from someone she could trust.

A woman screamed. Parker clicked on the Delete key. Too cliché. *A woman gasped.* That was a little better.

Parker shook his head and pushed back from his uncle's kitchen table, where he'd set up his temporary office. He needed a break.

He strode into the expansive living room, stopping next to the tall window beside the marble fireplace. He should be on top of the world. He was twenty-eight years old, and he already had a hit play on Broadway. The *Times* had dubbed him the brightest of Broadway's new stars, and he already had investors lined up to produce his second play.

That should have comforted him, but instead, it brought a pressure few people would ever understand. He'd won a Tony, for heaven's sake. On his first try. That didn't happen. Or rarely anyway. But instead of instilling confidence in him, it brought overwhelming doubts. What if he couldn't write a second play? What if the first one was the only good story he had in him?

He tried to shove his insecurities aside. The simple truth remained that, investors or not, his next play would never make it into any theater, on or off Broadway, if he didn't get it written. And for that to happen, he had to believe he was capable of writing something worthy of the stage.

He'd hoped a change of scenery would help him finish the play, but this week at his uncle's place in the Hamptons had yet to give him the inspiration he needed, despite the gorgeous views of the ocean and the stunning fall colors. Not that he could see anything at this time of night.

The solitude he'd craved closed in on him, the sound of the crashing waves on the beach carrying to him.

Maybe it was the silence that was slowing him down tonight. For the past week, his uncle Ian's beach house had been transformed into a mini writers' retreat. His aunt Phoebe and her friend Kimber had both spent their time working on their novels while he'd struggled with his play. Following Kimber and Phoebe's writing routine had helped him push through some of his writer's block, but they'd headed back to Manhattan this afternoon. Since their departure, he'd written exactly thirty-nine words. Not a very productive six hours.

Parker let out a sigh and strode past the thick columns that separated the formal dining room from the great room. He put his hand on the back of the sofa.

So many acting greats had visited this house; so many deals had been brokered in Uncle Ian's office down the hall. Uncle Ian was an icon in Hollywood; he was the actor all of America knew and the leading man everyone still wanted. The echoes of the past three decades should have filled Parker with inspiration. But they didn't.

Maybe he needed someone to talk to. That was it. Of course, with it already being eleven thirty at night, talking out plot ideas was going to have to wait until a more reasonable hour.

He returned to the kitchen and sat back down. One way or another, he needed to push through this scene tonight, or he was never going to make his deadline.

He read his last three words: *A woman gasped.* It was a start.

Chapter 2

Crime-scene tape already cordoned off one side of the hallway when Detective Colin Murray arrived at the scene, his partner, Derrick, trailing behind him. Another murder, but this one was in the studio of one of the most anticipated television shows of the season, a show that had debuted two weeks ago.

Colin hadn't seen it himself — he'd been far too busy with his own real-life drama in the form of a wrongful-conviction lawsuit brought against him and the police department. As if anyone else wouldn't have gone after the same suspect he had. And he wasn't alone in his belief that Wyatt Harvey was guilty based on the evidence presented. The jury had believed he was guilty too.

Everyone had wanted to find justice for the victim. Unfortunately, the clues had led Colin to an innocent man. Just the thought of someone successfully framing Wyatt caused Colin's gut to twist uncomfortably. The man had lost years of his life, and Colin had been partially to blame.

Shaking that thought away, Colin retrieved a pair of crime-scene gloves from his pocket and put them on. Then he approached the closest police officer. "What do you have?"

The officer lifted the crime-scene tape as Colin and Derrick ducked under it.

"White female, mid-thirties. Her wallet was still in her purse. ID shows her as Juliet Clark."

Colin entered the office where the victim lay on the floor, the coroner beside her. Another life cut short prematurely. Another tragedy.

As much out of habit as necessity, Colin shoved his emotions onto a shelf and focused on the task at hand. "Hey, Doc. What can you tell me?"

"Best guess, she was stabbed first and then hit her head on her way down," the coroner said. "The murder weapon has a sharp, narrow blade, narrow enough for the wound to look like a gunshot at first glance."

"But you're sure she was stabbed?" Colin asked the coroner.

"Yes, I'm sure. It's possible the head wound is what actually killed her, but I won't know until I do the autopsy."

"Has anyone seen any sign of the knife?" Colin asked.

"No, the killer must have taken it," the coroner answered.

"Estimated time of death?" Derrick asked.

"Between ten and eleven."

The officer standing at the door spoke. "The 911 call came in at 10:42."

"That gives us a nice, tight window." Always a good thing in a murder investigation.

The officer held out a cell phone in a pink case. "You'll want this too. One of the guards gave it to me."

Colin took the phone from him. "Who does that belong to?"

"A woman was here when the guard arrived," the officer said. "She dropped it when he tried to apprehend her."

Derrick stepped toward the officer. "Where is she now?"

"We're not sure. I have the guards checking the building," the officer said. "The screen is locked, but there was a driver's license and credit card in the case. They both belong to Tessa Seidel, twenty-five years old."

"I'll check out her apartment," Derrick said.

Colin nodded and moved closer to the

desk in the corner. A notepad and pen lay on the desk, and the chair was still in place, although it was facing the door rather than the desk.

He glanced at where the body lay again. He could visualize it all too easily: Someone had come to the door. The woman had turned to face the newcomer and then stood when the killer had entered.

"Looks like the victim knew her attacker," Colin said.

The coroner didn't respond. He was still preparing the body for transport.

Another officer approached carrying a red jacket. "We found this on the eighteenth floor. We think it belongs to our suspect."

The first officer nodded. "The guard mentioned that the woman he fought was wearing a red jacket."

"Maybe she took it off to make it easier to blend in," Colin said. "Canvass the area. Let's see if we can identify where our suspect went."

The two officers nodded, and the newest arrival spoke. "We're on it."

Tessa was out of breath and shivering when she reached the police station. Her body still shook from the adrenaline coursing through her, and for the first time in years, she wished she had someone to lean on. Too bad Kimber wasn't home. If she hadn't gone to that writing retreat in the Hamptons, Tessa could have called and asked her to come with her to make her statement. Of course, she'd need a phone to do that.

Eager to get out of the cold, Tessa rushed into the police station, the scent of body odor, disinfectant, and stale coffee tingeing the air. Tessa ignored the smell and focused on the warmth that now surrounded her.

Wide concrete pillars separated the waiting area from the reception area, and a middle-aged officer sat behind a long counter, a cup of coffee in his hand.

Tessa rushed past the first two pillars and stopped at the welcome desk. She gripped the edge of the counter. "I need to talk to someone. There's been a murder."

The officer barely raised an eyebrow. "Where was the murder?"

Tessa gave him the address and the floor for the studio.

He typed something into his computer. "We already have a unit on the scene." The officer retrieved a clipboard and handed it to her along with a pen. "Write down your statement here and then bring it back to me."

Another shiver worked through her body,

but she nodded. She took a seat in the waiting area two chairs down from an older woman clutching her purse in her lap.

Tessa set the clipboard on her lap and rubbed her hands together to fight the numbness. Then she proceeded to write everything she could remember — the scream, the woman on the floor, the man who attacked her.

Not sure what else to add, she carried the clipboard back to the front desk.

The man who had helped her earlier held a phone up to his ear. He reached out and took the clipboard from her. "Why can't Sally do it?" The man paused, clearly listening to whoever was on the other end of the phone. He set the clipboard down. "Fine. Then we'll do Chinese. Get everyone's order, and I'll call it in."

He was talking about food while Tessa couldn't stop shaking after what had happened.

A draft of cold air rushed over her, and she glanced at the open doors. A police officer walked in first, a second man stepping in beside him.

Recognition struck Tessa immediately. The man who had grabbed her!

She stepped behind the pillar closest to her, her pulse racing and her breaths coming in short gasps. What was he doing here?

Though tempted to peek around the pillar to confirm the man approaching was the same one she'd seen in the studio, she didn't dare, for fear that he might see her.

The footsteps grew closer.

The officer spoke as the two men passed the pillar and her. "It'll take a few minutes to record your statement. Then you can be on your way."

Take his statement? Tessa stared at the two men's backs and tried to grasp what was happening. Was this man pretending to be a witness?

"I'm just lucky it was you working tonight. Otherwise, I'd still be stuck at the crime scene, talking to those detectives."

"I guess that's one advantage of having a cousin on the police force," the officer said.

Great. The man who had attacked her was related to a cop.

She stepped out from behind the pillar and debated what to do next. The man couldn't hurt her here. They were in a police station. But what if the police believed her attacker instead of her?

She motioned to the clerk who was on the phone again that she needed the clipboard back. He handed it over, and she added the new information to her statement. Surely, the police would want to know that her attacker had come to the station and that his cousin was on the force. Once she made the addition, she handed it back to the desk clerk. Now what?

For the second time tonight, the question rushed through her mind: *What would Kimber do?*

Kimber. That was it. Kimber might still be in the Hamptons, but Tessa could take the train to see her. She didn't need a phone to do that. And it would get her out of the city, away from the person who had tried to hurt her. Once she reached the Hamptons, her former-CIA sister could help her decide what to do next.

Parker rubbed at his eyes to fight the stinging that came from staring at screens for too long. He should know better than to stay up so late, but after he'd finally given up on work for the day, he'd decided to fall into someone else's fictional world by watching a movie.

After a quick late-night snack, he headed to his room and checked his phone for messages. Six texts from his mom confirmed that he'd forgotten to take his phone off silent again — and that his mother was once again trying to set him up with a friend's daughter. That wasn't going to happen. He wasn't looking to get into a relationship his mother orchestrated. He'd prefer to meet someone on his own. Of course, he'd have to interact with people for that to happen.

After sending a quick text to his mom to let her know he was still among the living and wasn't interested in a blind date, he plugged in his phone, climbed into bed, and turned out the light. Shutting out his lack of progress for the day, he let his body relax and was just drifting into that blissful semiconscious state when the doorbell rang.

He shook his head and rolled over. He must already be dreaming. No one would show up at Uncle Ian and Aunt Phoebe's place in the middle of the night.

The doorbell rang again.

Now Parker sat up. "What in the world?"

He climbed out of bed and flipped on the light. Surely Ian would have told him if someone else was supposed to be coming to visit.

He turned on the porch light and peeked through the window beside the door. A woman who appeared to be a few years younger than he stood on the doorstep, wearing black jeans and a short-sleeved shirt. *Gorgeous* was his first thought. *Unbelievable* was his next. It couldn't be more than forty degrees outside.

The woman folded her arms and rubbed her hands over them as though trying to keep warm.

Curious about what she was doing here after midnight, Parker pulled open the door. "Can I help you?"

Surprise lit her brown eyes. "Sorry," she said, her teeth chattering. "Is K-Kimber here?"

"Kimber Frost?"

She nodded.

"She left this morning."

The crestfallen look that followed nearly broke Parker's heart. The woman looked like he'd just informed her of a death in the family.

"Why are you looking for Kimber?"

"Sh-She's my sister."

Parker had never met Kimber's sister, but he'd witnessed Kimber call her several times over the past week. He gestured her inside. "Come in. You're going to freeze to death dressed like that."

She hesitated.

"I'm Parker Sawyer. I'm Ian's nephew."

A shiver worked through her.

"Come on." Parker stepped back to give her easy access to walk in. "We'll turn on the fireplace, and you can tell me what brought you out here in the middle of the night."

After another brief hesitation, the woman nodded and stepped inside.

"What's your name?" Parker asked as he led the way into the great room.

"Tessa."

Parker grabbed the sherpa throw off the back of the couch and wrapped it around Tessa's shoulders. "Here. You look like you need this."

She lifted her hands to hold it in place, and her fingers brushed against his. The simple touch ignited an unexpected spark, and for a brief moment, time stopped. His gaze met hers, and the confusion in her brown eyes matched his own.

Tessa shivered again, and he snapped out of his stupor. "Please, sit down."

She pulled the blanket more firmly around her and sat on the couch.

Parker turned on the fireplace and lowered onto the couch beside her. "Want to tell me how you ended up out here at —" He looked up at the clock across the room. "Two o'clock in the morning?"

"I came to find Kimber."

"And why did you need Kimber in the middle of the night?"

"Because I think someone tried to kill me."

Chapter 3

Someone had tried to kill her. She'd spoken the words aloud for the first time, and now the trauma of the past few hours hit her full force. Tessa's eyes filled again. Saying the words made them more real somehow.

Parker shifted away from her as though needing to see her face more clearly. "I'm sorry. Did you just say someone tried to kill you?"

Tessa pressed her lips together and nodded.

"Why?" Parker asked.

"I found a woman —" Tessa struggled to find the right words. How could she even describe what she'd seen?

"You found a woman," Parker repeated her words. "What about the woman put you in danger?"

"I think she was dead." Tessa shivered again.

Parker rolled the ottoman in front of

where she sat and lowered onto it. He pulled out his phone. "We need to call the police."

"No!" She grabbed his hand before he could dial.

"Why not?"

"I already went to the police station." Her cold fingers remained on his, the warmth of his hand helping negate the chill in her body. "I saw the man who attacked me come in. One of the cops was his cousin."

Parker's eyes widened, and his gaze met hers. "Maybe it would help if you tell me everything that happened."

Tears spilled over and trickled down her cheeks. She withdrew her hand and tucked it beneath the blanket. She wasn't quite sure where to start, so she went back to the beginning. "I had to drop some clothes off on set for Ian's TV show."

"My uncle's TV show? That Ian?"

She nodded. "My boss is his talent agent."

"You work for Greta Meyer?"

"Yes."

He seemed to absorb this new information before he spoke again. "Sorry. Tell me what happened next."

She drew a deep breath, the feeling starting to return to her fingers and toes. "When I was leaving, I heard a woman scream. I thought maybe someone was taping, but then I saw the woman lying on the floor."

"Could you tell what happened to her?"

"No. There was blood in her hair, so I thought maybe she'd fallen or something." Tessa pulled the blanket up higher, the edge of it now tucked beneath her chin. "Then some guy showed up. I think he might have been the person arguing with the woman when I first got there."

"Wait. You think you were there when the actual murder was committed?"

More tears spilled over, and she nodded.

Parker reached for a box of tissues and held it out to her.

She looked down at it but couldn't bring herself to free her arms from the increasing warmth beneath the blankets. When she didn't take the tissues, Parker pulled one from the box and used the tissue to gently wipe the tears from her cheeks.

"What did the man say when he found you?" he asked.

"I don't remember exactly, but he grabbed me, and I ran away."

Parker furrowed his brow. "How did you get away if he grabbed you?"

She shrugged. "I just did. I hid in the stairwell, and then I took the elevator down to the lobby."

"If you saw the man who attacked you at the police station, clearly someone called the cops."

"Someone must have, but I don't know who." That thought caused her to pause. Who else would have known about the woman upstairs besides her and the killer? Unless her attacker had called and pretended to be a witness. That would make sense. "When I reached the lobby, all the security guards were gone, and there was a police car parked out front."

"The police will need a statement from you."

"I already turned in my statement. I just never talked to anyone about it." She relayed her experience at the police station.

Parker held up his phone. "We should probably call the station so you can follow up."

The mere thought of speaking to the police by herself caused her stomach to churn. Would they even believe her? Or would they believe the man who had grabbed her? "I need to talk to my sister first."

He creased his brow. "Why?"

Tessa hesitated. She'd promised not to tell anyone her sister used to work for the CIA. Sharing what she could, Tessa said, "My sister has dealt with law enforcement before. I just really need to talk to her."

Parker looked up at the clock. "Since it's after two, maybe you should wait until morning to call."

Tessa flexed her fingers. They were still frigid, but at least she could feel them.

Though all she wanted was to crawl into bed and hide in sleep, she asked, "Do you have a phone I can borrow to call a cab? I lost mine when I was getting away."

"I'm not sending you out in the middle of the night, especially after what you've been through." Parker stood. "You can stay in one of the guest rooms."

Stay here with a man she didn't know? Tessa glanced at the front door, debating.

"If it'll make you feel any better, I'll text my aunt and uncle to let them know you're here." He looked down at her purse. "And I'll find something for you to sleep in."

She should have declined, but the kindness in his eyes and the gentle way he'd helped her since her arrival swayed her. "Thank you."

His gaze met hers. "You're welcome."

Chapter 4

Brandon Hale slowed his steps as he approached the Manhattan high-rise. Three police cars were parked by the curb — not a normal sight for this part of town.

His girlfriend, Kimber, walked beside him and slowed her steps as they approached the entrance. "I wonder what the police are doing here."

"Probably someone trying to sneak onto set again." Brandon opened the door and waited for her to walk inside before joining her. "Why am I here again?"

"Because Ian wanted to meet for breakfast, and we don't want anyone to get the idea that Ian and I are anything more than friends."

The fact that both Brandon and Kimber considered Ian a friend still fell into the surreal category, especially since they'd met him for the first time only seven months ago, when Kimber was in the process of expanding her social media accounts as an up-and-coming author.

"You know Ian is old enough to be your father, right?" Brandon said.

"Yeah, but he's also been in the business long enough to know how wise it is to avoid rumors and the appearance of anything that could get them started."

"So I'm here for rumor prevention."

"That, and I like it when I'm able to spend time with you." Kimber squeezed his hand. "Plus, I thought you could take some photos for my social media. Haseeb has been hinting a lot lately that he wants me to beef up my content."

"That doesn't surprise me."

They stopped at the front desk, where an attendant was speaking with an older couple. Kimber grabbed the pen by the sign-in sheet and wrote down both of their names as well as the time. Then she continued to the elevator and pressed the Up button.

"Are you already on a first-name basis with all the security guards here?" Brandon asked.

Kimber laughed. "Not yet."

"That will change soon enough," Brandon said with certainty. Besides being a brilliant writer, Kimber had the full backing of Monroe Publishing's marketing team. The combination of the two was bound to launch her to the top. "Do they all know that by next year, you'll be a best-selling author?"

"Everyone at Monroe hopes I'll be a best-selling author." She held up both hands. "And for the record, it wasn't my idea to try to get famous."

That was true. Last March, when he'd gone undercover in the editorial department of Monroe Publishing, the CIA had helped Kimber join the publishing house as their promising debut author with a huge contract. Even after their assignment had ended, their superiors at the CIA had decided to leave both of them in place, him working as an editorial assistant and Kimber as an author who was a year away from publishing her debut novel.

The elevator doors opened, and they both stepped inside.

A surge of anxiety shot through Brandon. Despite his CIA training and more than seven years on the job, he couldn't deny that a couple of deadly incidents involving elevators had left him unsteady.

Kimber put her hand on his arm as the doors slid closed. "You okay?"

He gave a little nod. He didn't have to explain to her where his thoughts had gone.

She was more than just his girlfriend. She was also his partner. Trying to pick up their conversation, he focused on their cover stories. "Is the marketing director still hoping to get you more followers through your association with Ian?"

"Ian, Tyrone, Madison," she said, listing off just a few of the prominent actors she now considered friends. "And everyone else I've met through my sister and Ian."

"Haseeb and Amelia were going at it the other day about how Amelia wants you to focus on your next book," Brandon said as the elevator climbed far too slowly.

"Amelia knew I was in the Hamptons to finish polishing my next manuscript. Now that I've turned it in, hopefully she'll be okay with me taking a little break."

"I don't think Amelia believes in taking breaks."

They reached their floor and promptly stepped out into a wall of yellow crime-scene tape cordoning off one hall and a crowd of cast and crew members hovering in the other direction. Brandon's training kicked in, and he quickly assessed the scene. Ian was standing with a few of his colleagues on his side of the taped-off area, and the tension and faint smell of death suggested this crime scene had included a murder.

Not good.

Ian spotted them and quickly excused himself from the man he was speaking with.

When he reached them, Kimber asked, "What's going on?"

Ian leaned close and spoke in a low voice. "There was a murder last night."

Brandon replayed Ian's words. "A murder?"

Kimber gripped Brandon's hand. "Who was it?"

"One of the production assistants."

"Do they have any idea who did it?" Kimber asked.

"They do have a person of interest they're trying to find." Ian paused before he focused on Kimber. "Kimber, it's Tessa."

Kimber's jaw dropped, and she shook her head. "Tessa? My sister?"

"Yes. The police want to talk to her."

"Where is she?" Kimber asked frantically. "Is she okay?"

"We don't know." Compassion filled Ian's features. "No one has seen her since last night."

Brandon put his arm around Kimber's waist. He didn't miss the tremor that worked through her body. Hoping for some clarity, he asked, "Why would the cops want to talk to Tessa?"

"Tessa was here when the murder happened." Ian paused, and his gaze met Kimber's. "The police think she was involved."

Kimber grappled with Ian's words, unable to process them. Tessa didn't have a violent bone in her body, and if she had witnessed anything, surely she would have called Kimber. The fact that she hadn't put a new sense of fear into her. What if Tessa was another victim rather than a witness?

Emotions clogged Kimber's throat, and she struggled to find words. Quickly, she pulled out her phone and pressed the button to call her sister. The phone rang, both in her ear and from somewhere nearby. After two rings, the call rolled to voicemail. Her panic heightened.

"Why do the police think Tessa is involved?" Brandon asked before Kimber could manage to pose the question.

"She came by the studio last night. Apparently, she arrived a few minutes before the murder happened," Ian said.

Kimber held up her phone. "We have to make sure she's okay."

Kimber tried calling Tessa again. For a second time, a phone rang in near perfect time to the ringing coming through her cell. The sound grew louder before once again rolling to voicemail.

A man approached, his suit coat nearly concealing the slight bulge of a shoulder holster. "Kimber Seidel?"

Kimber tensed at the man's use of her given name. Except for Brandon, everyone in her world here in New York knew her by her pen name, Kimber Frost. She furrowed her brow and focused on the man in the suit. "I'm Kimber."

"I'm Detective Murray." He held up a pink cell phone identical to Tessa's. "Is this your sister's phone?"

"I don't know." Kimber's blood chilled. Her sister never went anywhere without her phone.

"Can you call her please?"

Kimber dialed Tessa again, praying the phone in the detective's hand wouldn't ring.

It rang.

Fear knotted in Kimber's stomach. "Where's my sister?"

"We were hoping you could tell us." Detective Murray continued to hold Tessa's phone in her view. "Surveillance footage from last night shows Tessa Seidel was here in the building when the murder occurred, and she fled the scene shortly after the victim was discovered."

"I need to go check her apartment." Kimber took a step toward the elevator.

"We had a detective search there earlier," Detective Murray said. "She wasn't home."

Panic burst through Kimber. Tessa would have told her if she'd gone out of town, and she wasn't dating anyone right now. Kimber glanced toward the police tape a short distance away. Someone had been killed. If Kimber's sister had been here, could she have seen the murder? Could the killer be responsible for Tessa's disappearance?

Kimber's panic multiplied.

Brandon put his arm around her shoulders, clearly sensing the turmoil swirling inside her. "What can you tell us about what happened last night?"

"And you are?"

"Brandon Hale. I'm Kimber's boyfriend."

"I'm afraid there isn't much I can tell you, except that Mr. Sawyer here confirmed that Miss Seidel called him last night."

Kimber turned to face Ian. "Why did she call you?"

"She was supposed to drop off some clothes for today's shooting. I guess the person in wardrobe left before she got here, and wardrobe was locked," Ian said. "She asked if she could put the clothes in my dressing room instead."

Of course. Tessa was in a bind so she

reached out to the one person she was close to on set: Ian. Kimber nodded in understanding even as she fought against her rising emotions. "So you gave her the code to your door."

"Yes."

"And that was at what time?" Brandon asked.

Ian pulled out his phone. "Ten twenty-eight."

"The security log for Mr. Sawyer's dressing-room door confirms that his code was used to open the door at ten thirty," Detective Murray said.

"Do you have a time of death for the victim?" Brandon asked.

"A guard found her with the body at approximately ten forty."

"Wait." Kimber's thoughts realigned. If Tessa had been spotted by the guard, then she'd likely arrived after the killer had left the scene. Kimber prayed that was the case. Bringing herself back to the conversation, she asked, "So you're saying my sister saw the victim?"

"Yes, and based on the initial findings, it appears she was present when the victim was killed."

"She saw it?" Kimber pressed her hand to her heart. If her sister had been there when the victim was killed, what danger was Tessa in now?

"She saw it," Detective Murray confirmed. "Or she's the killer."

Impossible. Kimber shook her head. "There's no way. My sister isn't a killer. Plus, I doubt Tessa even knew the victim, much less had any issues with her."

"We'll look into that, but the fact remains that she was clearly on this floor before the murder, and security cameras show her leaving after the police arrived." The detective pulled a business card from his pocket. "If you see or hear from your sister, I expect a call. Your sister is the key to us finding the killer."

Kimber clenched her jaw. Based on the detective's expression, he really was convinced that he'd already identified his killer: Tessa.

Brandon pulled out a business card of his own. "I'd appreciate it if you can let us know when you uncover any new leads."

"This is an active investigation," Detective Murray said. "I won't be able to share details."

Kimber glanced down the hall to where more crime-scene tape criss-crossed one of the office doors. Ian's dressing room was a good ten doors down.

Ian put his hand on her arm. "What do you say the three of us head out and get that breakfast I promised you?"

Kimber started to protest, but she caught a glint of something in Ian's eye that told her he knew more than he was saying in front of the detective.

Brandon spoke to the detective. "Is it okay for us to leave?"

"Yes, but stay in touch," Detective Murray said.

"We will." Brandon pushed the Down button on the elevator.

As soon the three of them entered the elevator car and the doors closed, Kimber asked, "What do you know?"

"We'll talk at my apartment." Ian pulled out his phone. "I'll have my driver pick us up."

Kimber fought back her impatience. Her sister was somewhere out there, and she had no idea if Tessa was okay or where she was. Kimber needed answers. And she wanted them now.

Chapter 5

Parker put the kettle on to boil. He should still be sleeping, but he'd awoken shortly after daybreak with an idea for his next scene and knew he wouldn't be able to sleep until he'd typed it out.

He retrieved his mug from the cabinet. As an afterthought, he pulled out a second one and set it beside his.

Out the window, the waves washed up on the beach that lay beyond the grassy knoll that comprised the larger part of his uncle Ian's backyard. This house had always been a source of peace, particularly when his parents had divorced and left him struggling to find his footing in an ever-changing world. Since the knock on the door last night, his world had definitely changed.

Tessa had yet to emerge from her room, although that was hardly surprising since she hadn't settled into her room until nearly three this morning. For a moment, when he woke up, he'd thought he'd imagined her presence, but the guest-room door remained closed, and his faded Yale T-shirt was decidedly missing from his closet.

Faint footsteps approached, and he turned as Tessa walked in, her brown hair tumbling over her shoulders, her eyes a bit wary, and his T-shirt looking much better on her than it ever had on him.

"Hey there. How did you sleep?" Parker asked.

"Okay, I guess." She stood at the edge of the kitchen, ill at ease. "It was hard to stop thinking about last night."

"I bet." Parker lifted the extra mug. "Would you like some tea? My aunt has a bunch of the herbal kinds."

"That would be great, thanks."

"Chamomile, peppermint, or peach?"

"Peppermint, please."

"Have a seat." He gestured to the large table by the window.

Tessa crossed to the table but remained standing, her gaze drawn to the surf and sand.

The kettle whistled, and Parker poured water into both of the mugs. After adding the tea bags, he carried the tea to the table and handed one to Tessa. "Here you go."

"Thanks." She took a mug from him and

held it in her hands as though she needed the mug to warm them. "It's so peaceful out there; it's like everything that happened last night can't be real."

"I haven't checked the news yet, but I can grab my laptop if you want to see what's out there so far."

She shook her head and lowered into a chair. "I kind of want to pretend that it didn't happen for a little longer."

Parker sat beside her. "What do you plan to do now? Are you going back to the city today?"

"I need to call my sister first."

Parker still didn't understand what Kimber could do to help Tessa. Unless maybe Kimber was the only family Tessa had. "What about your parents?"

"I'll talk to them after I talk to Kimber."

So her parents were still alive and in her life. He took a sip of his peppermint tea.

"How long have you been awake?" Tessa asked.

"A couple hours. I had an idea for a scene, and I needed to get it written before I forgot it."

"You're a writer?"

"A playwright." He lifted his cup. "Trying to be anyway." At this point, he was merely a one-hit wonder.

He expected her to ask one of the usual questions: What are you working on? What do you do for your real job? Or his favorite: Have you written anything I've seen?

Instead, she said, "I'm sorry I interrupted your work."

Oddly relieved that she didn't ask about his writing, he shrugged. "It's okay. In truth, I've been struggling a bit with this one."

"I know it can't be easy," she said. "I've seen how much my sister struggles sometimes when her story isn't working the way she wants."

He supposed being related to a writer would make her a bit more intuitive about the questions not to ask. Not that he usually minded. It was just hard to talk about his project when it wasn't working.

Tessa fidgeted in her seat. "Any chance you would mind letting me borrow your phone so I can call Kimber?"

"No problem. It's charging in my room, so let me get it for you."

"Finish your tea first." Tessa took a sip of hers. "Kimber won't even know there's a problem until I call her."

"I'm sure you're right."

Kimber fought the urge to ask Ian what else he knew about her sister as his driver took the two of them and Brandon to Ian's apartment overlooking Central Park. Her whole body trembled with the rush of adrenaline and overwhelming fear.

She might be an undercover operative for the CIA, but none of her training had prepared her for this crippling sense of helplessness now that danger was affecting her family.

Brandon held her hand, gently rubbing his thumb back and forth over it. The gesture was meant to soothe, but nothing was going to help until she knew her sister was safe.

Ian's driver dropped them off in front of Ian's building, and Ian led them inside. Another long ride up an elevator, this time to the thirty-second floor.

Ian escorted them into his apartment, and the moment he shut the door behind him, he said, "Your sister is safe."

Her shoulders drooped with relief. "Is she here?"

"No, but before I tell you where she is, we need to talk."

They continued past the wide entryway into the great room that boasted a wall of windows overlooking Central Park.

Ian's wife, Phoebe, hurried into the room through the door that led to the kitchen.

"What happened at the studio?" she asked. "The news isn't saying much except that someone was killed."

Ian crossed to his wife and embraced her. "We don't know much yet, except that it was Juliet Clark who was killed."

"Oh, that poor girl," Phoebe said, sympathy carrying in her voice.

Ian released her and gestured for everyone to sit down.

Kimber and Brandon sat on a love seat, and Phoebe and Ian chose the couch opposite them.

"I have to ask," Ian began. "If I tell the two of you where Tessa is, will you be compelled to inform the police?"

Kimber hadn't considered that possibility, but her position with the CIA would dictate she do exactly that. So would Brandon's. But outwardly, both of them worked in regular jobs. Their association with the CIA was a closely guarded secret, so why was Ian asking such a question? He would have no way of knowing she and Brandon worked undercover for the agency.

Ian must have sensed her confusion. "I hadn't planned to bring this up, but we've suspected for a while that the two of you are more than meets the eye." He gestured toward Kimber. "And then today, the detective confirmed that your real name isn't Kimber Frost."

Kimber looked at Brandon, his surprise and concern reflected on his face, likely mirroring her own expression.

"Kimber Frost is my pen name," Kimber said, addressing the easiest of Ian's comments. "I figured you knew my last name was Seidel since you know my sister."

"I wondered, but when we've been out at events, it has seemed like you avoid letting people know the two of you are related."

"I'm not sure what you mean," Kimber said.

"And why do you think we'd have to tell the authorities anything you share with us?" Brandon added.

"We were with you when the electrical problem happened at the theater." Ian lifted both hands and signaled air quotes when he said the words *electrical problem.* "I know it was really a bomb."

A sense of alarm shot through Kimber. How could he possibly know that? She swallowed before asking the question, "Where did you get that idea?"

"Someone in the crew overheard the two of you backstage." Ian lifted both eyebrows. "And we didn't miss the fact that you were nowhere to be found until after the authorities arrived."

Kimber didn't know what to say. She'd been undercover only since March. Never before had she faced such a situation. And even though Brandon had been undercover for his entire career, she doubted this was a common occurrence for him either.

Ian leaned forward in his seat, his gaze flicking from Kimber to Brandon and back again. "You don't have to tell us who you really work for, but I've done enough action movies to have a clue. I also know that if you know where Tessa is and don't tell the police, regardless of who you work for, you risk legal action. And if you do tell them where she is —"

Kimber's heart sank. Her concern about keeping her cover intact died beneath the more pressing reality. "If we tell the police where Tessa is, she could be arrested for murder."

Ian nodded. "I know the responsible thing to do is turn everything over to the police and let them sort through the evidence, but with Detective Murray leading the investigation, I'm not sure that's the wisest course of action."

"You know him?" Brandon asked.

"I know of him."

"Wait." Phoebe shifted her body so she

was facing Ian more fully. "Isn't he the detective from that wrongful-conviction case a week or two ago?"

"Yes," Ian said.

Kimber had heard of the case and the accusations that the police had ignored promising leads because they'd been so sure they had the right suspect. A man had lost years of his life behind bars for something he hadn't done. And that had been the second case this detective had been assigned in which an innocent person had been convicted. Could the same thing happen in a third case to Tessa? A sharp pain radiated from Kimber's chest and spread through her body.

Beside her, Brandon put his hand on hers. "If Detective Murray messed up that badly in two separate wrongful-conviction cases, why is he still working on the police force?"

"In the technical sense, he was doing his job for both of them," Ian said. "He followed the evidence, but he also neglected a lot of leads he could have followed. But since he wasn't the only officer involved, it's hard to make a case that it was all his fault. After all, the prosecutors thought they had the right suspects too."

A sickness rose up Kimber's throat. She couldn't let her sister end up in jail. She just couldn't. "How do we keep Tessa from suffering a similar fate?"

"I know where she is, and since right now she's simply a person the police want to talk to, I think it would be best if she stays out of town for a while."

Kimber turned to Brandon. "Maybe we should reach out to your friend with the FBI." Rafi Ebeid had worked with them during the case that had brought them both to New York. Surely he could help them now. Kimber hoped.

"That's not a bad idea," Brandon said.

Phoebe settled her hand on her husband's knee. "What about you, Ian? Won't you be at risk if you don't tell the police what you know?"

"Technically, the police didn't ask me where Tessa is or ask me to tell them if I see her."

"That's splitting hairs," Brandon said. "We don't want you at risk any more than we want either of us to get into legal trouble."

"I have an idea that may solve that problem," Ian said.

"Which is?" Kimber asked.

"I'll make sure the message gets to Tessa that she needs to relocate to somewhere else safe, and then I can tell the police what I do know."

"That's a good idea." Phoebe nodded.

"The real issue is finding who the actual murderer is." Ian patted his wife's hand. "Someone killed Juliet, and we all know it wasn't Tessa."

"We need a copy of the sign-in log," Brandon said. "That's the best way to see who was in the building at the time of the murder."

Kimber hoped their FBI contact could help them with that. With Tessa's future in jeopardy, they needed all the help they could get. "Do you think anyone we know would be able to get us a copy of the police file?" she asked Brandon.

"I can make a call," he said. "In the meantime, I think we should have Ian put his plan into motion so he can tell the police what he knows."

Ian nodded. "I think that's a very wise decision."

"Fine." Bringing in help on the legal front would hopefully help them point the police in the direction of more promising suspects than Tessa, but Kimber wasn't going to rest easy until she heard her sister's voice. "But first, I need to talk to Tessa. She needs to understand what's happening."

Ian retrieved his phone from his pocket. "I can make that happen, but I think we need to be creative about how we handle this."

"What do you have in mind?"

"I know someone who might be able to help Tessa disappear for a few days, but I'm not sure Tessa will trust him."

"Can *we* trust him?" Kimber asked.

"Yes." Ian hesitated briefly. "It's my nephew Parker."

Kimber looked at Brandon for a brief moment. Then she turned back to face Ian. Though most of the country rarely saw beyond Ian's accomplishments and fame, he had become a true friend over the past many months. Relying on the code her parents had created when they were children, she shared the two words that would ensure Tessa would know she could trust Ian's nephew. "Rocky road."

Ian shot her a confused look. "Rocky road?"

"Yes. If someone tells Tessa I said those words, she'll know that she can trust whoever gives her our code."

Understanding bloomed on Ian's face. "When the time is right, I'll make sure the message gets passed along."

"Good, but first, I need to talk to her. Can

we call her on your phone?"

"Are you trying to make sure the police don't know you and Tessa talked?" Ian asked.

"No. I just don't want them to have access to Parker's phone number if they pull up my call log," Kimber said. "We'll record the conversation for the police, and I'll say all the right things to keep us out of trouble."

"I can record it for you," Brandon offered.

"Thanks." Kimber caught the confused look on Ian's face. Offering what she could by way of an explanation, she said, "Even though we don't want her involved with the police at this point in the investigation, the police need to think she's willing to talk to them and that we're encouraging her to do so."

"That's a good idea," Brandon said. "Then maybe we can have Phoebe or Ian call and tell Parker and Tessa what they really need to do."

"My thoughts exactly," Kimber said. "Assuming Parker is really willing to help."

Ian nodded. "As long as he believes she's innocent, I'm sure he will."

Chapter 6

The ringing of a phone carried to Tessa along with Parker's approaching footsteps.

"Hello?" He reached the kitchen as he answered and then listened to the person on the other end of the call. Then he said, "Hey, Kimber. I assume Uncle Ian gave you my message." Parker fell silent for a moment. "Yeah. She's right here." He handed the phone to Tessa. "It's for you."

She lifted it to her ear. "Hello?"

"Tessa!" Kimber said. "I was so worried."

Relief flooded through Tessa. "I wanted to call you, but I lost my phone." Her sister's words caught up to her. "Why were you worried?"

"Because I got to the studio today to meet Ian, and I found out there was a murder while you were there last night," she said.

The image of the woman on the floor flooded Tessa's mind, and her body went numb. She was right. The woman really was dead. Hearing the words — from her sister, of all people — made this whole situation even more surreal.

Kimber continued, breaking into Tessa's thoughts. "I need you to tell me what happened, but I'm going to put you on speaker so Brandon can use his phone to record our call. Are you okay with that?"

"Why do you want to record our call?"

"It's always best to have a good record of a witness statement."

Had Tessa not known better, she would have sworn she was speaking to a law enforcement officer rather than her sister. Kimber sounded so calm and almost detached from the weight of what Tessa had gone through. But she must have her reasons. "I already turned in a witness statement at the police station," Tessa said.

"Really?" Surprise colored Kimber's voice. "The way the detective was talking, I assumed you hadn't spoken to the police."

"Technically, I didn't speak to the police. I just filled out the witness statement form."

"Either way, I want to hear what happened. We'll give this recording to the police for them to add to your statement."

"Okay." Tessa sat back down and let out a sigh. Just the thought of going back through the events of last night drained her energy.

But her sister needed to know what she'd been through, and hopefully, Kimber could help her make sure she would remain safely away from the man who had attacked her, despite his connection to the police.

Parker sat beside her and gave her an encouraging nod. He must have overheard Kimber's request.

Tessa skipped the preliminary details that led up to why she'd been at the studio and shared the pertinent information. "I was leaving the studio last night when I heard a woman scream."

"Where were you when that happened?"

"Just outside Ian's dressing room."

"Do you remember what time that was?" Kimber asked.

"I know I signed in at the front desk at 10:20. It was probably about ten or fifteen minutes later."

"What did you do after you heard the scream?"

"I went to see who else was still there," Tessa said, now realizing she should have simply called the police and steered clear of the crime scene. "I thought maybe someone was taping and that the scream was part of the show."

"When did you realize it wasn't?" Kimber asked.

"When I got to the office with the open door." Just the memory of the woman lying on the floor was enough to clog her throat. She took a moment to settle her emotions before she continued. "Kimber, she wasn't breathing."

Sympathy filled Kimber's voice. "I know."

Brandon's voice came over the line now. "Had you ever seen the victim before?"

"I don't think so," Tessa said. "I leaned down to check on her and tried to call 911 when this guy showed up. He grabbed me, and I freaked out."

"What did he look like?" Kimber asked.

Tessa closed her eyes and tried to bring the man's image into her mind. Using her years of working in the talent industry, she focused on the details she had absorbed during her brief interaction with him. "White, early thirties. He was taller than me by a few inches, maybe five foot ten. Broad shoulders. He definitely looked the sort who worked out."

"What else?" Brandon asked. "Hair color, eye color?"

"Medium-brown hair. I don't know what color his eyes were."

"What about his clothes?" Kimber asked.

That was way easier to describe than the physical features. "He was wearing a black polo shirt. It might have had a logo on it, but I didn't get a good look. I was too busy trying to get away."

"Anything else you can think of that might help the police?" Kimber asked. "Tattoos, piercings, jewelry?"

"Not that I remember."

"You said you tried calling 911," Brandon said. "Did your call go through?"

Tessa took another moment to replay that particular moment. "No. He grabbed me before I could finish dialing."

"So that's how your phone ended up at the crime scene?" Kimber asked.

"Yeah." Tessa drew a deep breath. "What do I do now? I don't know if that man is still out there or if he might know who I am."

"You need to talk to the police." Kimber paused. "But you should know that they're considering you a suspect."

"What?" Tessa pushed out of her chair so fast it nearly toppled over. It likely would have had Parker not grabbed it. "Why would they think I did it? I don't even know the woman who died."

"Yes, but they'll need to hear that from you," Kimber said gently. "Your phone with your ID was found at the crime scene. That proves that you were there."

"This is a nightmare." Tessa pressed her fingers against her forehead. "I was trying to help. I didn't do anything wrong."

"We know," Kimber said. "Where are you now?"

"I'm at Ian's house in the Hamptons. I thought you were still here for your writing retreat with Phoebe."

"Sorry I missed you. Phoebe and I drove back yesterday," Kimber said. "Why don't you take the eleven o'clock train, and I can meet you at Penn Station? Then we can go in to meet with the police together."

Go into the police station when they might put her in jail? She tried to wrap her brain around what her sister was suggesting. "You can't be serious. What if they arrest me?"

"Trust me. We'll do everything it takes to get to the truth of what really happened."

But her sister wouldn't have any ability to prevent her from being arrested if the police decided she was the real killer. Kimber wasn't even with the CIA anymore. And as much as she trusted Kimber, Tessa couldn't keep the doubts from seeping in. "Kimber, I don't know about this."

"You need to trust me."

Tessa wavered a moment longer. She did trust her sister, but this was her future they were talking about.

Kimber was former CIA. Surely she wouldn't put her own sister in danger of ending up behind bars.

Though reluctant, Tessa said, "Okay. I'll see you this afternoon." Tessa hung up the phone and handed it back to Parker. "I guess I should go shower and change back into my clothes."

Parker nodded. "Let me know when you're ready to go, and I'll give you a ride to the station."

"Thanks." Tessa headed down the hall to the guest room. Maybe she could get Parker to stop by a shop in town so she could pick up something clean to wear. Then again, if her trust in Kimber was misplaced and the police didn't believe her story, she could very well end up wearing an orange prison jumpsuit before the day was over. She cringed. She wasn't cut out for this kind of thing. And one thing was certain: Orange wasn't her color.

Chapter 7

Parker's first impression of Kimber Frost had been that she had a good head on her shoulders. Now he wasn't so sure. Did she really want Tessa to turn herself in, knowing that she could end up behind bars?

He supposed hiding from the authorities wasn't exactly a good idea, but he couldn't imagine facing a police interrogation.

His phone rang again; this time his aunt Phoebe's name came up as the caller. "Did you hear what just happened with Kimber's sister?" he asked.

"Yes, that's why I'm calling," Phoebe said. "Here. Your uncle wants to talk to you."

Ian's voice came on a second later. "I have a huge favor to ask."

Somehow, Parker doubted his uncle was about to ask him to change the water filter in the fridge. "What do you need?"

"I need you to help Tessa disappear for a few days."

Parker may not have liked Kimber's advice to Tessa, but that didn't mean he wanted to be in the middle of a possible manhunt. He shook his head. "You want me to hide a fugitive?"

"She's not a fugitive," Ian said. "Not yet anyway."

Ian's words could have come straight out of a script for one of his movies — or one of Parker's plays. "You're not making me feel any better."

"I know, and if you don't feel comfortable with this, you can just pass the message to Tessa that her sister said for her to come in because that's what she needed the police to hear when she turns over the recording of her phone call."

Understanding dawned. "But she doesn't want her to come in." This was more in line with the woman he'd spent the past week with at their writing retreat.

"No. Kimber wants some time for the investigation to progress beyond the police only looking at her sister as a suspect."

"Why do I get the feeling that there's more to this story?"

"The investigating officer is one who tends to fixate on a single subject," Ian said. "At least, that's what the article in the *Times* said last week."

"Which article?"

"It was about a wrongful-conviction lawsuit," Ian said. "A man spent six years in prison before new evidence emerged that proved he'd been telling the truth all along. Unfortunately, that was the second time this officer was involved in an innocent person going to prison."

A protective surge flowed through Parker. "We can't let that happen to Tessa." Not that he really knew the woman, but he couldn't stand the thought of anyone being locked up without cause.

"I agree. That's why I was hoping you could take her away somewhere," Ian said. "You have a car, and since your writing retreat ended yesterday, it will look natural for you to leave the beach house today without anyone realizing the two of you are together."

"If you want me to leave the Hamptons, I assume that means the police are going to show up sooner than later."

"My guess is that the locals will be sent out within an hour of Tessa not showing up on the train."

It also made sense now why Ian called on his phone to let the two sisters talk.

"Any suggestions on where I should take her?" Parker asked.

"I have plenty, but it's best if I don't know where you've gone in case anyone asks me if I know where she is."

"Good point." Parker paced the length of the kitchen before turning back to his temporary workstation. He hadn't been able to get much writing done here anyway, and he was the only person currently in a position to help Tessa. "I'll be sure to lock up the house before I leave."

"Thanks, Parker. Also, if Tessa has any concerns about going with you, tell her 'rocky road.' "

"Rocky road?"

"Yeah. It's what Kimber told us to tell her."

Parker had no idea why an ice-cream flavor would help put Tessa more at ease, but who was he to question this insanity?

"Oh, and for the record," Ian continued, "I'll reimburse you for anything you need to spend."

"I appreciate the offer, but I'll be fine." Parker might be a one-hit wonder, but he'd been paid handsomely for that one hit. He closed his laptop. "I'll text you tonight when I get settled."

"Just remember that you need to make sure nothing can be traced back to Tessa," Ian said.

"Understood." Parker ended the call, picked up his laptop, and walked into his room. For the next ten minutes, he packed his belongings, double-checking the outlets to make sure he had all his charging cords.

Before closing up his suitcase, he pulled out a simple blue hoodie and set it aside.

A few minutes later, Tessa emerged from the bathroom, her hair damp from the shower. She'd dressed again in the clothes she'd arrived in, and she held his T-shirt in her hand. "Here's this back for you."

"Hold on to it for now. You may need it." Parker picked up the hoodie. "And you'll want this. It's cold outside."

"Thank you." She took it from him and pulled it over her head. "I'll give this to Ian to make sure it gets back to you."

"Don't worry about it." Parker slid his laptop bag over his shoulder and grabbed the handle of his suitcase. "You ready?"

"Are you leaving too?"

"We're leaving together." Parker headed for the door.

"Wait. What?" Tessa caught up to him in the great room. "You're coming with me to New York?"

"No. We're going somewhere besides Manhattan," Parker said. "My uncle called and passed along a message from your sister. Kimber doesn't want you coming back until they have time to look for the real killer."

Tessa pressed her lips together, and Parker sensed her trepidation. "Your sister passed the message that if you didn't believe me, I should tell you 'rocky road.' " Parker shrugged. "I'm not sure what that's supposed to mean."

Something softened in her expression. "It's her way of telling me that I can trust you."

Parker stopped by the front door and turned to face her. "You *can* trust me."

She drew a deep breath and let it out on a sigh. Then she nodded. "Okay, but if I'm going to disappear, maybe it's best that we make it look like I'm traveling on my own."

"How do you plan to do that?"

"I thought I could take an Uber to the train station and then request another one to take me from the train station into town," Tessa said.

"You're giving the police a trail to follow." Parker nodded his approval. "Clever."

"I don't know how clever it is, but hopefully it will make it look like you and I aren't traveling together."

Another reminder that agreeing to help Tessa could land him in trouble with the law. His eyes met hers. Concern shone in the vibrant green. He suspected her concern was as much for him as for herself. He pulled his cell phone from his pocket. "Here. You can log in on my phone to make the requests."

"Thanks." She logged him out of his account and proceeded to log into hers. When she finished, she logged back out of her account and handed his phone back to him. "The first Uber will be here in a couple minutes. I already scheduled one to pick me up from the train station about fifteen minutes after I should get there."

"In that case, let's decide where we want to meet up in town."

"My ride will drop me off on Main Street."

"Great. I know just where to pick you up." He pulled up the Maps app on his phone and held it out to show her where they could meet.

His phone vibrated with a message from Uber. "Looks like your ride is almost here."

"I'd better go wait outside."

Parker gestured to her hood. "You'd better put that up. It's best if no one can identify you here." He reached for the door. "And it's cold outside."

Chapter 8

An inadvertent disclosure. Brandon wasn't quite sure what to do about Ian's revelation that he and Phoebe suspected Brandon and Kimber worked for the government.

This whole day had turned into a nightmare of epic proportions. Brandon guided Kimber out of Ian's apartment and toward their waiting ride. Ian had been kind enough to lend them his car and driver since filming had been canceled for the day.

Brandon's phone buzzed for the fifth time in the past five minutes.

"Is that Amelia trying to get ahold of you?" Kimber asked, referring to his boss at the publishing house.

Brandon checked his phone. Sure enough, he found Amelia's name. "You guessed it on the first try."

They reached the car.

"We should drop you off at your office first," Kimber said. "I think I'm going to head over to the FBI office. I have a bunch of research I need to do for my next book."

Brandon understood her words held far more meaning than most might think. She might use her meeting with the FBI to help with a future book, but undoubtedly, she was going to meet with Rafi Ebeid, their FBI contact, to request help for Tessa's case. Brandon cast her a look of approval. It wasn't so long ago that Kimber had struggled with the concept of misleading others to protect their role as undercover operatives, but she had grown into her new assignment exceptionally well. Not bad for someone who had started out as an overt employee working in finance.

They climbed into the waiting car, and their driver turned to face them. "Where to?"

Brandon gave him the address before he turned his attention back to Kimber. For the benefit of the driver, he asked, "What time will you need to meet your sister at the train?"

"Around two."

"Let me know if you need me to meet you down at the police station after she gives her statement."

"I will."

They fell silent until they reached Monroe

Publishing. Brandon leaned in and kissed Kimber. Even though they'd been dating for months now, the meeting of their lips brought with it a sense of wonder that he never tired of. Unable to resist, he kissed her a second time, this time drawing it out. When he eased back, he said, "Let me know how everything goes today."

Kimber nodded. "I'll talk to you later."

Brandon climbed out and made his way upstairs. He debated trying to slip into his office before meeting with his boss, but with the number of text messages he'd received over the past few minutes, he opted for a more proactive approach. Ignoring the curious glances from Mary and Regina — the two coworkers who had been less than thrilled when he'd originally been hired — Brandon knocked on Amelia's door.

"Come in," he heard through the door.

Brandon entered.

"Where have you been?" Amelia asked.

"With Kimber. Her sister was missing. It took a while to track her down."

Amelia flicked her hand in the air as if to brush away a trivial problem. "I've had a dozen calls from Patricia Banik this morning. Do you have any idea what she wants?"

A dozen calls in Amelia's world was likely no more than two, but Brandon kept that thought to himself. "It's possible she was calling to let you know that Kimber finished polishing her third manuscript. My guess is Patricia will have it submitted to you by next week."

"Call Patricia and make sure that's all she wanted."

Brandon should have reminded Amelia that he'd been promoted from her personal assistant to an editorial assistant, but his words weren't likely to negate her request. "I'll call right now."

"Before you go, do you have any idea what Kimber has planned next?"

Kimber had drafted loose outlines for a half dozen possible books, but Brandon followed the cover story Kimber had given him on their ride over. "I know she's on her way to meet with someone from the FBI as part of her research."

Amelia nodded her approval. "Good. I don't want her taking too much time off. As soon as she goes on tour for her first book, she's going to have a hard time creating."

"She's hoping to get another manuscript completed before that happens."

"Good. Make sure you keep her on track."

Brandon didn't need to keep Kimber focused on her writing, but he nodded anyway. "I'll let you know as soon as I talk to Patricia."

He left her office, not surprised when Mary stood. "So, did she fire you yet?"

"No. Sorry."

Mary shrugged. "Well, there's always tomorrow."

Brandon didn't respond. He continued to his office that lay just beyond the cubicle he'd used previously when serving as Amelia's personal assistant. He stored his computer bag under his desk, sat down, and dialed Patricia.

She picked up on the second ring. "Let me guess: Amelia wants you to figure out why I was calling."

Brandon smothered a laugh. "You are a very astute woman."

"It doesn't take much with Amelia to guess her motives," Patricia said. "And to answer her question, I'm actually calling about our mutual friend Phoebe Sawyer."

Kimber had introduced Phoebe to her literary agent two months ago, which had resulted in Phoebe's signing Patricia as her agent. "How is her manuscript coming along?"

"Very well, and like Kimber, she's interested in publishing with Monroe," Patricia said. "More specifically, she would like for you to be her editor."

Brandon straightened in his chair. "Me?"

"Yes. You and I are the only people she's worked with who have given her honest feedback."

"I just read through her manuscript and gave her some suggestions."

"Without worrying about sugarcoating things because of who her husband is," Patricia said. "The reason I was calling Amelia instead of you was so I could put in the request with her since you're already familiar with the manuscript."

"I'm flattered that Phoebe wants to work with me, but I doubt Amelia will let me take on an edit yet. So far, she hasn't had me do anything beyond submissions and copyedit work." And Brandon wasn't sure how Amelia would feel about Patricia making such a demand.

"I'll handle Amelia, but first, I need her to take my call," Patricia said. "Or look at Phoebe's manuscript."

"Let me talk to her, and I'll try to get her to call you back."

"Thanks, Brandon."

He hung up the phone and stood. Might as well face Amelia now.

Tessa was shopping and using a credit card, knowing full well the police would ultimately look for her here in the Hamptons. Of course, that was the point. Thankfully, her typical habit of splitting up her IDs and credit cards between her phone case and her purse had ensured that she still had a way to access her money.

And the use of her credit card would make it obvious that she'd been here before she — hopefully — disappeared from sight to wherever Parker planned on taking her. That thought was more than a bit disconcerting. But Kimber and Ian trusted Parker, and she was trying to follow their lead.

The Uber had dropped her off at the Walgreens on Main Street, one of the busier sections of town. Before she'd left, Parker had given her a time and location to meet so he could avoid being seen with her. She still couldn't believe his incredible kindness. Never had she expected to end up in a situation such as this, but Parker was an unexpected ally, one she already found herself relying on far too much.

Thoughts of her new hero pushed into her mind during the hour she'd spent walking in and out of stores as though she didn't have a care in the world. If anyone were to look closely, they might see the slight trembling in her hands, but so far, no one seemed to suspect that she was a person of interest in a murder case. Why would they? This sort of thing didn't happen in real life.

But it *had* happened — to her.

Once she finished her shopping at three different clothing shops, the local Walgreens, and the Beach Bakery Café, she left the hustle and bustle of Main Street. With her shopping bags laden with clothing, toiletries, and a few food items, she passed the library and made her way to the spot Parker had told her to meet him.

She approached his SUV, where he'd parked on a side street void of traffic cameras and the bustle of foot traffic in the main shopping district. She was nearly there when the trunk opened, so she loaded her bags into the back, keeping the bakery bag with her. Then she opened the passenger door.

Parker gestured toward the back seat. "You should probably get in the back and lie down until we're out of town."

She supposed that was one way to stay out of sight. She glanced behind her to make sure no one was nearby before she closed the front door and climbed into the back. She opted for the center seat and buckled her seat belt.

"I picked up some pastries at the bakery." Tessa passed the bakery bag to Parker between the two front seats. "Did you want one?"

"Yeah. Thanks." He fished one out and then handed the bag back to her before putting the car into gear and starting toward Main Street.

"Have you decided where we're going?" Tessa asked as she lay down as he'd instructed.

"I have an idea. I should know if it'll work out by the time we pass through Manhattan." He didn't expand on his answer, and Tessa fell silent.

She suspected she was destined to hide in the back seat for the duration of their drive, but Parker drove for only a half hour before he pulled over and turned back to look at her. "You want to come up front?"

"You think it'll be okay for me to be up there?"

"You should probably keep your hood up to hide your face, but I think we'll be all right now."

Tessa sat up to see that they were at a gas station.

Parker filled up the tank while she settled herself in the front seat. When he climbed back into the driver's seat, he navigated his way through a construction zone and back to the main thoroughfare leading to the city.

"Are there any more of those pastries in there?" he asked.

"Yeah." She hadn't been able to bring herself to eat anything yet. "You have a choice between a chocolate chip muffin and a bear claw."

"I'll take the bear claw."

Tessa used a napkin to pass it to him.

"Thanks."

The easy exchange made it feel like they'd known each other much longer than a handful of hours. And she couldn't deny that his willingness to help her had made an impossible situation almost bearable. Not to mention that he was also putting himself in jeopardy with his charity.

"Maybe you should just drop me off somewhere and go back to the Hamptons," Tessa said. "I don't want you to get in trouble because of me."

"It'll be fine," Parker said as though helping her were what he'd planned to do today. "And no one knows you're with me."

"I'm sure you have other things you need to be doing."

"I was stuck on my story anyway." Parker glanced over his shoulder before switching lanes. "Who knows. Maybe all this will give me some inspiration."

"That's one way to look for a silver lining." It was probably the only positive anyone had experienced through any of this ordeal.

Parker's phone rang, the name Micah popping up on the console screen. Parker clicked on the button on his steering wheel to answer it. "Hey, Micah. Any luck?"

"Yeah. My mom said you're welcome to the cabin. No one will be using it until Thanksgiving weekend."

"That's great." Parker flashed a smile at Tessa. "Thanks."

"I'll text you the code for the door."

"You're the best," Parker said. "And tell your mom I said thank you."

"Will do." Micah ended the call.

"Does this mean we have a place to stay?" Tessa asked.

"It does. My friend's parents have a cabin in the Catskills." Parker handed her the phone as a text message came in. "Can you put in the directions for me and see if you can find a grocery store along the way? Ideally, we'll want to pick up food right before we get to the city."

"Why before? Aren't the Catskills over two hours from Manhattan?"

"About two and a half hours, but if we buy our groceries before we pass the city, it will prevent anyone from knowing where I went after leaving Uncle Ian's house."

"Are you sure?" Tessa asked. "How will we keep the fridge and freezer stuff cold?"

"I can buy a cooler and some ice."

Tessa gripped her hands together. "Do you really think there's any way someone would connect me to you?"

"I doubt it, but the fact that you spoke with Ian last night could put me on the police's radar."

"Then I'll start a list." She picked up his phone and pulled up the notes app. "What do you want from the store?"

CHAPTER 9

Kimber waited in the lobby of the FBI's New York field office for nearly twenty minutes before Special Agent Rafi Ebeid emerged.

"Sorry to keep you waiting," Rafi said. "I had an interview that went long."

Kimber stood. "It's fine. I appreciate that you're able to squeeze me in."

"Come on." Rafi gestured for her to follow him. "We can talk in my office."

They walked down the hall until they reached the simple office that was little more than a desk, three chairs, and a four-drawer safe that doubled as a filing cabinet.

Rafi closed the door and sat at his desk while Kimber took the chair closest to him. "So what brings you here?" he asked.

"Officially, I'm here to research my next book."

Rafi lifted his eyebrows. "And the real reason?"

"It appears my sister was in proximity of a murder when it happened, and now the detective is hyperfocusing on her as the main suspect." Kimber's throat tightened at the gravity of Tessa's current situation.

Sympathy shone on Rafi's face, but he gave her the expected line. "The best thing she can do is cooperate with the authorities."

"Normally, I would agree, but the investigating officer is Detective Colin Murray." Kimber caught the look of understanding on Rafi's face. Though she wasn't about to admit that she was hoping Tessa got the message not to get on the train home, she concentrated on the crux of the problem. "Is there any way you can gain access to the police report for the murder? I'm especially interested in the surveillance feed and entry log for the building where it happened."

"I can stretch things to say it could be related to one of my cases." Rafi turned to his laptop. "Give me everything you know so far."

Kimber shared the name of the victim and the estimated time of death. Then she played the recording of her phone conversation with Tessa.

"I'll put the wheels in motion, but I'll be honest," Rafi began, "I've worked with Murray before."

"And?"

"If you really want to help your sister, I suggest you find a way to go undercover at the studio to help identify the real killer. Someone there must know something."

"I'm not sure Brandon could pull an undercover assignment while he's still working for Monroe."

"I wasn't thinking about Brandon. I was thinking about you." Rafi leaned back in his chair. "You have an established relationship with Ian, and you can use the same excuse at the studio as you're using with me today."

The fact that Rafi would even suggest she fill such a role signified how far she'd come. Six months ago, she'd stepped into her first undercover assignment, but that didn't mean she was adept at the skills needed to investigate a murder. "I wouldn't even know what to look for."

"I can help you focus your efforts. So can Brandon," Rafi said. "Of course, it would be better if both of you could ask around. It would look less obvious if it isn't just one new person being curious."

"I'll talk to him, but like I said, I doubt he can do much more than make a few visits."

"He's your boyfriend. That alone would warrant him coming to the studio if you can get approval to shadow someone there."

"I never thought I'd use my personal life to help with a cover story," Kimber said.

"More often than not, the best cover stories are the ones coated in truth."

"So I'm finding out." Kimber glanced at her watch. "I'd better get going. I promised Tessa I'd meet her at the train station."

"Have you already told Detective Murray that you spoke with Tessa?"

"Not yet."

"Do that now." Rafi pointed at her purse. "I want to hear how the conversation goes."

"Okay." Kimber retrieved the detective's business card and dialed the number.

"Murray."

"Detective Murray, this is Kimber Seidel. I spoke with you this morning about my sister, Tessa."

"Have you heard from her?" he asked eagerly.

"I spoke with her a little while ago," Kimber said. "From what she told me, she found the woman who was killed, and a man tried to grab her. She freaked out and left the building and went looking for me."

"Where is she now?"

"She was in the Hamptons, but she said she was going to catch the eleven o'clock train to come back into the city. I'm planning on meeting her at Penn Station at two."

"As soon as you find her, I want you to come straight to my office."

"I understand. Assuming the train is on time, I'll see you around two thirty."

"Good. I'll see you both then."

Kimber hung up. "Well, that's done."

"It's best that you stay on his good side." Rafi stood. "But I do have one more piece of advice."

"What's that?"

"Find your sister a good lawyer," Rafi said. "She may need one."

Parker pulled onto the narrow dirt road that led to the cabin where he'd be staying for the foreseeable future. Other than a quick stop at the grocery store, where Tessa had deliberately stayed in the car to avoid being seen, their drive to the Catskills had been uneventful, ordinary even. Had it not been for the fact that he'd just met the woman beside him, he could almost pretend they were longtime friends on their way to a shared vacation.

Tessa looked out her window toward the lake visible between the few trees separating the drive from the water. "This view is gorgeous."

"Yeah, it is." So many leaves already in

full color, the water a deep blue against an equally blue sky. And not another building anywhere to be seen.

Parker came to a stop beside a sugar maple, bright orange leaves hanging on the tree and scattered on the ground.

Tessa leaned forward to get a better look out the windshield. "This is where we're staying?" The tone of her voice suggested her surprise was good.

"This is it." The log cabin in front of them boasted a generous front porch as well as a fire pit in the open space between it and the water. The modified A-frame included wings on either side, where the bedrooms were located.

Parker climbed out of the car and met her at the back of the SUV. "If you can get your stuff, I'll get the rest."

Tessa looked in both directions. "If you're worried about me being seen here, I think you're being overly cautious. There's no one around here." She narrowed her eyes. "This really is crazy."

"What?" Parker cast a quick glance her way. "Going on a road trip with a complete stranger?"

"Yes. We just met, and we're staying in a house together in the middle of nowhere." Tessa glanced at the lake. "I mean, it's gorgeous here, but —"

"I know. It's all pretty strange."

"Yeah," Tessa said with a sigh. She collected her shopping bags from the back of the car. "I'm completely cut off from everyone I know and all my work. Last night, I found a murder victim, and now I'm avoiding the police because someone is misreading the situation."

"Yeah, that has to be unsettling." Parker grabbed his suitcase and his laptop bag and headed up the stairs.

Tessa followed him onto the porch. "Why are you helping me?"

"My uncle is convinced you didn't kill the woman you found." Parker shared that conviction. He glanced at her again. "I'm assuming Ian is correct, right?"

She cocked both eyebrows. "Yes, he's correct."

And Parker believed her. Everything about this woman screamed integrity. He couldn't imagine her lying to him, much less committing murder. "Then I'm helping because I don't want an innocent woman to end up in jail."

"Are you in the habit of rescuing people?"

Parker nearly laughed. "No. Not at all." His older sisters didn't think he could even take care of himself, and his mom wasn't much better. Maybe that was why he preferred spending time with Ian and Phoebe. They let him be himself, and they trusted him to make his own decisions.

He unlocked the front door using the code Micah had sent him and pushed it open so Tessa could walk in first.

She took a few steps before she stopped and stared. "Oh wow. This is even better than I'd hoped."

Parker set his suitcase beside the door and studied the space he'd visited a dozen times before. The wooden walls, the throw rug on the hardwood floor, the sofa and oversized chairs that faced the stone fireplace.

"The guest rooms are down that hall." He pointed to his left. "Yours is the second one on the right."

She set her shopping bags on the floor and continued into the kitchen, stopping to stare out the large window overlooking the lake.

Parker carried his suitcase and laptop into his usual room. When he returned to the living area, Tessa still stood beside the window.

"Tessa? Are you okay?"

She turned slowly. "No, but thanks for making my situation the best it can be."

Sympathy welled up inside him, and he put his hand on her shoulder. "You're welcome."

Brandon approached Amelia's office, the events of this morning still playing through his thoughts. For the past few months, he'd largely been able to pretend he was nothing more than an editorial assistant. Sure, he and Kimber had worked on a few intel projects together, but primarily, Kimber remained focused on her writing, and he worked toward excelling in his new editing career, which he had hoped to pursue after graduating from Brown years ago.

He reached Amelia's door and rapped his knuckles against it.

Without looking up from her laptop, she lifted her hand and waved him forward.

Brandon walked in and waited for his boss to look up. The wait lasted a full two minutes.

Finally, Amelia acknowledged him. "What does Patricia want?"

"She's repping another debut author who might be of interest to us," Brandon began.

Amelia scowled. "Are you trying to push one of your friends' work?"

Amelia was never a fan of people using their position at Monroe to fast-track manuscripts, particularly when it came to friends and family. Despite that knowledge,

Brandon opted for honesty. "I am, but only because you asked me to call Patricia. I didn't realize we were Phoebe's first choice until today."

"Phoebe?"

"Phoebe Sawyer, Ian Sawyer's wife." Not giving Amelia the chance to discount Phoebe's talent, he pushed on. "I did an initial edit for her. It's quite good."

Amelia's eyebrows lifted. "Ian Sawyer? As in the movie star?"

"That's the one."

Clearly pondering, Amelia tapped her manicured nail on her desk. "Get me the manuscript. I'll take a look at it tonight."

"I'll email it to you now." Considering the conversation a victory, he took a step back. "Would you like my initial analysis as well?"

"No. I don't want a biased opinion."

"Okay, but just so you know, the part that needed the most work was fleshing out the secondary characters, especially the female protagonist's best friend."

Amelia gave a curt nod. "Got it."

Brandon returned to his office. After a quick call to Patricia to make sure he had the latest version of Phoebe's manuscript, he forwarded the document to Amelia.

He checked his watch, noting that the time Tessa's train was due had already come and gone.

Though he often closed his office door to keep Mary and Regina from overhearing his calls, he left it open and dialed Kimber's number. She answered on the third ring.

"Hey, I just wanted to see if you want me to come with you and Tessa while she gives her statement," he said.

"Thanks for the offer, but I'm afraid Tessa wasn't on the train. She must have missed it."

Following their planned script, Brandon said, "I'm so sorry. This is so hard that she doesn't have her phone with her."

"It's driving me crazy." Kimber's sigh carried over the line. "The next train doesn't arrive for a couple hours. I think I'm going to head down to the police station and give Detective Murray the recording of our conversation this morning. That way, he'll have as much information as we can give him for now."

"That's a good idea." Brandon wished he could go with her, but he didn't dare irritate Amelia any further. "I'll give you a call as soon as I leave tonight. I thought we might want to order in."

"Thanks. I'll let you know if Tessa wants to eat with us. Her train should get in around five."

"I'll plan on it being the three of us," Brandon said. "You should probably set up an appointment with Detective Murray for Tessa to give her official statement tomorrow."

"I will. Talk to you later," Kimber said. "Love you."

"Love you too," Brandon said, the words still foreign to his ears even as the feelings behind them continued to grow and deepen. "And good luck with everything."

"Thanks."

Brandon ended the call and turned back to the work on his desk. Time to get caught up after his morning away, because he really didn't want to stay late tonight.

CHAPTER 10

Kimber walked into her apartment and pulled out her cell phone. She made it all the way to her list of favorites before she remembered. She couldn't call Tessa and give her an update. Tessa didn't have her phone. She set her purse and phone on the long counter that separated the kitchen from the living room.

This whole situation was beyond unreal. Her sister was one of the kindest, most vibrant people she knew. The mere thought of her being accused of murder put today into an alternate reality.

Kimber's phone rang, and she lifted it. It was Greta. "Hey, Greta."

"Kimber, have you talked to Tessa today?" Greta asked in her brisk, no-nonsense tone. "I heard there was a murder at Ian's studio last night, and I'm worried. Your sister hasn't been to the office yet, and she isn't picking up her phone. Please tell me it wasn't Tessa who was killed."

"Sorry. I should have thought to call you earlier." Kimber paused and searched for the right words to explain the unexplainable. Starting at the beginning, she said, "It wasn't Tessa. It was a production assistant named Juliet Clark."

"I don't think I know her, but that's terrible."

"Even worse is that the police believe Tessa was there when it happened."

"There?" Greta asked, her words coming rapidly. "In the building?"

"That's what it sounds like."

"Poor Tessa." Compassion carried over the line. "How is she doing?"

"She lost her phone, so I've only been able to talk to her once, but I have a feeling she may need some time off." Assuming Ian managed to get the message to Tessa to stay out of sight for the time being.

"Of course. I feel so bad. Had I not sent her to deliver the clothes last night, she wouldn't be in this mess."

"I'm sure everything will get sorted out, but it may take a little time," Kimber said, hoping the mess would not only get sorted out but that Tessa would soon be proved innocent too.

"When you talk to her, you tell her to take

as long as she needs," Greta said. "I'll hire a couple of temps to help out until she can get back to the office."

"I'm sure that will be a relief for her." Kimber didn't know what Tessa would do if she lost her job. She loved working for Greta. "Thanks so much, Greta."

"You're welcome. Let me know if there's anything either of you needs."

"I will." Kimber ended the call and dropped onto the nearest bar stool. Her sister's job was safe. Now she just had to make sure Tessa could clear her name so she could return to work.

Tessa strolled onto the private dock located down the hill from the cabin, her hands resting in the front pocket of the hoodie Parker had lent her. She supposed she should give it back to him, but it was so comfortable, and she hadn't wanted to change when they'd arrived.

She reached the end of the dock and leaned on the side railing. The scenery here really was stunning. Too bad she didn't have a way to take a photo to capture the image.

Then again, if she had her phone, it would likely be blowing up with calls and messages from her boss. She really hoped Greta didn't fire her, but she wouldn't blame her if she did. After all, Tessa's to-do list for today had a dozen tasks on it, none of which included ignoring work or ending up on a road trip with a handsome stranger.

And Parker was handsome. She supposed she shouldn't be surprised. After all, the man was related to Ian Sawyer, one of the biggest heartthrobs of his generation. But more than Parker's looks, Tessa still couldn't quite wrap her brain around his selflessness. It was as though taking the chance to help someone was his favorite way to spend his time.

A board creaked behind her, and Tessa turned.

Parker approached, his long-sleeved shirt and faded jeans showcasing his toned physique. "I made some chowder. It should be ready in about twenty minutes," he said. "I thought maybe we could sit out by the fire pit and eat our dinner while we watch the sun go down."

Watch a sunset. That was something she hadn't taken time for in far too long. "I'd like that."

He put his hand on her arm. "How are you holding up?"

She looked up at him. "Thanks to you, I'm doing okay." She couldn't begin to imagine how she would have managed without Parker's help.

"I just gave you a ride to where you needed to go." He dropped his hand and leaned against the dock's wooden railing.

"Are you kidding me?" This man really was too much. "Besides saving me from freezing last night, you dropped everything to keep me safe and out of jail. That's kind of a big thing."

"This has been good for me. I wasn't getting much done in the Hamptons. Maybe a change of pace will help me meet my deadline."

"I never realized playwrights have deadlines," Tessa said. "I guess I always assumed you just wrote your play and then tried to find someone to produce it."

"That's usually how it works." He shrugged. "But I ended up having way more success with my first play than I expected, and a group of investors wants me to come up with a new one for next fall."

She hadn't expected that. "How soon would you need to get it written for it to be ready to cast in time?"

"The investors want it in hand by March." He sighed. "Theoretically, that shouldn't be a problem, except I'm struggling to find a story that feels right."

"What kind of story are you trying to

write?" Tessa asked. "What genre?"

"My first one was a family drama, but I'd like to do a mystery this time."

"If you need insight into what a woman feels like when stumbling upon a dead body, I can help you with that."

"I was hoping you might say that." He tapped his hand against the railing. "How would you feel about walking me through everything that happened last night?"

Her stomach tightened, and she closed her eyes for a long moment. "I already did that."

Parker shook his head. "No. You told me about finding the woman who had been killed and about the man who grabbed you. I want to go back to the beginning."

"The beginning?" Tessa repeated.

"Yes. I want everything from why you were there, how you felt about it, who you talked to when you arrived at the building . . . everything."

"Why do you want all that?" Living through the nightmare once had been enough. She didn't want to keep revisiting it over and over.

"Starting from the beginning helps set the stage. And if I can write down your story, maybe I can alter it to make my own mystery."

"I guess I can do that." Not that she wanted to, but she could hardly deny this simple request from the man who had already done so much for her. Gathering her strength, she added, "It's the least I can do to thank you."

"You don't have to thank me." He gestured to his hoodie. "Just promise when all this is over, you'll remember to give me back my sweatshirt. It's my favorite."

"I can see why. It's so comfy." Tessa pointed at the house. "But if you want, I can give it back to you when we go inside."

A little smile played on his face. "That's all right. It looks good on you."

Tessa wasn't sure she'd ever been complimented for how she wore a sweatshirt three sizes too big, but she answered automatically. "Thanks." She glanced out at the lake again, the lowering sun sparkling on the water. "Can I ask you to do me another favor?"

"Sure. What?"

"Can you take a photo of the lake for me? It's so gorgeous, and I hate that I can't take a picture."

"That's easy enough." He pulled his phone from his pocket and lifted it, tapping the screen several times. "Come on. Let's take one of us together too."

"You sure you want a photo with me? I may be a fugitive before the week is out."

"I'm sure." Parker put his arm around her shoulders and held up the phone to take a selfie. A ripple of attraction skittered through her, and Tessa had to remind herself to keep looking at the camera instead of at him.

Parker took several more photos before he lowered his phone and released her. "If your bad luck turns into a hit play, I want a photo to remind us of where the idea started."

"I really hope that by this time next year, you'll be getting rave reviews and I won't be in prison."

"Not being in prison is a good plan, but I think you should work on raising the bar of where you'd like to be by this time next year."

"Honestly, I love my job," Tessa said. "What I really want is to be able to keep doing it without this whole disaster causing me to get fired."

"Maybe we need to put that in one of my early scenes," Parker said. "I can email it to my uncle Ian and let him do his magic to make sure you keep your job."

"What do you mean?" Tessa asked, uncertain how Parker's play could affect her employment.

"Uncle Ian reads through my pages for me whenever I ask. If I send him the scenes I write, I can mirror what happened with you and also include script notes about character concerns and questions."

"So your play really would mimic my life."

"Yes, and we can use it as a way to communicate back and forth without raising suspicions if anyone were to look at our emails or phone calls."

"We're supposed to be keeping our families out of my mess, remember?"

"I know, but I think this may be our best plan to keep your sister and my uncle in the loop while also giving them a way to send information back to us," Parker said.

Tessa couldn't deny the idea was a good one. "I think this week, you may be asking him to critique your work a lot."

Chapter 11

Every insecurity Kimber had ever experienced about lying flooded through her as she entered the police station. She may have become somewhat adept at misleading people when necessary for her job with the CIA, but straight-out lying wasn't one of her strong suits. And misleading a police detective would put all her newfound deception skills to the test.

Kimber checked in at the front desk. After receiving a visitor badge, she found her way to a row of desks where Detective Murray sat along with several other men wearing suits rather than uniforms.

The moment Detective Murray saw her, he stood. Then he scowled. "Where's your sister?"

"I don't know. She was supposed to be on the train from the Hamptons that arrived at two this afternoon, but she wasn't on it."

Detective Murray motioned toward the

chair beside his desk.

Kimber sat, bracing for the interrogation that was sure to follow.

"When did you last speak with her?" Detective Murray asked.

"This morning." She held up her phone. "My boyfriend recorded our conversation and sent it to me. I heard that it could be helpful to have a recording of a witness statement from the first time they talk about what they saw."

"Text it to me." The detective handed her another business card. Kimber took it and proceeded to forward the recording. "My sister also mentioned that she came here to the station and filled out a witness statement."

He furrowed his brow. "I have no record of that."

"She turned it in at the front desk. Her account is on the recording."

Detective Murray sat in his office chair and rolled it closer so he was very much in Kimber's personal space, then leaned toward her. "You understand that interfering with this investigation could end with you in jail for obstruction of justice, right?"

Kimber suspected Murray was attempting to instill fear in her, but all he did was succeed in sparking her anger. She lifted her eyes so her gaze was even with his. "I understand that I'm uncomfortable with you sitting this close to me."

The muscle in his jaw twitched. After a moment, he leaned back slightly.

Kimber simply stared until he rolled his chair back into place behind his desk.

Detective Murray pulled his keyboard toward him. "I'll need your contact information."

Great. Now this overzealous detective would know where she lived. She'd have to warn her next-door neighbor to keep an eye out. Brandon too. Thank goodness he lived just two doors down.

Kimber gave the detective her phone number, address, and email address.

He typed it all into his computer. "One more thing." Detective Murray looked up at her. "When you talked to your sister this morning, whose phone did she call from?"

"I'm not sure." Sure, she'd met Parker Sawyer, but she couldn't be 100 percent certain that she'd used his phone. "She stayed the night at a friend's house in the Hamptons and called from there."

"I'll need the number."

"I don't have it," Kimber said. "Tessa called my friend Ian."

"Then I need you to get the number from him."

"I'll see what I can do," Kimber said, fully prepared to stall. The longer she could keep Parker from talking to the police, the better. Not interested in enduring any more questions, Kimber stood. "The next train doesn't come in until five. I'll have my sister call you in the morning to set up a time to come in if you need to conduct an in-person interview."

Detective Murray stood as well. "We will definitely want to speak with her in person. And one more thing." He opened his desk drawer and pulled out the evidence bag that held Tessa's phone. "Do you have the code to unlock your sister's cell phone? Granting us access could speed along our investigation."

Kimber hesitated. The phone could help prove that Tessa was telling the truth, but it also contained the phone numbers of dozens of actors, models, and top entertainment professionals.

"What? Are you worried we'll find something in here to incriminate your sister?"

"No. I'm concerned that my sister has numerous contacts that are confidential." Kimber tilted her chin up. "I need your assurance that no information from her phone will be shared."

"It won't be unless it relates to the investigation."

"Fine, but I also want to see what's on the screen when you first open the phone." Kimber wasn't going to let this detective ignore evidence. And if what Tessa said was true, the numbers 911 should be the first thing they would see on the phone screen.

Detective Murray didn't look happy with her demands. He cast a quick glance at the detective seated at the next desk over, who gave a subtle nod. "Whatever." Detective Murray opened the bag and pushed the button on the side to bring the phone to life. "Do you know the code?"

Kimber wanted to say no, but Tessa always used the same code for everything, including the lock on her apartment. Kimber stepped closer so she could see the screen before she gave him the six-digit passcode.

The phone opened. Sure enough, the phone app filled the screen with the numbers 91. Apparently, Tessa hadn't managed to dial the last number.

Relieved that at least one piece of evidence had fallen in Tessa's favor, Kimber gestured to the phone. "It appears my sister's phone backs up her story that she was trying to call 911 when a man arrived and tried to detain her."

The muscle in the detective's jaw twitched. "That may be, but it doesn't change our need to speak with her in person."

"Understood. In the meantime, I suggest you ask your front desk staff about her statement."

"Oh, I will." He took a step forward. "But with or without the statement, I expect to see her tomorrow. I report in at nine."

"One of us will call you at nine, then."

"See that you do."

Kimber turned and walked toward the elevators. She really didn't like that this man was trying to pin a murder on her sister.

Colin had a feeling Kimber would protect her sister. And no matter what had been said on the recorded phone call, he seriously doubted the two women wouldn't find a way to communicate. He also doubted Seidel would be on the next train, despite the evidence that she'd tried to call 911.

He picked up his phone and dialed. "I need a couple of undercovers on Kimber Seidel. I'm hoping she'll lead us to her sister." Colin passed along Kimber's address. After he hung up, he turned to Derrick, his partner. "Did you check with the front desk about Tessa's statement?"

"Yeah. No sign of it."

As Colin had suspected.

"What do you think about the attempted call on her phone?" Derrick asked.

"It's hard to say. It could be that she didn't mean to kill Juliet Clark and had a moment of remorse before she realized the victim wasn't going to make it." Colin shrugged. "Or she could have tried to call to throw us off."

"Maybe." Derrick passed Colin a file. "Also, the financials just came in. It shows multiple charges last night and this morning. A taxi in the Hamptons. Then this morning, there were two charges for Uber. The first was from Ian Sawyer's house in the Hamptons to the train station."

Excitement stirred. If Tessa was using her credit card and ride shares, she'd be easy to track. "Can you track down Ian's house? I need the locals to check it out to make sure Seidel isn't still there. And where was the second ride?"

"I already have the address. And the second ride was from the train station in the Hamptons to the Walgreens in Southampton."

"Anything after that?" Colin asked.

"There were some charges at various

stores in the area, but nothing else for transportation. And the place she was dropped off is a good six miles from Ian Sawyer's place." Derrick leaned back in his chair. "It's not likely that she walked it."

"Someone has to be helping her, then." But who?

"I'll ask the local police to check out Ian's place and see if they can also get us the traffic cam footage for the area where she was shopping."

"Thanks." Colin tapped his finger on the arm of his office chair. "You keep trying to track her movements forward. I'll try to find her through her friends and family."

"What about the victim? Have you found anything that connects her to Tessa?"

"No, but in the entertainment world, everyone crosses paths eventually."

"That may be." Derrick cocked his head to one side and stroked his beard. "But crossing paths is a lot different from murdering someone."

"My guess is there's a cheating boyfriend somewhere in the middle of this," Colin said. Jealousy could be a powerful motivator to make someone act irrationally, even to the point of committing murder.

"I haven't found any common numbers in their phone records," Derrick said.

"Then one of them must have a second phone."

"I'll keep looking, but maybe the sister is right. Maybe Seidel is just a witness, not the killer."

Colin stiffened, and the need to defend himself rose inside him. "If she's innocent, why hasn't she come forward?"

"I have no idea, but my guess is she's scared."

That was what Kimber had said, but Colin wasn't buying it. Nor was he buying her story that Tessa had come to the police station last night.

"In our business, we need more than guesses. We need evidence," Colin said. "And if she were so innocent, I don't know why she would have dumped her jacket upstairs before sneaking out of the building."

"That has me curious too," Derrick said.

Colin gestured toward Derrick's phone. "Let me know what you find out from the Hamptons PD. Until we find Tessa, we aren't going to find the answers we need."

"Got it." Derrick picked up his phone and dialed.

Colin turned back to his computer. No common phone numbers. There had to be a connection between the two women somewhere. And he was determined to find it.

Chapter 12

Parker settled on the couch beside the fireplace and opened a new document. He'd briefly considered modifying the play he'd already started, but at this point, a blank page might work to his advantage. No expectations, no concern about what the investors might think. Just him and Tessa and her story.

Tessa walked in from the kitchen with an ice-cream bar in her hand and held it up. "Do you want one?"

Parker shook his head. "Maybe later, after I get the first bit written."

"Okay, but you're missing out." She sat on the love seat across from him and stretched her legs out on the cushion beside her. "Where do you want to start?"

"How about why you were at the studio last night."

"That's easy. One of the designers Greta works with was providing a few pieces for

Ian's show. Greta said I had to get them there last night."

"Is this a usual occurrence for you?"

"Kind of." She took a bite of her ice cream, taking a moment to eat it before she continued. "I mean, I'm constantly carrying clothes around the city for one reason or another, but having to drop something off that late at night isn't common."

"Were they supposed to be shooting last night?"

"No. That's why I wanted to wait until morning, but Greta said I had to make the delivery before eleven." She shook her head. "Then when I arrived, the wardrobe manager wasn't even there."

"But she was supposed to be?"

"That's what Greta said." Tessa held up her ice cream and shook her head. "I really hope Greta doesn't fire me for disappearing."

"I'm sure Kimber will think to let her know, and Greta will understand."

"I hope so."

Parker jotted down notes of everything she'd told him so far, including her concern about losing her job. "What did you do when you got there and found out that the wardrobe person wasn't there to take delivery?"

"I tried calling Greta, but she didn't answer. She went to a play that night, so my guess is that it wasn't over yet, or she hadn't turned her phone back on," Tessa said. "That's why I called Ian. He gave me the code to his dressing room so I could drop off the clothes."

Parker typed up some more notes. "Okay, so obviously, someone else was there when you arrived. Otherwise, the woman wouldn't have ended up dead."

"Yeah. I heard some people arguing when I first got off the elevator."

Parker looked up from his laptop. "You didn't mention that before."

"I didn't?" Tessa furrowed her brow. "I'm sorry. I can't remember what I told you, what I told Kimber, and what I've blocked out."

Logically, Parker understood how stress could affect a person's memory, but he'd never witnessed it firsthand in quite this way before. "What exactly did you hear?" Hoping to jog her memory, he added, "Men, women? Could you tell how many voices? Did you see any of them? Could you hear what they were saying?"

Tessa held up her half-eaten ice cream. "Slow down. One question at a time."

"Okay, let's start with what you heard,"

Parker said. "I want every detail you can give me."

Tessa took another bite of ice cream. "Are you sure you want me to go through every detail?"

"Last I checked, neither of us has any plans."

"Good point."

Brandon slowed his steps when he approached the jewelry store down the street from his apartment. The display had changed several times since he'd moved to New York last February, but recently, an engagement ring in the center display had caught his attention.

A brisk breeze ruffled his hair that was in need of a trim. He couldn't explain how he kept visualizing that ring on Kimber's finger after only six months together, but all too easily, he could imagine what it would be like to share his life with her beyond what they had now. Whether she was ready to move to the next step in their relationship, he wasn't sure. And he definitely didn't look forward to the potential backlash an engagement could cause at work. Mary and Regina already believed he'd started dating Kimber because of the size of her publishing contract. He had no idea what Amelia would think if she learned he was thinking about marriage, but if he had his way, that ring would be on Kimber's finger come Christmas.

He turned the corner and did his customary glance around the area. Pumpkins and illuminated skeletons glowed in the windows of the Italian restaurant down the street from his building. A family of tourists stood on the opposite corner, the dad staring at his phone as though trying to figure out which direction to go. Hovering a short distance from them, a man leaned against the wall of the building across from Brandon's.

Brandon's senses heightened. The man's keen awareness of his surroundings matched Brandon's; the slight bulge beneath the man's jacket suggested he was armed. Criminal or cop? Brandon wasn't entirely sure.

He forced his gaze away from the man and crossed the street toward him. When he reached the side where the man still stood, he continued past and entered the pizza place just beyond him. With no specific dinner plans, Brandon ordered several slices of pizza, enough to feed him and Kimber and some extra for Tessa. Even though she would undoubtedly miss dinner with them, it would be best to make it look like they expected to see her tonight.

With food in hand, he walked back outside. The man he'd noticed remained where he'd been when Brandon had entered the pizza place, and from this angle, there was no doubt. He was definitely armed. Unfortunately, nothing in his countenance indicated whether he was a cop on a stakeout or someone waiting to do something illegal.

Brandon passed him and reached the corner. When the light changed to green, he crossed the street and scanned the area in front of his building. The sidewalk was busy with people walking by. A single person remained stationary on his side of the street, the woman standing beside the entrance to the deli next door. Her purse hung across her body, and her hand rested on top of it, the zipper slightly open. If Brandon was right, she was a cop and the man across the street was her partner.

Brandon walked into his building and bypassed the crowd waiting for the elevator. Today, he'd rather not hang out in an open lobby when it would likely take two loads to get everyone to their respective floors.

He walked up the eight flights to his apartment.

Trudy, the middle-aged neighbor who

lived between him and Kimber, opened her door as he passed.

"Hey, Trudy." He tilted his head toward the front of the building. "Any idea why the cops are staking our place out?"

"Probably watching out for Kimber to see if she'll lead them to Tessa."

"Did she tell you what happened?"

"No, but Rafi called me."

Brandon should have known. Trudy might have retired from the FBI years ago, but she was still very much plugged in to everything happening in her corner of New York.

"What do you think?" Brandon asked. "Should I tell Kimber or hope she doesn't notice?"

"I'd tell her." Trudy gave him a sly smile. "And after you two finish your pizza, I think you should go for a nice walk and see if they follow."

The corners of Brandon's lips twitched up. "It is nice out."

"And after everything that's happened today, it would be good for Kimber to unwind a bit."

Brandon cocked an eyebrow. "Even if it means being followed by the police?"

"Even then." She took a step back. "And maybe if you're lucky, the spice cake I'm making will be done by the time you get back."

Brandon grinned. "I like the way you think." He also knew that Trudy baked both for the love of it and to make sure they would stop by and keep her informed of their day-to-day activities. "We'll stop by later."

Trudy disappeared into her apartment, and Brandon continued to Kimber's. He knocked on the door.

She opened it and looked down at the pizza in his hand. "I guess I don't have to worry about figuring out what to order for dinner."

"Picking this up was a last-minute decision." Brandon leaned in and greeted her with a kiss. "But Trudy invited us over for dessert after our walk."

"I'm not sure if I'm up for going out tonight."

"I know it's been a rough day." Brandon set the pizza on the serving bar that separated her kitchen from the living room. Then he slipped his arms around her. "I'm sorry about that, but I kind of want to see if the cops outside follow us when we leave. Or more specifically, if they follow you."

"The police are watching me?"

"Detective Murray probably put a couple

of undercover cops downstairs to see if you would lead them to Tessa."

"I really don't like him."

"You don't have to like him," Brandon said. "But we need to figure out how to work around him. Did you have any luck with Rafi?"

"I haven't heard from him yet, but he said he's going to put in a request for the surveillance feed and sign-in log for the studio and also get us the police report."

"It's a start." Brandon sat at the kitchen counter. "Come on. Let's eat before the pizza gets cold."

Kimber took the seat beside him. "Rafi also suggested I go undercover at the studio to do some poking around."

Kimber poking around where there was an unsolved murder and when the police were watching her? Brandon's protective instincts kicked in. "I don't love that idea."

"It may be the only way to find who really killed that woman."

"Yes, but having you in there without backup isn't a great plan." And Brandon didn't particularly trust anyone else to be her backup.

"Rafi was hoping you could figure out a way to go undercover with me, but I don't know how you can swing that without taking leave from your current job." Kimber held up her slice of pizza. "I still need to figure out how to get myself into the studio without raising suspicions."

Brandon's conversation with Patricia pressed into his thoughts. "Actually, I may have an idea. What do you say we head over to Ian's after dinner? We can see if the police follow us, and we can also ask about getting one or both of us a position to ask around without raising suspicions."

Kimber nodded. "The sooner we put this in motion, the better."

"I agree."

CHAPTER 13

Tessa had never considered herself a good storyteller, but with Parker asking simple questions, the details of last night were becoming vivid in her mind — a little too vivid.

"So that's when you lost your phone?" Parker looked up from his laptop and propped a foot on the coffee table. "When the guy grabbed you?"

Sitting on the couch beside him, Tessa nodded. "I was trying to call 911."

"You were trying to, or you did?" Parker asked. "Did the call actually go through?"

Tessa closed her eyes for a second. "I don't think so, but the screen was still open. If the guy chasing me didn't clear it, it should show that I was dialing 911."

"That's good. Hopefully, the police will see that and put it on record that you tried to call for help."

"Now you're sounding like a defense attorney." And Tessa was starting to wonder if she should start researching how to find a good one. Not that she had access to the internet at the moment, not without borrowing Parker's phone or laptop.

"I'm just thinking about how these types of stories usually play out." Parker finished typing something before he looked up at her. "These are the types of details that can help show intent. Besides the fact that you didn't know the victim, you trying to call 911 is consistent with what a normal person would do when coming across the victim of a crime."

"I didn't even realize she was a victim when I first went into the office," Tessa admitted. "I was just trying to see if there was something I could do to help."

"Again, that's a normal response."

The rush of adrenaline she'd experienced last night resurfaced. Had it really been last night when she'd gone from a woman who had everything she wanted at her fingertips to a runaway with no idea what her future would hold? She clasped her hands together. "Nothing about my life feels normal right now."

Parker lowered his foot and set his laptop on the coffee table before he straightened and faced her. "I guess you don't want me to tell you that feeling that way is normal, huh?"

She cocked an eyebrow. "Not particularly."

"What if I tell you I'm thinking about taking a break to make some hot chocolate?"

Take a break and spend time not thinking about the mess her life had become? That was exactly what she needed. A wave of appreciation flowed through her, and she managed a small smile. "Then I'd say we should go out and sit by the firepit. It'll make this all feel more like a vacation instead of an escape."

Parker returned her smile. "We can do that." He stood and walked into the kitchen.

Tessa followed him. "I know I've already asked you this, but why are you being so nice to me?"

He retrieved a kettle from a cabinet and filled it with water. "Have you ever considered that I'm just a nice guy?" He turned on the stove and set the kettle on the burner.

"I know a lot of guys, but unfortunately, most people in my world are only nice when they want something."

"Then you don't know the right people."

"Maybe that's true." Tessa considered her usual interactions. "And there are a lot of exceptions. Your uncle is one of them. He has been an amazing friend to my sister."

"How did they meet?" Parker asked. He retrieved two mugs from a cabinet. "My uncle tends to be pretty selective when it comes to his inner circle, and Kimber has definitely claimed that status."

"It was rather comical actually." Tessa smiled at the memory. "Kimber's publisher wanted her to build up a bigger social media presence, so I took her to Madison Peters's birthday party at the Met."

"The actress?"

"Yeah. My boss, Greta, suggested we give Kimber a head start on her social media by putting her in the same space as a lot of people with big followings."

"Uncle Ian isn't usually the type to jump in if he knows someone is trying to use him to build up their own name."

"You're right." Tessa smiled. "I'd just suggested that I take some photos of Kimber with some of the people at the party to do just that when your uncle showed up. We didn't even see him behind Kimber, but Kimber said something about how it didn't feel right to use people that way. Then your uncle came up and introduced himself."

"Now, that makes a lot more sense." Parker scooped hot chocolate into the mugs.

"Uncle Ian is far more likely to offer help when someone isn't trying to take advantage."

"You're telling me. He spent the whole night introducing Kimber to everyone at the party," Tessa said. "He really helped her launch her social media campaign."

"It's obvious that she's become close to both my uncle and my aunt."

"They're good people," Tessa said. "Ian signed with my boss shortly after we first met him. He's been a dream client for Greta."

Steam rose from the kettle, and Parker poured the hot water into the mugs. "Sounds like everyone came out on top after Uncle Ian met you."

Tessa couldn't help but smile. "I like to think so."

Parker stirred the two cups of hot chocolate and handed one to Tessa. "Here you go. Now we can go outside and pretend we're on a date."

Her eyes widened. "A date?"

"Yeah." Parker took her hand in his, a tingle rippling over her skin. He took a step closer, and his gaze lowered to hers. "You know, two people spending time together for no other reason than to get to know each other?"

Her heartbeat quickened, and for a moment, she lost herself in his gaze. This man was too good to be true, but she couldn't deny that she wanted to know him better. She swallowed before she attempted to respond. "When you put it that way, let's go on a date."

Parker grinned and leaned forward to brush a kiss across her cheek. "I thought you'd never ask."

Kimber hadn't considered what she wanted to write next, but one way or another, she needed to include a television studio in her story — assuming Ian could help her gain permission to work behind the scenes for the next week or two.

She could also include what it felt like to be tailed by the police. Brandon's and Trudy's suspicions that she was their person of interest had proved correct. She and Brandon had barely walked out of the building when the woman she'd noticed earlier had abandoned her spot and fallen in behind her and Brandon on the sidewalk. She suspected the female cop and her partner were stationed outside Ian's building at this very moment.

Brandon knocked on Ian's door. "Does it still feel weird to you that we're on Ian's friends-and-family list for his building?"

"A little." Admittedly, the first time she met Ian, she'd been awestruck, but it hadn't taken long for her to see him as a friend rather than a movie star. "The stranger thing is trying to pretend we don't know him very well to keep Haseeb from trying to use him in my social media all the time."

"Yeah, marketing can get pretty demanding."

Phoebe opened the door. "Come on in." She ushered them inside. "Ian's in the kitchen."

Kimber checked her watch. It was already after seven. "Are we catching you at dinnertime?"

"No. Ian has his heart set on pumpkin bars for dessert," Phoebe said. "He just finished making the cream cheese icing."

They walked into the kitchen at the exact moment Ian lifted an icing-covered spoon to his lips.

"Ian! Stop eating the icing," Phoebe said.

He gestured to the pan of pumpkin bars, dollops of icing evenly spread on top. "I already put the icing on." He gave a boyish grin. "Sort of."

Phoebe just shook her head and extended her hand toward him. "And this is what I've had to live with for the past twenty-five years."

Ian scraped his spoon along the inside of the icing bowl, then held it out to Phoebe. "I'll share." He cast an apologetic glance at Kimber and Brandon. "I'd offer to share with you, too, but Phoebe's the one I have to live with."

"That's okay," Kimber said. "We're actually here to ask for a different kind of favor."

Phoebe took the spoon from Ian. "How about you three go into the living room while I finish icing these? Then everyone can have their icing on top of a pumpkin bar."

Ian leaned in and kissed Phoebe's cheek. "I love you."

Phoebe rolled her eyes, but her lips twitched into the beginnings of a smile. "I love you too." She waved toward the doorway leading to the living room. "You go talk with Kimber and Brandon. I'll be out in a minute."

"Yes, dear." Ian took them into the living room. After everyone sat down, he asked, "So, what is it I can do for you?"

"Is there any way you'd be able to get me access to the studio to do some research for my next book?" Kimber asked. "I really need to get a feel for what it's like to be behind the scenes."

Ian raised his eyebrows. "You're going to write about a TV show in your next book?"

Kimber supposed she should maintain her cover despite Ian's earlier observations about her and Brandon being more than they seemed, but she needed his help, and the more involved Ian was, the more likely it would be that she'd succeed. "Officially, I want access to the studio to do research."

"And unofficially?" Ian asked.

Kimber glanced at Brandon, silently asking for his approval to bring Ian into their need-to-know circle.

Brandon gave a subtle nod.

She turned her attention back to Ian. "I want to see if I can figure out who had motive to kill Juliet Clark."

Ian rubbed his chin. "I know you want to help your sister, but shouldn't we let the authorities do their job and see what they come up with?"

"I can't sit by and do nothing," Kimber insisted. "Not when there's a chance the police are trying to prove Tessa guilty instead of finding the real killer."

Brandon gave Kimber's knee a squeeze. "Even though I'm not thrilled with Kimber poking around, she can take care of herself."

Kimber put her hand on Brandon's, appreciating his support. "Ian, I wouldn't ask if I were sure the police could find the truth on their own."

Ian fell silent for a moment, as though pondering. Then he focused on Kimber again. "How would you feel about a temporary job that would give you access to the studio?"

"What do you have in mind?"

"My personal assistant stayed behind in LA when we moved here. She still takes care of all my fan mail and my calendar, but it would be easy to justify bringing on a second assistant to help me on set."

Brandon leaned forward. "That actually could work really well." He took her hand. "It would give you easy access to the different production assistants as well as the actors."

Another undercover assignment. Kimber fought back a sigh. "I guess since no one knows I'm an author yet, that would work."

"And it will save you from endless questions about how you got an agent, how to break into the book business, and everything else that goes with getting a publishing deal," Ian said.

"I wouldn't think people working in the TV industry would focus on publishing."

"You'd be surprised," Ian said. "Phoebe

has deliberately kept her writing journey private because of what she's seen me experience with people hoping I would give them a leg up in their acting careers."

"If you think this would be my best entrance into your world, I'd love to be your new assistant."

"Great. I'll text you the call sheet for the rest of the week." Ian rubbed his hands together. "This will be fun. I've never helped with solving a real-life murder before."

Brandon released Kimber's hand and straightened. "Ian, we appreciate you getting Kimber in the door, but we don't want you to involve yourself." Brandon tilted his head toward Kimber. "Kimber has extensive martial-arts training. Your experience in protecting yourself is a bit more limited."

"Don't worry. All I plan to do is keep my ears open." He waved in Kimber's direction. "Kimber can do the heavy lifting."

Phoebe entered the living room holding a plate of pumpkin bars and a stack of napkins. "What did I miss?"

Ian gestured to Kimber. "Meet my new personal assistant."

"Kimber?" Phoebe stopped in the middle of the living room. "Are you sure you have time for this?"

"If my editor asks, we're calling this research."

"And if anyone else asks, she's my new assistant," Ian added.

"Great." Phoebe handed everyone a napkin and let them take a pumpkin bar off the plate. As soon as she settled beside Ian, she said, "Your first job is to take the extra pumpkin bars home with you."

"What?" Ian shot his wife an indignant look. "We made those so I could snack on them."

"Yes, and your new assistant can put the extras in her freezer and bring you one every day to keep you from making yourself sick on them."

"One a day? How about three, one with each meal?"

"Two. That's my final offer."

"Fine."

Brandon leaned closer to Kimber and whispered, "I think you're going to have your work cut out for you."

Kimber couldn't help but laugh. "In more ways than one."

Chapter 14

Parker sat in the Adirondack chair beside Tessa, the flames in the firepit casting a warm glow over the circle surrounding it. A comfortable silence had settled between them, but Parker couldn't deny that he enjoyed knowing he wasn't alone. He'd spent far too much time in his own company lately.

"I forgot how nice it is to just sit still for a while," Tessa said.

"With your job, I doubt you have time for this sort of thing very often."

"No, I don't. It seems Greta always has a client who needs some extra help. And then there's the travel."

An unexpected pang of disappointment surfaced. "You travel a lot?"

She nodded. "Especially in the spring. Fashion week, the awards shows. Everything kind of runs together." She sighed. "I should be helping get Greta ready to fly to LA next week. I really hope she doesn't have to replace me."

"Considering why you're in this situation, I'm sure she'll hold your job for you."

"I hope you're right, but I can't help but wonder if some temp will prove they can do the job as well as me."

"I doubt that's going to happen." Parker shouldn't pry, but he couldn't help it. "So is your schedule the reason you don't have a boyfriend? Because you're too busy?"

"How did you know I don't have a boyfriend?" Tessa asked. "Is it that obvious?"

Parker caught a hint of insecurity in her questions, though where it came from, he had no idea. Tessa was beautiful, intelligent, quick-witted, and kind. The only reason he could imagine she didn't have a boyfriend was that she didn't want one.

"Your sister actually told me you weren't dating anyone during our writers' retreat," Parker said. "She mentioned that one of her old coworkers has been crushing on you for a while now, but you never have time to go out with him." Now that he spoke the words, he wasn't sure how he felt about Kimber trying to set Tessa up with someone else.

"Kimber must have been talking about Mark." She shrugged. "He's sweet, but I don't want to go out with someone in the CIA."

"The CIA?" Kimber had never mentioned having that particular background. Which was odd since she wrote thrillers.

Tessa lifted her hand to her mouth. "I'm sorry. I shouldn't have said that."

"Why?"

She let out a sigh. "Can I trust you?"

"Of course." Parker held out both arms. "In case you haven't noticed, you are staying with me alone in the woods. I think trust between us is implied at this point."

"True." She drew in a deep breath and let it out in a rush. "So my sister has this big publishing contract."

"With Monroe Publishing. I know."

Tessa gripped the arms of her chair. "Well, what most people don't know is that right after she signed with Monroe, she quit her job with the CIA."

"Why hide that?" A dozen possibilities raced through his overactive brain. "Was she undercover?"

"No. And I had the same question," Tessa said. "According to Kimber, the agency asked her not to share her background because they didn't want me or Kimber to become a target."

His imagination hadn't stretched quite

that far. "They think some terrorist organization might try to take you hostage or something?"

"Something like that." Tessa shook her head. "Sounds crazy, huh?"

"Yeah, but lots of crazy stuff happens in the world."

"I guess so. It's weird though," Tessa said. "Half the time, when we go out with my friends, Kimber doesn't even want me to mention that we're sisters."

"Why not?"

"Because my last name isn't Frost."

So Kimber was former CIA, and she was using a pen name. Interesting. "What is your last name?"

Tessa bit her lip.

"You work for my uncle's agent. It wouldn't be hard for me to find out."

"I guess that's true." She let out a sigh. "Seidel. My last name is Seidel."

Unable to resist, Parker took her hand. "I think I like getting to know you better."

She lifted her eyebrows. "You think?"

Parker smiled. "Okay, I know."

Something thumped in an erratic rhythm, like footsteps on glass. Tessa startled from her semiconscious state to fully awake and sat up in bed before she looked around. It took her a moment to remember where she was — a cabin in the woods, isolated and alone. But she wasn't alone. Parker was here.

The thumping continued, a scratching sound accompanying it. Shadows played over the room, and it took Tessa another moment to recognize what was causing them: tree branches swaying beneath the moonlight and hitting against the window.

Tessa pressed her hand against her racing heart. Her entire body vibrated with nerves, and she pushed out of bed. No way would she be able to get back to sleep until her emotions settled.

The chill in the air sent a shiver through her, and she grabbed Parker's sweatshirt off the trunk at the end of the bed, where she'd left it.

After pulling it on, she donned a pair of socks and headed to the living room. To her surprise, the light was on, and a fire burned in the fireplace.

Parker's laptop lay on the coffee table, the screen illuminated, but Parker wasn't anywhere to be seen.

A few seconds later, he appeared in the doorway leading to the kitchen, a mug in his hand. He spotted her and jumped. "Whoa." Dark liquid sloshed over the rim of the cup. "I thought you were sleeping."

"I was. I tried anyway." She pointed at the spill on the floor. "Sorry. I didn't mean to startle you."

"It's not your fault." He stepped back into the kitchen and returned with paper towels. He leaned down and mopped up the spill. "What time is it anyway?"

Tessa shrugged. "I have no idea."

Parker discarded the paper towel in the trash and pulled out his phone. "It's already four?"

Tessa took in his clothes — jeans and a long-sleeved shirt, the same clothes he'd been wearing when she'd gone to bed hours ago. "Have you been up all night?"

"Yeah." He took a sip of his drink and set it on the coffee table.

She lifted her eyebrows. "Please tell me you aren't drinking coffee at four in the morning."

"I'm not." He gave her a sheepish look. "I'm drinking hot chocolate."

"That's not likely to help you sleep either."

"Yeah, but I got on a roll, and I don't want to lose my momentum until I hit a good stopping place."

And she'd just interrupted him. "I'm sorry. I should leave you to it."

"No, it's okay." He sat on the edge of the

sofa. "In fact, I'd love your help for a minute, if you don't mind."

"What do you want my help with?" Tessa sat beside him. "I'm not a writer."

"No, but I remembered you talking about hearing a man and a woman arguing." Parker picked up his laptop and rested it on his thighs. "What happened to the man?"

"My guess is he's the guy who grabbed me." She thought for a moment. "Or he could have been the guy in the elevator."

"What guy in the elevator?" Parker looked at her. "You didn't mention that."

"It was when I was trying to find a place to put the clothes." At least, she was pretty sure that was when she'd tried to get the man's help. "He was heading for the elevator, and I tried to get his attention, but I wasn't fast enough."

Parker typed something on his computer before he asked, "What did he look like?"

"I barely caught a glimpse of him. He had dark-brown hair, and he was wearing casual clothes. I'm pretty sure his shirt was dark colored."

"Tall, short? Thin, heavy-set?"

"Average for both."

"Age?"

"I don't know." Tessa worked in an industry where people constantly changed their appearance to look older or younger than they actually were. Taking her best guess, she said, "Maybe late thirties, early forties."

"And how soon did that happen before you found the murder victim?"

Judging time was even harder than guessing someone's age. "Five minutes. Maybe ten."

"I'll add that in." He tapped on his keyboard.

Tessa yawned.

"You look like you could use some more sleep," he said.

"I know, but I'm afraid if I try to close my eyes, I'll just wake up to another nightmare."

"Do you want to lie down out here?" Parker suggested. He patted the cushion between them. "You can have the couch. I'll move over to the love seat."

"How much longer are you going to stay up?"

"I don't know, but I'll send what I've got so far to Uncle Ian in the next hour or two," he said. "I want to make sure he gets these pages before he leaves for work."

The prospect of having someone nearby brought comfort, but she asked, "Are you sure you don't mind my being out here?"

"It's fine."

She stood. "Okay, I'm going to get a pillow and a blanket."

"Do you want me to make you a cup of hot chocolate?" Parker asked.

"No, thanks." She tilted her head toward the couch. "I'm still hoping to get some sleep tonight."

CHAPTER 15

The predawn light peeked through the window as Parker sent his first few scenes to his uncle. He hadn't written through the night in longer than he could remember, but after talking to Tessa last night, he couldn't seem to stop.

He set his laptop aside and rubbed his eyes. Tessa had fallen asleep within minutes of settling onto the couch, one of her arms raised above her head as though trying to keep her hair out of her eyes. Her face was free of makeup, but the lack didn't make her any less beautiful. He almost felt guilty that her misfortune had thrown her into his world. But only almost guilty.

He plugged his laptop in to charge.

Tessa stirred, and her eyes fluttered open. "You're still here."

"Yeah, I was just heading to bed."

She propped herself on one elbow. "Maybe I'll try to sleep in bed for a while too."

"That would probably be more comfortable than the couch."

"Actually, it wasn't too bad." She swung her legs over the edge and stood. "Of course, I'm a few inches shorter than you."

"Yeah, but I've spent a few nights crashing on it anyway."

Tessa glanced out the window. "Is the sun coming up?"

"It's about to."

"I haven't seen a sunrise in forever." She wrapped the blanket around her and crossed to the window.

Parker's desire to go to bed took a back seat to sharing the sunrise with a fascinating woman. "Want to go out front to watch it?"

She nodded. "I'll grab my shoes."

He stepped into his shoes that he'd left by the door and put on his jacket.

Tessa walked back in, her blanket still wrapped around her.

He opened the door and waited for her to walk out first. Then he stepped into the brisk air.

"Oh my gosh." Tessa shivered. "It's freezing."

"Here." Parker stepped behind her and put his hands on her arms. Then he rubbed his hands up and down to help warm her.

"Thanks."

He started to lower his hands, but then something incredible happened. Tessa leaned back against him, her back against his chest. What was he to do but slip his arms around her waist and enjoy the warmth of the moment?

They stood there in silence for several minutes.

Then Tessa lifted her hand and pointed. "There it is."

Parker lifted his gaze to the spot where the first rays of sunlight now filtered through the trees. "It's beautiful."

"It really is." Tessa remained in place for a minute longer. Then she stepped free of his embrace. "Come on. We both need to get some sleep, especially you."

"Yeah, I guess so." But he wouldn't have minded a few more minutes holding Tessa against him.

They walked back inside, and she stopped and looked up at him. "Do you think you'll wake up in time for us to have another date tonight?"

Parker didn't try to stop the smile that spread across his face. "I'll be sure of it."

"Good." She stepped toward her bedroom. "I'll see you later."

"Good night." Parker paused. "Or good

morning."

Tessa returned his smile. "Sweet dreams."

"You too."

Brandon hit the Pause button on his laptop and rubbed at his eyes. He really hated watching security feed. When he and Kimber had returned to Kimber's apartment after visiting Ian, the links for the studio security feed from the night of the murder had been in both his and Kimber's inboxes along with a list of employees who were authorized to be on the sixteenth floor.

Kimber had taken the task of reviewing the personnel list, while Brandon had made a list of his own, noting every person who had come in or out of the building during the hours before and after Juliet Clark was killed.

On the couch beside him, Kimber reached out and put her hand on his neck, rubbing at the tense muscles there. "Do you want me to take over for a while?"

"No, it's okay." Brandon let his head fall forward to give Kimber better access to his neck. "I don't have much left."

"See anything worth noting?"

"Not really. I can see when Tessa arrived and when she left, but both are in the window for the time of death."

"So all that does is prove she was there."

"Yes." Brandon didn't mention the panicked look on Tessa's face when she'd exited the building.

"Is there anything that can prove Tessa's innocence?"

"Nothing so far, but she wasn't the only person who was still in the building when Juliet was killed." Playing devil's advocate, Brandon added, "The timing of when Tessa was in the building lines up with the window of the murder, and they know she was on the studio's floor, so at this point, the police have reason to list her as a primary suspect."

"Even if she dialed 911?" Kimber shook her head. "That's really pushing it."

"The 911 call didn't go through before the guard showed up. We only have her word that she was trying to make the call."

"Yes, but when I was at the police station today, I helped Detective Murray unlock Tessa's phone. The nine and first one had already been dialed when Tessa dropped her phone."

"I didn't see that in the police file."

"Maybe he hasn't updated it yet."

"Maybe." Or maybe the detective was leaving out information that would paint his prime suspect in an innocent light. Brandon held up his hand. "Obviously, I don't think it's feasible that the murder happened when Tessa was in the victim's office, but unfortunately, it is possible."

"It might be possible if Tessa were a cold-blooded killer, but she isn't." Kimber set her laptop aside. "And she didn't even know the woman who was killed."

"Let's hope Murray doesn't manage to find a connection between them."

"He not only needs to find a connection, but a connection that would also cause enough conflict to motivate violence." Kimber lifted both hands. "Tessa has a stable job, so robbery wouldn't be a motive. She gets along with everyone, so the likelihood of her killing someone in a fit of rage certainly doesn't fit. She doesn't even have a boyfriend, so the whole killing someone over a man doesn't fly."

Brandon furrowed his brow. "You bring up an interesting point though. Why would someone want Juliet Clark dead?"

"I don't know, but that's on the top of my list of questions when I get to the studio tomorrow."

"Maybe you should ease into that sort of question," Brandon suggested. "Finding out who her friends are and if she was dating someone would help a lot."

Kimber nodded. "Fingers crossed that I can find someone who knows the answers."

Chapter 16

Kimber stifled a yawn and slid into the back of the car where Ian waited, his driver, David, already behind the wheel. She shouldn't have stayed up so late studying the cast and crew bios, but she didn't want to go to the studio unprepared.

"Good morning," Ian said.

"Morning." Kimber clicked her seat belt into place. "You know, I really appreciate you picking me up, but you didn't have to."

"Can't have my new assistant being late for her first day on the job." Ian handed her a paper coffee cup with a heat guard encircling it. "I picked you up a hot chocolate on my way."

Kimber accepted the offering and narrowed her eyes. "Are you trying to bribe me?"

"I just think it wouldn't hurt for you to accidentally bring another pumpkin bar tomorrow."

Kimber laughed. “You’re trying to get me in trouble with your wife.”

“Not exactly.” Ian lowered his voice. “And I think both of us know how to keep secrets.”

“That’s true, but I’m not bringing you an extra pumpkin bar.”

“It’s official.” Ian huffed out a breath. “Everyone is more afraid of my wife than they are of me.”

“It’s not that I’m more afraid of her,” Kimber corrected. “I just know she wants what’s best for you.”

Ian shot her an indignant look. “Limiting my sweets is not what’s best for me.”

“I’ll let you two argue about that.”

Resigned, Ian pulled several pages out of his soft-sided briefcase and passed them to her. “I do have something for you.”

“What’s this?”

“Pages from my nephew’s next play,” Ian said. “I thought you might be willing to read through them and give him some feedback.”

“If you want, I’d be happy to, but Brandon is better at editing than I am.”

“Brandon might want to take a look at them too.”

Kimber started skimming the first page. It took a moment for her to catch on. The pages from Ian’s nephew weren’t just scenes from a play. They were a recounting of Tessa's experience.

Conscientious of the driver in the front seat, Kimber asked, "Is this based on a true story?"

"It is." Ian wiggled his eyebrows. "I thought maybe with your help, we could coauthor this particular play. That is, if you wouldn't mind drafting up what you think the next scene should be."

The next scene, or rather, the details of their investigation.

"I've never written a play before, but I'd love the chance to try." And bless Parker for coming up with a way for them to communicate during the investigation.

"Great. When I'm on set, feel free to use my dressing room any time you need a little privacy."

"Thanks, but I have a feeling today is going to be spent primarily trying to learn everyone's names."

"I can help you with that," Ian said. "Although, I'll likely need you to help me with my lines too. The writers on this show are notorious for making last-minute changes."

"I'm happy to help wherever I can."

"Good. Now about those pumpkin bars . . ."

Kimber laughed. "Don't push your luck."

The driver pulled up in front of the studio. "Do you know what time you want to be picked up tonight?"

"Not yet, but one of us will call you," Ian said. "Speaking of which, I'll send you Kimber's number."

Kimber opened the door and waited for Ian to join her on the sidewalk.

"Thanks for the ride," she told David.

He nodded. "Have a good day."

"You too."

Ian led Kimber to the entrance. "You ready for this?"

Ready to go undercover again? Not really, but she straightened her shoulders and lifted her chin. "I'm as ready as I'm going to get."

"Great." Ian lowered his voice. "Let's go find a murderer."

Colin strode into his precinct, anticipation humming through him. This was the day. He could feel it. The murder at the studio was already trending on the news, and if he could make an arrest quickly, he'd finally be able to redeem himself after that nightmare of a trial last month. It was time the public associated his name with getting it right instead of getting it wrong.

Derrick already sat at his desk, his phone

to his ear. "You sure about that?" He paused and looked up at Colin. "Yeah, I'll tell him."

As soon as Derrick hung up, Colin asked, "Tell me what?"

"Just got the report on Kimber Seidel, aka Kimber Frost."

"And?" This really could be his day. "Did they find the sister?"

"No, but she did go out last night and again this morning."

Colin sat down and rolled his desk chair forward. "Where?"

"Last night, she visited the building where Ian Sawyer lives." Derrick took a sip of his coffee. "One of our undercovers checked with the doorman. Turns out, she and her boyfriend are both on the close-friends-and-family list."

"Meaning, they can come and go into that building whenever they want."

"Yep."

Interesting. This case was getting more high-profile by the minute. That could be good. "Where did she go this morning?"

"Ian Sawyer picked her up, and then they went to the studio together."

"She's at the studio again?" He gripped the edge of his chair. "Why?"

"I don't know, but maybe it's worth chatting with her to find out."

"Yeah." Colin stood back up. "Maybe so. Any updates from the Hamptons on Tessa Seidel's movements?"

"The locals canvassed the area near where she was dropped off by her Uber yesterday," Derrick said. "She was spotted in several shops. Then she just disappeared."

"What about Ian Sawyer's place out there?"

"No one was home. The locals said they walked the perimeter and didn't see any signs of life," Derrick said. "One of the neighbors said they saw a man leaving an hour or so after Tessa was picked up."

"So a man at the house had a car, but Tessa took an Uber to the train station." Colin tapped his finger on his desk. "Interesting that he wouldn't just give her a ride."

Derrick frowned. "You think she wanted us to be able to track her?"

"If this guy is helping her, what better way to make it look like they aren't connected?" And if she was crafting a false trail, she must know there would be a reason for them to be looking for her.

"Maybe. Or maybe their schedules didn't line up." Derrick leaned back in his chair.

Though Colin hated to step away from such a promising suspect, he said, "Maybe it's time to look beyond Tessa Seidel for suspects." Colin lifted a hand. "After what happened with the Wyatt Harvey case, it wouldn't be a bad idea to show that we considered other possibilities."

Derrick shot him a look of disbelief. "The guard caught her standing over the body."

"Yes, but when we unlocked her phone, it was obvious she was trying to make a call. The numbers 9 and 1 had both been entered." Which was an odd tidbit that played in Seidel's favor.

Derrick held out both hands. "This wouldn't be the first time a killer called 911 to throw suspicion elsewhere."

"Yes, but why call and then run away?"

"Obviously, the guard spooked her." Derrick put his hand on a file on his desk. "And from the security feed, she's the only person who was on the floor at the time Juliet Clark was killed."

"Assuming no one used the stairs," Colin said. "Those doors are coded for entry into the studio. There's no way to be sure if someone with access couldn't have slipped out of there and hidden on another floor."

"If you want to follow that angle, go ahead."

Colin pushed back from his desk. "I will, but for now, I'm going to pay a visit to the studio to see what Kimber Seidel is doing there."

"Maybe I should come with you."

Though tempted to take backup with him, he shook his head. Time to divide and conquer. "You start running down other possible suspects. I think I can handle Kimber."

Chapter 17

Brandon had no doubt Kimber could handle herself, but they were a team. And like it or not, he had to trust his partner and focus on his own tasks.

This morning, he'd spent the better part of his time going through the last bits of security feed from the night of the murder. Best he could tell, there were a half dozen people from the studio who had exited after the majority of the others had left for the day. In addition to the victim, another production assistant had remained behind as well as the producer, the director, a video editor, a screenwriter, and one of the actors.

Brandon made a list, typing the names and positions in an email to Kimber. He then noted when each of them left. Unfortunately, with the exception of the victim, all the people on his list went down the elevator before Tessa arrived.

Though he hated sending Kimber bad news, he forwarded the latest information to her and sent her a quick text so she'd know to look at her email.

The sound of Regina's and Mary's voices carried to him, probably the two of them complaining about the promotions they didn't get last spring. It really was too bad Mary hadn't scored the job she'd wanted in London, although it was a bit of a toss-up as to which of the two women resented him more for taking positions they felt should have belonged to them.

"I'm sorry. There's just no way," Regina said.

"That's what I heard."

Brandon's phone chimed with an incoming text. Amelia. *My office. Now.*

He really wished Amelia would hire a new assistant. Or that HR would hire her one who could last more than a few days. Not that he could blame the last five for failing to keep up. Amelia could be a bit challenging at times, and Mary and Regina were known for sabotaging whoever took that position.

Brandon stepped out of his office.

Regina and Mary both stopped talking, waiting until he passed before Mary's whispered voice carried to him.

"I'm telling you, this might be the thing that finally gets him fired."

Great. Something else had upset Amelia, something he didn't know about.

He knocked on Amelia's open door.

"Come in." She looked up long enough to identify who had entered before looking back at her computer screen. "Close the door."

Brandon did as he was told.

"What is this about Phoebe Sawyer wanting you as her editor?"

"Sorry." Brandon had hoped Patricia wouldn't pursue that particular idea. "Patricia mentioned something about Phoebe wanting me, but I think it's mostly to do with me being honest with her," Brandon said. "She had a lot of people just tell her how good her manuscript was rather than offering useful feedback."

"I see." Amelia tapped her fingers on her desk.

Hoping to get her off this particular topic, he asked, "Are you considering making Phoebe an offer?"

"It's already in the works." She gestured toward her phone. "It was during negotiations that your name came up."

"Where do negotiations stand now?"

"Legal is working up the contract. The

manuscript is solid." Amelia leaned back in her chair. "Not Kimber Frost level, but with Ian Sawyer's name attached to the project, I think it will sell well enough."

Brandon tried to consider how Phoebe's unique situation would play out and how she would feel about using her husband's fame to create her own success. "Knowing Ian, he'll do everything he can to help his wife succeed." Brandon hesitated.

"I sense a 'but' coming."

"But Phoebe will want to earn her spot on her own merits."

"Which is exactly what Patricia said and why they're requesting you." Amelia tapped her fingers against her desk again. "This is highly unusual, but given the circumstances, I think it's best we work together."

"Work together on the edit?"

"Yes. You'll do the initial edit and work with Phoebe. Then I'll do a second sweep, and you can help Phoebe incorporate my suggestions."

Shocked that Amelia would even consider letting him be involved at that level, Brandon opened his mouth and closed it before he managed to find his voice. "That sounds great."

"I'll email you my initial notes. Then I

want you to put this at the top of your to-do list."

"Above getting you coffee and picking up your lunch orders?" Brandon asked.

"I'm supposed to be getting a new assistant tomorrow. Let's hope this one lasts longer than the last five."

"Oh, I am."

Kimber made her way to wardrobe less than ten minutes after her arrival at the studio. She'd located the clothing Tessa had left in Ian's dressing room and now carried it to the open doorway. She entered the room filled with racks of clothing and shelves of accessories, annoyed that no one was in sight.

Hangers scraped along a metal rod. Maybe the room wasn't empty after all.

"Hello?" Kimber said.

"Be right there." A woman stepped out from between two racks on the left side of the room, a dress draped over her arm. Her silver hair was cut short, and she couldn't have been more than an inch over five feet. She seemed to gather her strength before she asked, "What can I do for you?"

"Are you the costume manager?" Kimber asked.

"Yes." She hung the dress up at the front

of the nearest rack before offering her hand. "I'm Elena."

"Kimber." Kimber hung the clothing she carried on the nearest rack. "Ian asked me to bring these clothes to you. They were dropped off after you left a couple nights ago."

"Ian?" Elena furrowed her brow. "You work for him?"

"Yes, I'm his new assistant."

"He finally broke down and hired one." Elena nodded absently. "It's about time. That man has worked long and hard enough to have some help."

"I agree." Kimber took a closer look at the woman in front of her. Judging from the shadows beneath her eyes, she'd either not slept well recently or had been crying. When Elena sniffled, Kimber guessed it was the latter. "You look upset. I'm so sorry. You must have known the woman who was killed."

Elena pressed her lips together.

Acting on instinct, Kimber put her hand on Elena's arm. "I'm sure this has been so hard for everyone here."

Tears filled her eyes. "I still can't believe she's gone."

"Were you close?"

Elena nodded. "We used to eat lunch

together all the time."

"Do you have any idea who might have done this?"

"No. Juliet got along with everyone." Elena grabbed the edge of the hanging rack beside her as though needing the extra support to remain steady on her feet. "I didn't even know she was working late that night."

"So she wasn't the person who was supposed to take delivery of these clothes?"

"Are they the ones from Adam Hamilton?" Elena took a closer look. "How did you end up with them?"

"Apparently, you'd already left on Tuesday night when they were dropped off, so Greta Meyers's assistant asked Ian if she could leave them in his dressing room."

"Tuesday night?" Her eyes widened. "Was Ian here when Juliet was killed?"

"No. He was home, but Greta's assistant called and asked for his help." Hoping she wasn't pushing too hard, Kimber asked, "Did you know the clothing delivery was scheduled that night?"

Elena shook her head. "I was told it would come either Tuesday or Wednesday, but I had no idea someone was coming in after hours." A tear spilled onto her cheek. "Maybe if I'd known and stayed late, Juliet would still be —"

"Don't think like that." Kimber squeezed her arm. "What happened to Juliet wasn't your fault."

A woman in her mid-twenties entered the room, a clipboard in her hand. "Elena, do you have the new wardrobe for Allison?"

"Yes. Kimber just gave me the new delivery." Elena turned to the clothing rack and began sorting through the items Kimber had brought to her.

Kimber turned to the woman who had just arrived. Like Elena, she had that shell-shocked look of unexpected grief.

"Hi, I'm Kimber. I'm Ian's new assistant." Kimber offered her hand.

"Nicole. I'm a production assistant here."

"Hey, I heard about your friend Juliet. If there's anything I can do for you, please let me know."

"Thanks, but for now, I need to get the clothes delivered." Nicole took the clothes from Elena. "See you later."

Kimber stepped aside and watched her go. Two women who were clearly distraught with Juliet Clark's sudden death. Would the killer also show grief, or would the person responsible not care about the result of taking a woman's life?

Chapter 18

Tessa walked along the edge of the lake, the birds chirping, a squirrel scurrying up a nearby tree, and the water gently lapping against the dock. The scene was so peaceful and a little too quiet.

She could almost pretend she was out here all alone, except for one fact: She had a date with Parker — another date.

Just the thought of spending more time with him sent little butterflies fluttering inside her. Which didn't make any sense. Up until Tuesday night, she hadn't even known he existed.

In truth, she couldn't remember the last time she'd gone out with anyone unless it had had to do with work. Granted, she had offers often enough, but she didn't particularly want to date any models or actors who Greta represented. If things didn't work out, it would be too difficult.

Not that her situation wouldn't get complicated if she and Parker dated for real. His uncle was one of Greta's biggest clients and a friend of her sister's. That could most definitely get awkward if things went south. Not to mention, they were stuck together right now, and acting on her growing attraction would be far too awkward if Parker didn't feel the same way.

She shook that thought away. This whole situation was so out of the ordinary, and she had no idea what his life was like when he wasn't busy rescuing her. For all she knew, he could be dating a half dozen women, and she was simply one of them. Or he could plan to ignore her as soon as she was able to go back to her real life.

She really hoped that didn't happen.

She considered the possibility that she had formed an infatuation because of the unusual circumstances that had thrown them together, but she immediately discarded that idea. She might have endured a trauma unlike anything she'd ever experienced before, but she knew her own heart and mind. And she'd spent plenty of time in proximity to good-looking men. No, there was something different about Parker and the connection she felt to him.

Restless, she headed back inside the cabin. She hadn't heard from him since he'd gone to bed early this morning. That had been seven hours ago.

With little to do on her own without access to a phone or a computer, she'd taken the time to do her laundry, including Parker's T-shirt and sweatshirt she'd borrowed, but she hoped he'd let her hold on to them until they went back to New York. His T-shirt made the best pajamas, and his sweatshirt had quickly become her favorite outerwear.

A door down the hall opened. A moment later, the bathroom door shut. Finally, she would have someone to talk to.

Suspecting Parker would be ready for something to eat, she pulled out the box of pancake mix he'd picked up at the store. Even though she'd had a yogurt for breakfast, that had been hours ago, and she was ready for some comfort food. Pancakes would fit that bill. And bacon. She definitely needed bacon.

A quick search of the cabinets was all it took before she had the supplies needed for her intended lunch.

The shower turned on in the bathroom. With any luck, the food would be ready just in time for Parker to join her.

Kimber matched the names from Brandon's

email with the people she'd met. Nicole, the production assistant who had shared an office with Juliet Clark, had crossed paths with Kimber several times today, tears always close to the surface. From what Sheridan, the producer, had said, the two women had been close friends, and Nicole was struggling with the unexpected death. Kimber suspected the same was true for many at work today.

Eli, one of the camera operators, had wiped at his eyes more than once between takes. And several of the actors had messed up their lines, causing the director to restart the various scenes multiple times.

Already, Kimber had more notes in her phone than she'd thought humanly possible in a two-hour period.

With Ian currently on set, she had taken refuge in his dressing room to read through Brandon's email again and look over the first scenes of the play Parker had written.

Her phone rang. It was Rafi.

"Hey." Kimber lowered her voice. "Any luck on that report we were waiting on?"

"Just got it," Rafi said. "Based on the security guard's statement, it looks like the person who Tessa thought was attacking her was actually the guard trying to detain her. So that's good."

"And bad." Good that Tessa didn't have someone actually trying to hurt her. Bad that the man wasn't a viable suspect. "Did he mention seeing anyone else in the area in his statement?"

"No, but he did say there were still several people in the building."

"I don't suppose there's a list you can send me."

"As a matter of fact, there is," Rafi said. "I'm emailing it over to you now."

"Thank you. I'd like to match it against the list Brandon made to see if we're missing anyone."

"One more thing."

Praying for good news, Kimber asked, "What's that?"

"Murray wasn't thrilled when I asked for the police report."

She opened her email on her laptop. "We expected that."

"Yeah, but I wanted you to have a heads-up. Make sure he doesn't know you have access to it."

"Understood." She was already on Murray's bad side. She wasn't about to give him another reason to be annoyed with her. After thanking Rafi again, Kimber ended the call and opened the email from him. She downloaded the attachments, then pulled up the list of people known to be in the building at the time of the murder. All forty-three of them, the same number of suspects on Brandon's list.

She forwarded the email to Brandon and texted him to let him know so he could make sure all the names lined up with his initial investigation.

With the new information about the guard's interaction with Tessa, she debated whether it would be helpful to share that with her sister or if it would matter.

With the scenes from the play sitting on Ian's desk, Kimber considered an unusual way to share the details without making direct contact.

She grabbed a blue pen from the pencil holder on Ian's desk and proceeded to mark up the scene Parker had written in which the character representing Tessa was attacked.

She then typed up inserts on her laptop, adding an inserted scene from the guard's point of view.

The dressing-room door opened, and Ian walked in. He rolled his shoulders and tilted his neck from one side to the other.

"You okay?" Kimber couldn't remember seeing him quite so worn out before.

"Yeah. Just an intense scene." He held up

his hand to reveal several sheets of paper. "And I hate to interrupt whatever you're working on, but I need your help learning new lines. The director changed up the next scene." Ian separated the pages in his hand and handed half to Kimber.

"What do you need me to do?"

"You read Lydia's part."

Lydia, the character played by Allison Linton. "Got it."

Ian settled onto the couch across from her.

"How long do you have to learn these lines?"

"An hour." He glanced at his watch. "With the lunch break, maybe an hour and a half."

"Seriously?"

"It could be worse."

"I'm happy to help wherever I can." Kimber held up the play pages. "When you have a minute, though, I need your help with something."

"Does this have to do with Tessa?"

She nodded. Kimber explained her idea to edit Parker's play as a way to send information back to him.

"That's brilliant." Ian gestured to his computer bag. "Hand me my laptop. We'll do that now."

"Shouldn't we work on your lines first?"

"This won't take long."

"Okay." Eager to get the information into Parker's and Tessa's hands, she passed Ian his bag. "I'll email you the additional scene I typed up."

Together they added their notes to Parker's play, and then Ian emailed the play back to him.

"Great. Now that we have that taken care of, you ready to help?"

"I am."

He held up his script. "Great. From the top."

Parker stepped out of the shower and inhaled the scent of bacon and pancakes. Breakfast he didn't have to make himself. Was he still dreaming?

He dried off and rubbed his towel over his damp hair one more time before he dressed in Levi's and his last clean T-shirt. He really needed to do some laundry today.

His appetite stirred. He'd do laundry after breakfast. Or lunch. Whatever meal this was.

He hung his towel on the hook behind the door and made his way to the kitchen.

Tessa stood at the counter beside an electric griddle, a spatula in hand. She turned and smiled. "Hey. I hope you're hungry. I may have made too many pancakes."

Tessa fixing him something to eat was a simple task, but the thoughtfulness behind it caused his chest to swell with unexpected emotion. "You can never make too many pancakes." He eyed the plate beside her that already had a half dozen pancakes on it. Four more were cooking on the griddle. "But maybe you should take a break and eat with me before you make any more."

"I will. As soon as this batch is done." She flipped one over.

"Do I smell bacon?"

"Yes. It's in the oven. It should be about ready."

His smile was instant. A beautiful woman. His favorite breakfast food. He could get used to this. "I'll grab the plates and the syrup."

"Can you get the butter too?" Tessa asked.

"You got it." Parker proceeded to set the table while Tessa pulled a foil-lined cookie sheet from the oven and transferred the sizzling bacon onto a plate.

She carried the plate to the table and set it in the center. "Breakfast is served."

"This looks great, but please tell me you didn't skip breakfast so you could eat with me."

"Okay, so this is more of a lunch for me, but there's never a wrong time of day to eat pancakes."

He couldn't agree more.

Tessa transferred two pancakes onto her plate and passed the others to Parker. "Did you manage to get some sleep?"

"I did. Thanks." He served himself and poured syrup on his pancakes. "I'm actually looking forward to getting back to work today."

"Is that an unusual occurrence?"

"It has been lately." He took a bite and was instantly transported to a simpler time when he still lived at home and his biggest concern was to enjoy life. "Mmm. This is good."

"Glad you like it." Tessa picked up a piece of bacon. "Is there anything I can do to help?"

"Actually, I was hoping you'd be willing to help me enhance the scenes I already have." Parker paused as his own words startled him. To have Tessa help him would mean letting her see his pages in their rough-draft form. He wasn't sure he was ready for that. Words formed on his tongue to recant his suggestion, but then he looked at her. She had shared everything with him about a moment that had changed her life.

Surely, he could manage letting her read his words.

She lifted her gaze to his, and an unexpected bond of trust rushed through him. Trying to pick up their conversation, he said, "Maybe if we work together, we can figure out who the real killer was."

"I already told you about him." She took a bite.

"You told me what happened when he found you, but we don't know why he killed that woman or why he stuck around and went after you." And Parker needed the man's motivation both for his story and to help Tessa clear her name.

"I don't know how you expect to figure that out."

"We can brainstorm ideas."

Tessa leaned back in her chair, and her shoulders slumped. "If you want."

Parker sensed her lack of enthusiasm. "You don't have to if it's too hard for you."

"No, it's okay." She speared a bite of pancakes with her fork and waved it in the air. "It's just, I don't know how any of this will help convince the police that I'm innocent. We can't do anything from over a hundred miles away from the city."

"No, but I'm sure my uncle and your sister are doing everything they can to encourage the police to look into other suspects."

She sighed. "You're right."

They finished eating their meal, and Parker leaned back in his chair. "I am so full."

"Me too." Tessa stood and began clearing the table.

"Oh, no." Parker rose to his feet. "You cooked. That means I should clean up."

"You don't have to." She opened drawers until she found a plastic container to store the leftovers in. "It won't take long."

"I insist." Parker took the container from her.

She lifted her eyebrows and stared for a moment before giving in. "Okay. Then I'm going to get the rest of my laundry out of the dryer."

Which was a good reminder that he needed to get his own started. "Do you have any more to do?"

"No, I'm all done." She disappeared into the adjoining laundry room. A moment later, she passed back through the kitchen with a basket of clothes. "I'll be right back."

Parker finished putting away the food and set the dishes in the sink to soak. Then he retrieved his first load of laundry and started it before moving back into the kitchen.

Tessa had already returned and held a dish towel. "Do you want to wash or dry?"

"I can do both."

"Yes, but it'll go faster if we work together."

"Fine. I'll wash." He squirted some dish soap on the dirty dishes. Within minutes, they completed their task and moved into the living room to work on his play.

He opened his email and skimmed a message from Ian. "My uncle sent me some notes on what we sent him."

Tessa leaned back on the couch and propped her feet up on the coffee table. "Anything interesting?"

He skimmed through the first few notes again and then came across an added scene. "There's a new scene in here."

"Let me see." Tessa put her feet down and moved closer to him on the couch. "Go up to your last scene so I'll have the context."

Parker scrolled up. He watched Tessa read his words. The awkwardness he'd expected when she read his work didn't surface.

He sensed the moment when she reached the new scene Kimber had inserted, Tessa's body stiffening.

She drew a sharp breath and pointed at the screen. "Is this saying what I think it's saying?"

“I think so.” Parker turned his head, and his gaze met hers. “The man who grabbed you wasn’t the murderer.”

Tessa’s cheeks colored. “No. He was the security guard.”

Chapter 19

Colin had planned to arrive at the studio hours ago, but prepping the Juliet Clark file to share with the FBI had forced him to inventory all the evidence he'd planned to deal with later. And then a double homicide a few blocks away had taken priority. That particular case hadn't required any brain power to identify the killer. A woman and her new boyfriend had been shot to death shortly after her ex-boyfriend had shown up. Three witnesses had seen the man leaving the area with a gun in hand. All they needed now was to find him. But the beat cops could handle that.

Now, finally, he was at the studio and on his way upstairs to find out exactly why Kimber Seidel was hanging out at his crime scene.

He stepped out of the elevator, a red light glowing on the wall along with an illuminated sign that read Recording in Progress.

To his left, the crime-scene tape across the victim's office remained in place, the door closed and sealed with more tape. He glanced up at the security cameras mounted to the ceiling at regular intervals, cameras that would have captured the movements of everyone in this hallway the night of the murder. Yet when they'd requested the security feed from the building's security team, this particular footage had been noticeably absent.

The light on the wall blinked off, and a door opened down the hall. A woman walked out carrying a water bottle and turned away from him. It took him a moment to identify her as Allison Linton, the actress who played one of the lead roles. Ian Sawyer followed and then Kimber, the two of them speaking quietly.

"Miss Seidel," Colin called out. He waited for her to stop and then closed the distance between them. "What are you doing here?"

"I work here."

"You work here?" He shot her a look of disbelief. "Is that why you were here yesterday?"

Kimber gestured to the actor now standing beside her. "I came to meet with Ian."

"And Miss Seidel, what exactly is your role here at the studio?" Colin asked.

"I'm Ian's personal assistant," Kimber said.

That would explain why Kimber was at Ian's building last night.

"You didn't mention that yesterday."

"You didn't ask," Kimber pointed out. "And I was a little rattled by the fact that you had my sister's cell phone."

What Kimber said made sense, but sympathy wasn't part of Colin's current job description. He needed answers. "Have you heard from her?"

"No." She shot him a repentant look. "And I'm sorry I didn't call you earlier. I keep hoping she'll show up, but so far, we have no idea where she is."

Sure, she didn't. Focusing on Kimber's boss, Colin moved to a new line of questioning. "Mr. Sawyer, your neighbors told us you had someone staying at your house in the Hamptons, but when the police stopped by, no one was there."

"Yes, it was my nephew. He left yesterday after he made sure Tessa was set with a ride to the train station."

"Why didn't he drive her himself?"

"I don't know." Ian shrugged. "If I had to guess, Parker didn't have time."

"Where is your nephew now?"

"Last time I talked to him, he was going

somewhere to work on his next play, but he didn't mention where."

Another person not sharing the whole truth with him. Great. "So your nephew just conveniently happened to be at your place the night your assistant's sister showed up after potentially murdering one of your work associates, and then he left the next day."

"If you were to ask me, I'd say it was darn inconvenient," Ian said. "Had he come back to the city with Kimber and my wife the day before, he wouldn't have been woken up in the middle of the night or have you asking about him."

That much was true.

"Can you give me his phone number?" Colin asked. "I'd like to take his statement."

"I'll have to check with him first," Ian said. "When he's writing, we mostly communicate by email."

Or they were trying to hide Parker's location from him. Colin would just have to put in a search to find the man's phone number.

Kimber put her hand on Ian's arm. "Maybe you can give Parker's email address to Detective Murray. Then he can ask for his phone number directly."

"That's a good idea." Ian spelled out Parker's email address, and Colin typed it into his phone. "I'll message my nephew and let him know to look for your email so he doesn't think it's spam."

"I appreciate that," Colin said. He couldn't count how many times people claimed they didn't think his phone calls and emails were really from a police officer.

Kimber glanced at her watch. "I'm sorry, Detective, but I really need to help Ian prep for his next scene. He has a lot of lines to memorize."

Colin gave a curt nod. "If you hear from either Tessa or Parker, please let me know."

Kimber nodded. "We will."

Colin watched them go before he went in search of whoever had control of those security cameras.

He opened the door that led into the studio and approached a brunette woman who looked like she knew what she was doing. "Excuse me."

"Who are you?" the woman asked impatiently.

"Detective Colin Murray." Colin retrieved his badge from his pocket and held it up. "Can you tell me who can give me access to the security cameras in the hall on this floor?"

"That would be our security team. If you give me your information, I can make sure it gets sent to you," the woman said.

"Thanks." Colin pulled a business card from the little pocket behind his badge and passed it to her. "And you are?"

"Sheridan Maxwell. Producer."

"Thank you, Ms. Maxwell. I appreciate your help."

"No problem." Sheridan turned to the woman beside her. "Nicole, go let Allison know we need her on set in ten."

The young woman nodded and hurried away.

"Any idea how long it will take to get that security footage?" Colin asked.

Sheridan held up her phone. "I'll call security for you right now."

"Thanks. I appreciate it." He didn't care to wait until the woman had a spare moment. He took a quick glance at the handful of people making adjustments to the set, the lighting, and the camera angles. So much effort when viewers would only spend an hour watching the fruits of their labor. Personally, he'd prefer to just see the finished product rather than the bits and pieces that occurred behind the scenes.

Brandon finished syncing his laptop to the television so he could view the last of the security feed on a larger screen. Throughout the day, he'd gone through about half the files that showed the elevator interiors and the lobby.

A knock sounded on his door, and he crossed to answer it. Kimber stood on the other side, the scent of Chinese food wafting on the air.

She lifted a brown paper bag. "I picked up dinner."

"Thank you." He ushered her inside. "I had to skip lunch again."

Kimber set the food on the kitchen counter. "Amelia's making you do your old job again, isn't she?"

"Yes, but her new assistant reports tomorrow."

"Do you think this one will last?"

"I don't know, but I'm going to do everything I can to make sure she does." Brandon waved toward his laptop. "I made up a cheat sheet for all of Amelia's favorite restaurants, what she orders, and all the key people she'll need the new assistant to call."

"I hope the new person trusts you instead of Mary and Regina."

"Me too." Brandon retrieved plates from his cabinet and poured both of them some water. "If she does, maybe she won't get sabotaged like the last five assistants who were supposed to replace me."

"Let's hope." Kimber dished some cashew chicken onto her plate and then passed the container to Brandon before dishing out some of the lo mein. "Are we watching more security feed tonight?"

"That's the plan." Brandon spooned food onto his plate and carried it to the sofa. "I did identify when the different people left who were still in the building."

"I don't suppose any of them went running out right before Tessa?"

"I'm afraid not," Brandon said. "There were three who left around the time Tessa got there, but no one looked suspicious."

"I guess if it were that easy, Detective Murray would have already figured it out."

"Probably." Brandon twirled some noodles on his fork. "Oh, I did have an interesting thing happen today."

"What's that?" She sat beside him.

"It looks like Phoebe is going to sign with Monroe, and I get to be the initial editor."

Kimber's face lit up. "Brandon, that's great." She set her cup on the end table. "Both for you and for Phoebe."

"I'm excited about it, especially since I've already worked with Phoebe."

"Yeah. It's nice to know your author actually wants you to make them better."

"Agreed." He set his plate aside and

picked up his laptop. "Any preference of which camera view you want to start with?"

"Yeah. I'd like to see the feed from the hall outside the victim's office. That's the most logical place we'd see the killer for certain."

"I don't have that."

"Are you sure?"

Brandon did a quick search. "Yeah, it's not here."

"You don't think Murray would withhold evidence from Rafi, do you?"

"No, but the feed I've been going through has primarily been for the elevators, the lobby, and the street view," Brandon said. "It's possible the security cameras on the sixteenth floor are controlled by the studio."

"That must be it, but I'm sure Murray has already asked for it." She took a sip of her water. "He stopped by the studio today. That may have been why he was there."

"I'll reach out to Rafi tomorrow and ask if he can request any new info that Murray has obtained since he sent the file over."

"Thanks for doing that." Kimber settled her plate onto her lap. "How much more do we have to go through?"

"Not a lot. Maybe thirty minutes."

"After we finish, I think we should start digging into the backgrounds of the people who were in the building on Tuesday night."

"Besides your sister."

"Yes, besides her."

Chapter 20

Tessa tucked her legs beneath her on the couch, her doubts and thoughts churning. The fire crackled in the fireplace, and Parker sat beside her, his features even more handsome now that she'd gotten to know him better. It would be the perfect setting for their quiet date at home if it weren't for one thing — the laptop Parker had resting on his lap.

Her stomach clenched at the thought that the man she'd fought with had actually been a security guard. She'd been so sure the man had been the killer, but looking back now, she supposed she should have known better. It only made sense that the murderer would have cleared out of the area as quickly as possible.

Even though Tessa didn't want to talk about the situation that had dropped her in Parker's life or the fact that she'd run from a man whose job it was to protect people, she asked, "Is there anything in what Ian sent you that says when the victim died?"

"Her name is Juliet Clark." Parker slid his finger over his mousepad. "And yes, it says she died between ten and eleven."

"Since I heard a woman arguing with a man around ten twenty, and I tried to call 911 around 10:40 —"

"The actual call to 911 came in at 10:42."

"Right." Tessa nodded. "Then my guess is she died right after I heard the scream."

"I already have that detail in the script."

"I'm not sure what else we can do." Despair pressed in on her. "We already know the guard wasn't the killer."

"We think he wasn't the killer," Parker said. "For all we know, he stuck around to throw off suspicion."

So maybe Tessa wasn't crazy to have run away. "But why would a security guard kill her?"

"Why would anyone want her dead?" Parker asked, expanding her question. "That's what we should look at tonight."

"Okay, so why would someone commit murder?" Tessa asked. "It's hard to imagine why anyone would do such a thing."

"It's hard to imagine because you aren't a killer." Parker set his laptop beside him and stretched his arm out behind her. He rested his hand on her shoulder and pulled her closer, sitting in silence as though lost in thought. After a moment, he spoke again. “From what I’ve seen, the common themes are money, love, jealousy, revenge, or hiding a secret.”

“From what you’ve seen?” Tessa asked. “Were you a homicide detective in your previous career?”

“No, but I’ve done a lot of research, especially when I was preparing to write my second play.”

Tessa could imagine him in a library with stacks of books around him. Curious about his life before success, she asked, “What did you do before your first play was produced?”

“I worked as Uncle Ian’s estate manager.”

“Estate manager?” Tessa asked. “Are you some finance whiz or something?”

“Not exactly. I mostly made sure that his financial advisers were managing his assets well, and I still spend time at each of his houses to take care of the upkeep.”

“How many houses does he have?” Tessa asked. “I know about his apartment in New York and his place in the Hamptons. And I’m assuming he still has a house somewhere in the LA area.”

“Yes. And he has a cabin in Vermont. It’s where they like to go to get away.”

"I thought that's what the place in the Hamptons was for."

"The Hamptons house gives them the beach and a place to entertain away from the city. The cabin gives them solitude and close proximity to skiing."

"I'm surprised you didn't want to go to your uncle's cabin instead of here," Tessa said.

"I thought about it, but I didn't want to risk the police tracking us there."

The gravity of Parker's choices pressed in on her. Tessa stood. "Maybe you should go. Or you should drop me off somewhere so you won't get in trouble."

"I'm not going to do that." He rose to his feet and took her hand in his as though to keep her from backing away. "I know you didn't kill Juliet Clark. Together we'll prove it."

Her chest tightened from the enormity of her situation — the risks Parker was taking to help her, the possibility of going to jail, being away from her work and her friends.

Tears welled up in her eyes, and she blinked against them.

"Hey, come here." Parker pulled her into a hug.

Unable to resist the comfort his embrace offered, Tessa wrapped her arms around him and rested her head against his shoulder.

Parker lifted his hand and cradled the back of her head.

Goose bumps rippled over her skin, and a jolt of attraction rose within her. But Parker wasn't holding her because he was interested in her. He was just a nice guy.

"I can't imagine what you're feeling right now, but we're in this together." He leaned back and stared down at her. She lifted her eyes to meet his as his gaze lowered to her lips. Butterflies erupted in her stomach.

Okay, so he was a nice guy she wanted to kiss.

She tilted her chin up. Parker leaned in.

And then his phone rang.

Parker bit back his frustration and straightened. Whoever was on the phone had better have a really good reason for interrupting what he'd hoped would be his first kiss with Tessa.

She eased out of his arms. "You should get that."

"Yeah." He pulled his phone from his pocket. "It's my uncle." He hit the Talk button. "Hey, Uncle Ian."

"How's the writing going?" Ian asked.

"You tell me." Maybe his uncle was calling to tell him the police had found the real killer. That would leave him and Tessa free — to do what, exactly?

Ian interrupted Parker's fragmented thoughts of his future relationship with Tessa. "Did you see the notes I sent back?"

"I did. That was an interesting idea, having the attacker be a security guard instead of the killer."

"I thought you might like that twist," Ian said. "I also wanted to let you know a Detective Murray may be reaching out to you."

"Why?"

"Seems he wants to talk to you about Tessa and what you know about where she is now."

With the way Ian was speaking, Parker suspected he was worried someone might access their phone call at some point. Playing along, he said, "You know she took an Uber to the train station."

"Yes, but apparently, she then took another Uber to Main Street in Southampton."

"Interesting."

"Anyway, I didn't feel comfortable giving out your phone number, but I gave him your email address."

Parker had hoped the police wouldn't take

any interest in him. He should have known better, but he couldn't deny the cold stone that sank in his stomach at the prospect of speaking with the detective. "I didn't see anything, but it may have ended up in my spam folder."

"Good luck with the play. I'm looking forward to reading the next few scenes."

"I'm working on possible motives for my murderer now," Parker said. "I don't suppose you have any suggestions."

"Not off the top of my head, but I'll let you know if I have any brilliant ideas."

Which meant he and Kimber hadn't made any real progress on finding another suspect yet. "Thanks, Uncle Ian."

"You take care of yourself."

"You too." Parker hung up the phone.

"What did he say?" Tessa asked.

Parker buried his concerns and tried to sound casual. "Apparently, the detective investigating the murder wants to talk to me."

Tessa took a step back. "I really should go."

"No." Parker looked down at his phone. "But I do think we should go for a drive tonight." He looked down at Tessa. "Or I should."

"Where?"

Parker held up his phone. "To somewhere the police will expect me to be, somewhere we can ensure that I won't lead them to you."

Tessa's face paled. "You think the police would try to trace your location through your phone?"

"My phone. Or my car."

"You won't want to be without your phone and car."

"No, but there's an inn a couple miles down the road. I can check in there and then use one of my friend's four-wheelers to drive back."

"What about your phone? If we lose internet or power up here, we'll be completely cut off."

"There's a landline in the office for emergencies."

Tessa gave him a skeptical look. "You sure about this?"

Parker nodded. "Positive. We need time, and if you do get arrested, it will actually help your case if you don't have access to the news."

"But it won't help you." Tessa's eyes shone with fresh tears. "I can't have you getting arrested for aiding a criminal."

"You aren't a criminal. You know it. I know it." Parker scooped his keys off the side table. "Before long, the police will know it too. But we need time without worrying about whether you're about to be falsely accused."

Tessa put her hand on his shoulder and pressed a kiss to his cheek. "You really are the nicest person I've ever met."

Parker's heart swelled, and warmth seeped through him. Part of him wished he and Tessa could hide out here indefinitely and explore the sizzle of attraction sparking between them, but for now, they had a task to accomplish. "Come on." He took her hand. "Let's go gas up the four-wheeler."

"Before we do that, you should go grocery shopping," Tessa said. "We'll want to stock up in case we're here longer than we expect."

"Good idea. I'll head to the store, and when I get back, you can drive my car down to the hotel. I don't want you to get lost trying to drive off-road through the woods."

CHAPTER 21

Colin should be on his way home by now, but the receipt of the preliminary autopsy report and the prospect of getting the new security feed was enough to push him into some overtime hours. With the printed autopsy report in hand, he walked to his desk and scanned the summary. "This is odd."

Derrick looked up from his desk. "What?"

"Cause of death was a precision wound to the heart."

"Sounds like our killer got lucky." Derrick pushed his keyboard forward on his desk and leaned back in his chair. "I have more news on the Clark case."

Colin shrugged out of his suit jacket and draped it over the back of his chair. "You found Seidel?"

"No, but I finished going through Clark's phone records. I also spoke to her sister."

"And?"

"Most of the calls and text messages are to people she works with, with somewhat regular phone calls to her family."

"No boyfriend?" Colin asked.

"Based on the phone records, there isn't an obvious partner, but according to her sister, she was dating a man who worked in her building. A guy by the name of Heath Quentin." Derrick passed him an 8 x 10 photo of a man in his thirties. "And guess where he was on Tuesday night?"

Colin tapped his finger on his desk. "You're about to tell me he was in the building at the time of the murder, aren't you?" He hated having multiple suspects.

"I am. Heath Quentin didn't leave until a half hour after the murder." Derrick's eyes sparked. "Not only that, but he's a security guard, and he was patrolling the floors at the time Clark was killed."

And as a security guard, he would have access to all the floors, including the television studio. This wasn't the news Colin wanted. "Have you talked to him?"

"Not yet. I was about to head out to question him. Want to come?"

"Maybe." Colin didn't really want to spend his overtime sitting in the evening rush-hour traffic, but the sooner they could check this suspect off the list, the better.

Derrick took a drink from his water bottle. "The studio also wants to know when we plan to release the crime scene."

"I want to take one more look at it tomorrow, but if forensics is done, we can turn it back over to the studio tomorrow afternoon."

"I'll let them know."

Colin's phone rang, but it was a phone number instead of a name. He hit the Talk button. "Murray."

"Detective Murray, this is Parker Sawyer. I received an email from you asking that I call."

"Yes. Thanks for getting back to me." Colin rolled his chair closer to his desk. "I just have a few details I need to clarify with you."

"Details about what?" Parker asked, sounding completely at ease. Maybe the guy wasn't involved with helping Seidel. Or maybe acting abilities ran in the Sawyer family.

Colin pulled his keyboard closer and opened a file to take notes. "I understand you were at Ian Sawyer's home in the Hamptons on Tuesday night when Tessa Seidel arrived."

"Yes. Well, it was more like Wednesday morning when she showed up."

"And what time was that?"

"I'm not sure exactly. It was well after midnight. Probably around one thirty or two."

"And did she say why she was there?"

"She was looking for her sister. She didn't know Kimber and my aunt Phoebe had already driven back to the city earlier that day."

"And why was she there in the middle of the night looking for her sister?"

"She was delivering some clothes to the studio where my uncle works when she heard someone scream. When she went to see what was wrong, she found a woman on the floor."

"Did she mention seeing anyone else?"

"Yeah. When she tried calling 911, a man showed up and grabbed her," Parker said. "She thinks it was probably the guy who was arguing with the woman who was killed."

"How did you know the woman was dead?"

"Tessa told me. She said she checked her for a pulse but couldn't find one," Parker said. "And I'm guessing that since you're asking questions, Tessa was right about that."

"When was the last time you spoke with Tessa?"

"She took an Uber to the train station on Wednesday morning. That was about an hour before I left, so it must have been around ten."

"Any particular reason you didn't offer her a ride?"

"I offered, but she needed to leave before I was able to. That's why I lent her my phone and let her use it to set up her Uber."

"Thanks for your help. Is this a good number to reach you if I have any more questions?"

"It's best to email me first. I usually turn off my phone when I'm working."

"Thank you, Mr. Sawyer." Colin checked his notes before asking one last pertinent question. "Also, where are you now, Mr. Sawyer? I assume you're no longer in the Hamptons."

"I'm still in New York. I'm just staying in a hotel while I write."

"I see." If Parker Sawyer was going to be this vague on his location, Colin would use other ways to find him. "Well, thank you again for your time." Colin ended the call and entered a request to ping Parker's phone. He then added Parker's phone number to his notes.

"Anything helpful?" Derrick asked.

"Not really. He said he let Tessa use his phone to order an Uber. If he's to be believed, she must have set up both Uber rides at the same time."

"Or she could have asked the driver to modify her trip."

"Can you do me a favor and track down the Uber driver?"

"Already way ahead of you. I left him a message to call me."

"Let me know what you find." Colin turned back to his computer and pulled up his email. He first spotted the approval to ping Parker's phone, so he wasted no time in starting that process. Seconds later, it popped up. The man was indeed staying in a hotel in New York. In the Catskills, to be exact. Colin skimmed through the next few emails. "Looks like the security feed finally came in from the studio."

"Good." Derrick rolled his chair closer. "This should tell us if there was anyone else there that night."

"Let's start at the time of the murder." Colin identified the file that included the feed from the camera nearest to the victim's office. "Here we go."

Colin played the video, fast-forwarding it until they reached the spot when a woman came into view. "That must be Tessa."

The woman entered the open door that led into the office where the victim had been found.

Less than two minutes later, a man entered.

Colin pointed. "That's the guard."

Seidel reappeared in the hall at a full run. Colin hit the button to freeze the image on his screen. The young woman's face was fully visible, and there was no doubt she was running from the scene of the crime. "Gotcha." He turned to Derrick. "Time to put in for the arrest warrant."

"What about the boyfriend?"

"List him as a person of interest in the file and interview him. That shows we considered someone besides her." Colin rewound the recording. "I'm going to watch the rest of the feed, going back to when Clark was last seen entering her office. I want to make sure I'm ready when I interrogate Seidel."

"You have to find her first."

"I'll find her."

Tessa peeked through the woods in the direction of the hotel down the street. To prevent her from being seen, Parker had taken the car the rest of the way to the hotel with the intent of walking back on foot to this spot.

The sun had nearly set when he'd come back from the grocery store. They'd put away the items that had needed to be stored in the fridge or freezer before they'd headed back out. Now here she was, the temperature cooling, and darkness nearly complete. And Parker wasn't anywhere in sight.

What was taking him so long?

She shivered and tucked her hands into the pocket of Parker's hoodie.

Behind her, footsteps crunched against fallen leaves. She whirled toward the sound.

"It's just me," Parker said.

The familiarity of his voice soothed her nerves and chased away the panic that had resulted from the surprise approach. He quickly appeared from behind a cluster of trees.

"Are you going to be able to find the way back in the dark?"

"There's a light on the four-wheeler, and I've driven through these woods a lot." Parker climbed onto the four-wheeler and motioned for her to take the spot behind him.

Tessa climbed on and scooted forward. At first, she put her hands on his waist, but Parker took both of her hands and pulled them forward so she was hugging him, her body pressed against his back. "Hold on tight."

"Okay." And she wasn't going to think about their nearness or the way the smell of the fall leaves mixed with the musky scent of Parker's aftershave.

He turned the key, and the engine roared to life. Then he flipped on the light and drove forward. Less than twenty yards later, Parker turned onto a path barely wide enough for them to travel on, leaves strewn across it.

Something bounded through the trees, likely a deer startled from their approach. The ride would be beautiful if it were light out, but the headlight shone only a short distance in front of them.

With each turn, Tessa held on tighter, her tension increasing. A bump over a protruding root caused her to bounce off the seat, her hold on Parker the only thing keeping her from flying off the vehicle.

By the time they reached the cabin, her back was tight, and her muscles screamed for relief.

Parker pulled up beside the shed. "Can you open the doors for me?"

"Yeah." Assuming her legs didn't collapse when her feet hit the ground. They didn't, but it was a close call. Her legs definitely felt more like jelly than functioning limbs.

Tessa opened the shed and stood back while Parker drove the four-wheeler inside and cut the engine. He came out and closed the shed, taking time to lock the doors.

A brisk breeze rushed past them, and Tessa shivered.

"Looks like we need some hot chocolate again tonight." Parker slipped his arm around her waist, the gesture feeling so natural.

They weren't a couple. And they were together solely because of a bad situation. But that didn't stop the warmth from spreading through Tessa as they walked up the steps to the porch.

Parker released her and opened the door for her.

She stepped into the warmth of the cabin and toed off her shoes, setting them beside the couch.

Parker closed the door, and she turned to ask what he wanted to do tonight. But when she looked up at him, her mind went blank.

His gaze lowered to her lips, and for the second time today, she couldn't help but wonder what it would be like to kiss him.

Parker leaned forward until his lips were a mere whisper from hers.

Her heartbeat quickened. Their breath

mingled, and he lifted his hands to frame her face. Then he closed the distance between them, and she didn't have to wonder anymore.

Her eyes fluttered closed, and myriad colors burst into her mind. Goose bumps rippled over her skin, and every nerve ending came alive. The chirping of crickets carried into the room, along with the faint sound of the wind rustling through the trees.

Their moments together, his kindness, his humor — all of it combined to bring an unrecognized truth to the forefront of her mind: Parker was the one bright spot in her life this week, and she didn't want this to end.

He trailed his fingers down her neck before he pulled her closer. The goose bumps multiplied, and a kaleidoscope of butterflies took flight.

His lips lingered until he finally pulled back and pressed his forehead to hers. "I've been wanting to do that all day."

Her lips curved into a smile. "Me too." She stepped back. "But we should get the rest of the groceries put away and start another fire."

"If I help you with that, will you let me kiss you again?"

Her smile widened. "If you make me hot chocolate, too, I think that can be arranged."

"Deal."

Chapter 22

Kimber was glad they hadn't received the additional security feed until this morning. If she'd seen it last night, there would have been no way she would have slept.

Ian sat beside her in his dressing room, Brandon standing behind the two of them.

"This can't be right," Kimber said. "There's no way Tessa killed Juliet Clark."

"I agree, but the video doesn't show anyone besides Tessa walking in there." Brandon put his hand on Kimber's shoulder. "Is it possible there's another way into that office?"

"I don't know." Kimber looked at the heating vent in the ceiling. "The vents aren't big enough for a person to fit through, and I haven't seen any offices that have more than one door."

"I don't think any of them do have more than one door," Ian said.

"Rafi is supposed to be meeting me here

at one," Brandon said. "That's when the police are releasing the crime scene."

"Finally." Kimber had been eager to see the room since she arrived, but she hadn't dared break through the tape. Sneaking around and asking questions was one thing. Tampering with an active crime scene was another. She turned to Ian. "Do you think you can spare me for a while when Brandon comes back?"

"I'm sure I can. It might even hit right around our lunch break." Ian pointed at Kimber's computer screen. "Can you play that again?"

"Yes, but I'm not sure I want to see it a second time," Kimber said. "Once Detective Murray sees this, an arrest warrant is inevitable."

"Humor me."

She let out a sigh and hit the Replay button. The image began with an empty hall, the time stamp clearly visible. Tessa appeared and walked down the hall, her back to the security camera. A couple of minutes later, she came back, her face clearly visible as she ran toward the stairs.

"Rewind it again," Ian said.

"Why?"

"I don't know. There's something off, but I can't put my finger on it."

Kimber moved the feed back to when Tessa appeared.

When Ian wanted to watch a fourth time, Kimber shifted her laptop toward him so he could manipulate the controls himself.

She swiveled her chair around so she was facing Brandon. "What are we going to do? This makes it look like Tessa is the killer."

"Everything in Tessa's story checks out perfectly," Brandon said.

"Except that she's the only person who went into the room at the time of the murder," Kimber said.

"Which means we must be missing something."

Ian leaned back in his chair. "Can you get me a copy of the video files?"

"I suppose." Brandon furrowed his brow. "But why do you want them?"

"Just following a hunch." Ian stood. "If it turns out to be right, I'll let you know."

"This isn't the time to keep your thoughts to yourself," Kimber insisted. "What are you thinking?"

Ian seemed to debate for a moment before he leaned forward and rested his elbows on his thighs. "The lighting seems off in the security feed. I think someone may have tampered with it."

Just hearing Ian voice a logical explanation about the evidence against Tessa brought with it new hope. "How do we prove it?"

"I may be able to help," Ian said. "That's why I want the files."

"We'll get them for you," Brandon said. "And I'll make sure our friend at the FBI takes a look too." He leaned in and kissed Kimber's cheek. "I'd better get to the office. Amelia's new assistant reports today."

"I'm surprised they're having her start her new job on a Friday," Kimber said.

"Technically, she started working on Monday, but HR wanted her to go through some extra training before she reported to Amelia."

Ian chuckled. "Sounds like they're getting tired of hiring new assistants."

"I'm sure. Which is why I'm going to pick up Amelia's morning coffee order on my way so the new girl can see that I'm not lying to her when I say Amelia likes Starbucks rather than the coffee shop across the street."

"Good luck," Kimber said.

"Thanks." He took a step toward the door. "I'll see you back here around one."

Brandon left, and Ian stood. "Make sure you send me those files."

"I'll do that right now."

"Great. I'd better get ready for my first scene." Ian grabbed the clothes off the hanging rack on the far wall and walked into the small changing area at the back of his dressing room.

She'd seen similar changing areas in a couple of the other dressing rooms. Was it possible one existed in Juliet Clark's office? She'd find out soon enough, but just in case, she played the video feed again; this time she started two hours earlier and continued until the police arrived.

Ian emerged from his changing room. "I thought you didn't want to look at that again."

"I didn't, but I just wondered if there was any way someone else could have been in the room when Tessa got there and then left after Tessa and the guard ran out of there."

"Any luck?" Ian asked.

"No. I could see where Juliet and another woman left the room together and then Juliet returned alone with what looked like her dinner," Kimber said. "A few people passed by, but no one was seen entering the office until Tessa walked in."

"Sorry." Ian tightened his tie. "It looks like we have a true mystery on our hands."

"Yes, and my sister's future depends on us solving it."

"Then we'll solve it. The truth is bound to come out." Ian grabbed his water bottle off his dressing table and took a sip. "But for now, we have work to do. And after I learn my new lines, you have a new scene to write."

"I'm not looking forward to writing this one," Kimber said.

"I know. I'm sure Parker won't be thrilled to read it either."

Parker hadn't intended to include a love story in his new play, but he couldn't help adding in the novelty of what he'd discovered with Tessa. Whether he wanted to admit it, little by little, he was becoming a big part of the story, both on and off the page. He glanced over at where Tessa lay on the love seat, her eyes closed as she slept.

Tessa shifted from her back to her side, curling up as her blanket slid to the floor.

Parker set his laptop aside and crossed to where the blanket had settled. He spread it over her, pulling it up over her shoulders.

Unable to resist, he leaned down and pressed a kiss to her forehead. Warmth flowed through him, building in his chest.

He stepped back and stared at Tessa's lovely features, her eyelashes dark against her skin. There was no doubt that she was one of the most beautiful women he'd ever seen, but she was so much more than her appearance — kind, smart, caring.

He couldn't deny that he'd found fulfillment in those early moments after he'd met Tessa. He'd never really had anyone rely on him before, anyone who had let him take care of them.

Ironically, he equally appreciated her independence. Maybe it was the contrast between the different sides of her that had drawn him in so quickly. He'd met her only three days ago, and already he looked forward to spending time with her each day.

He sat back down on the couch and read through the last few lines of his play. For today's scenes, he'd included a lost phone for one of the characters in the hope that Ian would understand he no longer had access to his.

After Parker was satisfied with his efforts, he copied today's scenes into a new document and opened his email. A message from Ian topped his inbox.

Parker clicked on it and read the note included with the attachment.

> Enjoying the story so far. See attached for suggested changes. I'm also going to

look into who else is good at editing.

— Ian

Parker opened the attachment. He skimmed through the notes, a handful of them clarifying details of the investigation. Then he skipped to the new scene at the bottom. In it, the narrow-minded detective viewed security footage that made it clear that the only person walking into and out of the victim's office the night of the murder was the main suspect — the character representing Tessa.

Hoping and praying good news would follow the bad, Parker gripped the side of his laptop and kept reading. A handful of character sketches had been added, all of them little more than names and titles: an actor, a producer, a director, a screenwriter, a video editor, and a production assistant. On each, a time of departure was listed, each one relative to the time of death of the victim. And in each case, the suspects listed had departed before the murder.

Still lying on the loveseat, Tessa stirred. Her eyes fluttered open, and she sat up. "I'm sorry. I didn't mean to fall asleep."

"It's okay. I was just cleaning up a few things on my script."

"Any word from Ian?"

"Just a few minor corrections on the timeline and some of the people who were at the studio before Juliet was killed."

Tessa's eyes lit with hope. "How many were still there when it happened?"

"None." Parker studied Tessa. Regardless of the evidence, his instincts and the instincts of his uncle convinced him Tessa wasn't capable of murder. "The killer must have come from another floor."

"The stairwell doors have coded alarms on the studio's floor," Tessa said. "Maybe the police need to look at whose code was used that night."

"That's a good idea." He furrowed his brow. "How do you know there are keypads in the stairwell?"

"I saw them the night of the murder." Tessa set the blanket aside. "I didn't need one to leave, but since they had the keypads inside the stairwell, my guess is that you need one to enter."

"I'll pass that along in my next submission to Uncle Ian." Not wanting to face the harsh picture painted within the play right now, he closed his laptop and stood. "Want to go for a walk? It looks like it's warmed up outside."

"I'd like that."

Parker stood and offered Tessa his hand.

She placed her hand in his and let him pull her up.

She tipped her chin up, and Parker took the gesture as an invitation. He leaned down and pressed his lips to hers. His heart soared, the novelty of this spark between them encompassing his very being. He lingered over the kiss, Tessa's hand still in his.

When he drew back, she smiled. "I'm really glad I met you."

"I'm glad I met you too." Parker's gaze remained locked on hers. He was falling for her, and if new evidence wasn't uncovered soon, he could lose her before they had a chance to see where this relationship could lead.

Chapter 23

Brandon stood beside Rafi inside the office where Juliet had been killed. Three desks took up most of the wall space along with a four-drawer filing cabinet.

He turned in a circle. No closets to hide in, no additional exits or vents large enough for a person to fit through. The only evidence that they were in the location where the murder had been committed was the bloodstain on the carpet.

"I'm sorry, Brandon," Rafi said. "I don't see how anyone else could have gotten in or out of here without being seen by the cameras."

"This is not what Kimber's going to want to hear."

Rafi peeked out the open door before he lowered his voice and said, "I hate to ask this, but are you sure Kimber's sister couldn't have been involved?"

"I'm sure." Although seeing that security

feed had shaken his confidence. "She had no motive, no connection to the victim, and she's never shown any kind of violent tendencies."

Footsteps approached, and a man's voice sounded behind them. "Who are you, and what are you doing here?"

Brandon turned to face a man in his forties who sported a closely trimmed beard.

Beside Brandon, Rafi reached into the pocket of his suit jacket and produced his ID. "I'm Special Agent Rafi Ebeid with the FBI."

The man leaned forward to inspect Rafi's badge before he straightened again. "Why is the FBI involved with a murder case?"

"I'm sorry, but I'm not at liberty to say." Rafi slid his badge back into his pocket. "And you are?"

"Gabriel Perez. I'm the show's director." He turned his attention to Brandon. "Wait. Haven't I met you before?"

Hoping the man wouldn't connect him to Kimber or Ian, he said, "I was here the morning after the murder."

Before Gabriel could respond, Rafi asked, "What can you tell me about the victim?"

"She's worked with us since we started taping this show, but I don't know a whole lot else about her."

"Family? Friends? Boyfriend?"

"She's closest to Nicole."

"Any chance you can let Nicole know I'd like to speak with her?" Rafi asked.

"Yeah, sure." Gabriel took a step back. "How much longer until we can get the cleaning crew in here?"

"We'll be finished here within the hour."

Gabriel nodded and disappeared from sight.

Brandon turned in a circle and took in the neatly organized desk to his right. On the next desk, papers were stacked haphazardly, and the third didn't look like it was being used.

A woman around his and Kimber's age appeared in the doorway, her body tense. Her dark hair hung past her shoulders. "I'm Nicole. I was told you wanted to see me?"

"Yes." Rafi gestured for her to enter. "I'm Special Agent Rafi Ebeid. I just wanted to ask you a few questions about Juliet Clark."

"But I already talked to the police."

"I know," Rafi said, "but *I* want to hear everything from you."

Nicole looked down at the bloodstain on the floor, and her eyes watered.

"I'm sorry," Rafi said. "I know this must be difficult for you, but we really need to know more about Miss Clark."

"Can you tell us if she was seeing anyone?" Brandon asked.

Nicole looked away, and her cheeks flushed.

Brandon recognized the signs of avoidance and guessed at the cause. "I know friends share secrets, but those secrets died with her. The best thing you can do to help us find her killer is to share with us what you know."

"So was she seeing someone?" Rafi pressed.

Nicole nodded. "They'd been together for a few months, but last weekend, Juliet saw her boyfriend with another woman."

Which could create a conflict that could lead to murder. "Any idea who the other woman was?" Brandon asked.

"Since both of them were wearing wedding rings, she guessed that he was married but was hiding it from her," Nicole said. "According to Juliet, he never wore a ring at work."

Now Rafi stepped in. "Did she confront her boyfriend about it?"

A tear spilled over and trickled down Nicole's cheek, and she nodded. "They fought about it on Monday. That's when she broke things off with him."

"What's his name?" Rafi asked.

"Heath Quentin. He works as a security guard here." She swiped at the moisture on her cheek. "He said he was getting a divorce, but Juliet didn't want anything to do with him after she found out he cheated on his wife and never told her he was married."

"What else do you know about Heath Quentin?" Rafi asked.

"Not much. He usually showed up after the rest of us left."

"How do you know that?" Brandon asked.

"I forgot my jacket one night, and he was here when I came back," Nicole said. "That's the only time I met him."

Rafi gestured to the desks. "Which one of these desks was Juliet's?"

"That one." She pointed to the neatly organized one. Nicole furrowed her brow.

"Is something wrong?" Brandon asked.

"Her laptop isn't there. Neither is her planner."

Rafi made a note. "The police probably took those into evidence."

A woman in her late thirties walked in, her clothing stylish and her hair barely skimming her shoulders. Irritation laced her voice when she took in the scene in front of her, and she zeroed in on Nicole. "What are you doing in here? I need those call sheets."

Nicole tensed. "Sorry. I was told to come

talk to Agent Ebeid first."

"Who are you?" Rafi asked.

The woman tilted her chin up a fraction of an inch. "I'm Sheridan Maxwell. I'm the producer of this show."

"Great. You're one of the people I need to talk to."

"I don't have time right now." She waved at Nicole. "If you want to meet with me, Nicole can help you make an appointment."

Brandon glanced at Rafi, not sure how he would react to being dismissed by the producer.

Rafi simply nodded and retrieved a business card from his pocket. He handed it to Nicole. "Since Ms. Maxwell isn't available to meet with me right now, please make sure you set up an appointment for her to come to the local FBI office before the end of the week. Oh, and I get off work at five."

Nicole took the card, and Sheridan shot him an indignant look. "Today's Friday. It's already the end of the week. I don't have time to leave the studio today, especially not after being shut down on Wednesday."

"I did offer to meet with you now."

"Fine." Sheridan bit off the word. She waved at Nicole. "Tell Gabriel I'll be in as soon as I can and to start without me."

Nicole nodded.

Brandon moved to the door and opened it wider for Nicole. "Thank you for your help."

She looked up at him and swallowed hard. "I hope you find who did this."

"We will."

Chapter 24

Colin climbed out of the unmarked police car in front of the studio, a freshly issued arrest warrant in his pocket. Not one to take chances, he'd also managed to secure the authorization to track Parker Sawyer's cell phone and finances as well as a search warrant for Kimber Seidel's electronic devices. He'd tried to gain a warrant for Ian Sawyer's phone and laptop, too, but the judge hadn't been inclined to sign off on that one, not without clear proof that Ian was directly involved with the suspect.

Based on what they'd learned from the Uber driver this morning, Tessa had indeed requested a ride to the train station and had scheduled a second ride to take her into town. Whether the trips with Uber were a decoy or not still remained to be seen.

Derrick slammed the driver's-side door and locked the car. "You sure you want to do this here?"

"This is the only place we'll be able to see Ian Sawyer's reaction to the news that Kimber's sister is being arrested."

"You're hoping he'll call and warn his nephew?"

"If his nephew is helping her hide and he knows about it, yeah." Plus, this was the best way to take the opportunity to search any of Ian's belongings. After all, as Ian's personal assistant, Kimber would certainly have some of her electronics in Ian's dressing room. He hoped.

Derrick let out a sigh. "Then let's get this over with."

They entered the building, flashed their badges as they passed the security desk, and entered the waiting elevator that was already half full.

Once the doors opened to the sixteenth floor, Colin led the way to Ian's dressing room. He knocked on the closed door. No answer. He knocked a second time. Again, nothing.

A door opened down the hall, and voices carried to them. Less than a minute passed before Kimber and Ian came into view at the end of the hall.

They spotted him at the same time, and both of them exhibited the typical flash of confusion. But beyond that, he didn't sense any concern or hesitation from them as they continued down the hall.

"Detective Murray." Ian shook his hand. "I didn't expect to see you today. Is there something I can do for you?"

"I'm here to ask if either of you have heard from or seen Tessa Seidel."

"No," Ian said without any signs of lying. Then again, the man was one of the most talented actors of his generation.

"Have you had any luck finding her?" Kimber asked, genuine concern in her voice. "I'm so worried about her. She's never gone this long without talking to me before."

"Maybe that's because she's never killed anyone before."

"Excuse me?" Kimber shook her head. "My sister didn't kill anyone. She couldn't. It's not possible."

"Whether you think it's possible or not, we have video evidence that she's the only person who entered the office in the window of the time of death."

Kimber folded her arms. "Then your time of death is wrong."

"Or your video feed has been tampered with," Ian added.

Colin had heard it all before, and he was prepared with the facts. "The preliminary autopsy report was conclusive."

Kimber's stare met his. "And how long until you get the final autopsy report?"

Odd that she would know to ask such a question. "Two to three weeks."

"Until then, I suggest you keep looking," Kimber said. "Because there's still a killer out there, and it isn't my sister."

With a degree of satisfaction, Colin pulled out the search and arrest warrants. "A warrant has been issued for the arrest of Tessa Seidel." Colin held it out.

Kimber leaned forward, but her expression was more resigned than surprised. "Have you found my sister's police statement yet?"

Colin narrowed his eyes. As if he were buying the story that Seidel had really been at the police station the night of the murder. "No one has seen it. I suspect she was never at the station that night."

"Has anyone thought to check the security feed of the police station lobby from Tuesday night?" Kimber asked. "Surely, that wouldn't be hard. And it would prove whether she turned in a statement or not."

Colin hadn't checked. He hadn't seen the need to. Annoyed that this woman was questioning his methods, he folded the arrest warrant back up and produced the search warrant. "And this is my authorization to search your electronics, Miss Seidel."

"What?" She turned to look at Derrick. "Is this for real?"

"I'm afraid so, miss." Derrick gave Kimber one of his sympathetic looks, much like a wet puppy sitting in the rain. "We'll need to take custody of your laptop, cell phone, and any other electronic devices with communication capability."

Kimber clenched her jaw before she turned to Ian. "Ian, will you please call Brandon and let him know what's going on?"

"Yes, happy to." Ian pulled out his phone and dialed before moving a few yards down the hall.

"Who's Brandon?" Colin asked.

"He's my main point of contact at Monroe Publishing."

Derrick asked the obvious question. "Why do you need to inform a publishing company that you're being served with a search warrant?"

"Because they have the exclusive rights to over a million dollars of my intellectual property contained on that laptop," Kimber said. "I'm sure they have protocols to follow in situations such as these."

"Whatever their protocols are, they don't

supersede this warrant." And Colin really didn't need some personal assistant trying to pull strings. He held out his hand. "Cell phone, please."

She hesitated before she reached into her pocket and took out her phone. "How long until I'll get this back? I need it for work and, obviously, to stay connected to my friends and family."

"We should have it processed by Monday or Tuesday," Derrick said.

Colin gestured to Ian's dressing-room door. "Open it."

Ian joined them again, his phone still in hand. "Brandon is on his way over."

"Thanks."

His patience wearing thin, Colin pointed at the keypad on the door again. "I said, 'Open it.' "

Kimber put her hand on Ian's arm. "I'll do it."

Brandon had barely met Amelia's new assistant, Candace, when Ian had called. And Brandon could already see the plotting looks on Mary's and Regina's faces. With no time to lose, he pocketed his phone, grabbed the survival kit he'd prepared for the new assistant, and handed it to Candace.

"Everything you need to figure out Amelia's food and drink preferences is in here." He tilted his head toward Mary and Regina. "And no matter what they say, Amelia doesn't like spicy food, and she wants her coffee from Starbucks."

Mary shook her head. "He's trying to mess with you so you'll get fired like the last three assistants."

Brandon didn't have time for Mary's antics, nor did he mention the two other assistants who had quit before Amelia could fire them. "Your first order of business is to go up to see Sheila in finance to get a company credit card." He leaned closer to Candace. "And have Sheila print out my credit-card receipts from when I was Amelia's assistant. It'll prove that I'm not the one trying to sabotage you."

He headed for the elevator and cast a glance over his shoulder. "Good luck."

Taking advantage of his previous assignment as Amelia's assistant, Brandon called the executive elevator to his floor. He didn't have time to waste.

Kimber shouldn't use her CIA knowledge to protect her sister, but at the moment, Tessa was only one consideration. If she let Detective Murray take her electronics, his search might very well reveal that her laptop was government issued. And she couldn't let him blow her cover.

She approached the cipher lock. Besides learning to break the codes on these types of locks, her time at the farm had also given her the knowledge of how to lock them down.

She keyed in the eight-digit override code, and the system beeped twice, once flashing a green light and then flashing red.

She tried the door handle, but it only rattled when she pushed down on it. "Sorry. I must have put in the wrong number."

She keyed in the code again, this time sticking to the typical four-digit code. The light on the keypad flashed red.

Detective Murray gestured to Ian. "Mr. Sawyer, would you open it, please?"

"Yes, of course."

Kimber moved aside to give Ian access.

Ian punched in the code. As expected, the keypad flashed red yet again, and the door remained locked.

"This isn't amusing." Detective Murray gestured to the door. "Put in the correct code. Now."

Ian held out his hands. "I did." He tried a second time before turning back to the two detectives. "I'm sorry. I have no idea why it isn't working."

Detective Murray turned to his partner. "Go get the producer or the security chief or whoever can override this lock."

The other detective nodded. "I'll be right back."

The producer tried first. Then a member of the security team. Kimber hated putting this wrench in everyone's plans for the afternoon, but she needed Brandon to arrive to run interference. Assuming he even could.

If nothing else, she hoped he would be able to claim her second cell phone as his.

She glanced at her watch. Best case, he would get here in twenty minutes, but that was assuming it didn't take him long to leave the office.

The producer and security guard left, and a few minutes later, another guard arrived.

A dozen more failed attempts and twenty minutes later, an emergency repairman arrived from a local locksmith.

"What seems to be the trouble?" the repairman asked.

"The code stopped working," the security guard said. "We tried resetting it, but nothing is fixing it."

"Let me see what I can do."

Kimber looked down the hall. Where was

Brandon? He should have been here by now. And if this locksmith had any experience at all, it would take him a matter of seconds to determine the problem.

"Looks like the override system kicked in," the locksmith said. "It'll take me a minute to reset it."

Sure enough, he used one of his tools to reset the code and proceeded to open the door.

"Thank you." Detective Murray stepped into the doorway and turned to the locksmith and the security guard, who remained in the hall. "That's all we need from you two for now." He then turned to his partner. "Come on, Derrick."

Kimber tried to follow them into Ian's dressing room, but Derrick held up his hand and blocked their entrance.

"Sorry, miss. You need to wait out here."

Detective Murray glanced over his shoulder. "Which laptop is yours, Miss Seidel?"

Her laptop that had both her stories and encrypted files. She wanted to point to Ian's, but she couldn't. Ian's computer had the scenes from Parker's play, while she had deleted the scenes from her laptop every day.

Family or country. She hated when she had to choose between the two. She pointed at her laptop. "The silver one."

Footsteps rushed toward her, and Kimber turned. Brandon!

"They're taking my laptop, and they already have my phone." One of her phones anyway. Thankfully, they hadn't searched her to discover her CIA-issued cell tucked in her blazer pocket.

Brandon leaned close. "Rafi is on his way."

Which meant they needed to stall.

The two detectives walked back out into the hall. The nicer detective handed Kimber a sheet of paper. "This is a receipt for the confiscated items. We should have these processed and back to you sometime early next week."

"So you're taking my ability to work to the police station and holding it hostage through the weekend?"

Brandon stepped forward and produced a business card. "I'll need to come with you to make sure the intellectual property on Kimber's laptop is properly secured."

Detective Murray shook his head. "I'm sorry. That's not how this works."

"But —" Kimber started.

Rafi rushed down the hall toward them. Before he reached them, he already had his badge out of his pocket. "Detectives, I'm Special Agent Rafi Ebeid with the FBI. I'm afraid I'm going to need to take possession of Ms. Frost's laptop."

"What?" Detective Murray shook his head. "I have a warrant."

Rafi produced a paper from the inside pocket of his jacket. "So do I."

Chapter 25

Tessa finished cleaning up their lunch, her thoughts on her regular routine and how far from it she was right now. She couldn't help but feel guilty that her situation had left Greta relying on temps to do Tessa's job, nor could she deny the niggling fear that the job she loved would no longer be hers when this ordeal was over. She couldn't imagine ever finding a better boss or a job that would give her more fulfillment. And the thought of having to start over somewhere else was more than she could bear.

Though the pit of uncertainty filled her, Tessa tried to focus on the peace of the countryside instead of the bustling city she should be navigating. Trying to leave her doubts behind, she walked into the living room, where Parker sat on the couch, his laptop balanced on his legs once again, his fingers on the mousepad rather than on the keyboard. She'd spent enough time with

Kimber to recognize avoidance when she saw it, and Parker was definitely avoiding.

She sat beside him and glanced at his blank screen. “Are you starting a new scene, or are you stumped?”

“I’m not stumped . . . exactly.” Parker looked away briefly as though trying to avoid talking to her.

“Is something wrong?” Tessa asked.

“No. It’s just that it’s hard figuring out who could be behind this when we don’t know much about the players.”

Tessa scooted closer and took his hand. “Is there something you aren’t telling me?”

He blinked rapidly several times.

More avoidance, but this time, it wasn’t just the story.

Her gut twisted uncomfortably. She drew a deep breath and let it out before she tried again. “Parker. Tell me.”

“There’s new security footage.” He squeezed her hand. “It shows that you’re the only person who went in or out of the victim’s office during the window when she could have been killed.”

Tessa pulled her hand away and stood. His words repeated in her mind. “You don’t think I really killed her, do you?”

“No, of course not.”

Tessa took a step back. “But you aren’t

really sure. After all, you just met me a few days ago."

Parker rose to his feet. "I only had to know you five minutes to know you aren't capable of murder." He closed the distance between them and settled his hands on her arms. "I know you're innocent. But I'm worried."

"You think I'm going to get arrested."

He clenched his jaw, clearly fighting against his own emotions, but he was honest enough to nod.

The sinking feeling inside her magnified. "My whole life, I've never had so much as a traffic ticket. And now, because I was in the wrong place at the wrong time, I could end up spending the next few decades in prison?" She pressed her lips together and tried to fight back the threatening tears.

Parker rubbed his hands up and down her arms. "I hate to ask this, but is there anyone who would want to frame you for this?" Parker's gaze intensified. "Maybe we should be looking for someone who has a connection to you who could have had access to the studio and the victim."

"The only person I know who would have a connection to me who could have gotten into the studio easily is your uncle, and we both know he didn't do it," Tessa said. "Besides the fact that he would never do something like this, I talked to him on the phone right before Juliet was killed. If he was in the studio, I likely would have heard his phone ring."

"It's still worth posing the possibility that there's someone else who knows both of you."

A heaviness pressed in on her chest, the ramifications of what could happen to her crashing over her. And Parker. The potential of him facing criminal charges by helping her multiplied. "You need to leave here. You need to get as far away from me as possible."

"No. We're in this together."

"Parker. Don't you understand?" She pulled free of him. "You could end up in jail for helping me."

"Technically, all I've done is leave out the part about knowing where you are when the detective called."

"Which is grounds for them to arrest you."

"Give your sister and my uncle some more time to look into this." Parker drew Tessa into his arms. "No one is going to find us here. I promise."

Parker gripped the edge of his laptop and let the ramifications of his actions roll through his mind. Tessa was right. He could go to jail. Giving a false statement, obstructing justice, harboring a fugitive. Although the last crime wasn't valid until he officially learned that an arrest warrant had been issued for Tessa and he didn't turn her in. He couldn't turn her in. The mere thought of her in police custody made his stomach curl.

She snuggled next to him on the couch. "Is there anything else in Ian's scenes today that you haven't told me about?"

"Not really, but your sister did expand the details on the character list a bit." Parker pulled up the part of the file that listed the characters, or the bio information on the potential suspects.

"Since whoever came into the studio area must have used the stairwell to avoid being seen by the elevator cameras, maybe we should focus on those who left last from there."

"We have six: Gabriel Perez, Sheridan Maxwell, Lisa Cooper, Daniel Kent, Eli Masterson, and Nicole Armstrong." Parker pointed at his screen. "My uncle doesn't seem to think Nicole was guilty."

"Your uncle is a pretty good judge of character. What about the others?"

"It looks like Lisa and Nicole — they're

the screenwriter and the production assistant — left together," Parker said.

"Which makes it unlikely that they killed her." Tessa reached behind her and pulled the afghan off the back of the couch. "They would have had to be in on it together."

"I wish we had a better idea of what the motive could be," Parker said. "Someone had to have a reason to want Juliet dead."

Tessa spread the afghan over her legs. "I keep thinking it had to be one of the people arguing when I got there."

"Did you recognize either of the voices?"

She seemed to ponder the question. "I don't remember experiencing any sense of familiarity."

"If Juliet was the woman speaking, logically, that makes our killer the man who was there."

"I don't know. I saw a man getting on the elevator, but that was before I heard Juliet scream."

"So it could have been someone who wasn't involved in the argument at all." Parker raked his fingers through his hair.

"Which means it literally could have been anyone in the building that night."

"According to what Uncle Ian sent us, there were forty-three people there when it happened."

"Maybe we should see if we can stalk the suspects on social media — assuming Kimber can get us a list."

"I can write that idea into the next scene, but for now, let's get back to possible motives." Parker typed in a search and pulled up the obituary for Juliet. He angled his laptop so Tessa could see the screen. "According to this, the funeral is tomorrow."

"I wish we could go to see who else is there."

"We can't risk going, not with the police wanting to talk to you, but maybe we can get Uncle Ian to go."

"That's a good idea. He would have known her since they worked together."

"Exactly." Parker put his fingers on his keyboard. "Want to help me write a funeral scene for my play?"

"Can your new scene include your uncle figuring out who the killer is?"

The thought of his uncle in proximity to a murderer chilled his blood. "Only if he can do it without putting himself in danger."

Tessa nodded. "You should definitely spell that part out for him."

"I agree."

Colin didn't need an FBI babysitter, and he had no idea what he'd done to get stuck with one. He stormed into his office, irritated on principle that Special Agent Ebeid had insisted on transporting the evidence they'd secured with their respective warrants. At least Ebeid hadn't fought him when Colin had insisted Derrick ride with Ebeid and the guy from the publisher.

Colin secured the conference room, and a minute later, Derrick entered with their two guests.

Colin shut the door. "Now that we're here, want to explain why the FBI's involved?"

Ebeid put his hand on Brandon's shoulder. "Can you do me a favor and wait outside for a minute?" Ebeid placed the clear plastic bags holding Kimber Frost's cell phone and laptop on the conference table. "We won't break the seals on the evidence bags until you're back inside."

Brandon nodded and stepped out of the room.

"Well?" Colin asked.

"This investigation has some ties to national security," Ebeid said. "I'm here to make sure we don't have any classification breaches."

National security? Colin narrowed his eyes. The information he had on Kimber was that she was an aspiring author writing under the name Kimber Frost. "How does Kimber Seidel fall into the picture?"

"I'm not at liberty to say." Ebeid put his hand on top of the laptop. "Mr. Hale will be present any time you are searching documents related to Miss Frost's intellectual property. I will be present for everything else."

"Fine." If the FBI didn't interfere, Ebeid could sit in the corner for as long as he wanted.

"One more thing: The evidence will need to be held at the FBI offices, but you're welcome to reseal the evidence bags before transport."

Colin shook his head. "That's ridiculous."

"That's nonnegotiable, and it's clearly stated in my warrant," Ebeid said.

"If you're going to insist on that, then one of us needs to accompany you to make sure it's secured properly." Colin wagged his finger between himself and Derrick.

"Not a problem," Ebeid said. "One more thing though."

"What's that?"

"I need an evidence list of everything you took into custody on the night of the murder, and I'd like the opportunity to inspect the planner and laptop secured from the scene."

Colin narrowed his eyes. "We didn't take any laptops or planners."

"Then the killer must have taken them because Nicole, the victim's office mate, said both were missing."

"So when we find Tessa, if she still has those with her, we'll have proof that she's the killer."

"Or if you look at the security footage again, you'll see that she didn't have anything in her hands when she left."

So where were the missing items?

Ebeid opened the door and invited Brandon back inside. He handed the bag holding the cell phone to Colin. "Shall we begin?"

"Yes." Colin broke the seal and pulled it out of the bag. He turned to Derrick. "We need to contact her cell phone manufacturer to get past the security code."

"No need," Brandon said. "I know the code."

Chapter 26

Tessa couldn't sit still. She'd already cut up the onions and cooked the hamburger for the chili she planned to make for dinner tonight, even though dinnertime was still several hours away. Now she was debating between making some cornbread to go with it or going for a walk outside.

She peeked into the living room, where Parker sat in the oversized chair beside the fireplace, his fingers tapping away on his laptop. His brow was furrowed, and the look of intense concentration was one she'd seen on his face several times over the past few days. With how quickly he was typing, she guessed the words were flowing freely.

The fact that he was clearly in the zone made the decision for her. Even though no one knew she was here, she couldn't bring herself to venture outside without Parker by her side. At the moment, she could barely imagine doing anything without him. That was a scary thought.

A week ago, she had been adventurous, always willing to go out and explore on her own. How much had changed in just a few short days. The familiar unsettled feeling rose inside her, and with it came a sense of desperation.

Tessa pressed her hand to her stomach. She needed to get back to her normal self, to go back to the illusion that she had control of her own destiny. Assuming she could ever go back to that state of mind.

Turning back to the kitchen, she retrieved the items she would need for the cornbread. The simple task of measuring ingredients calmed her, but when she finished mixing the dry ingredients, she was once again faced with what to do with her time. She wouldn't want to bake the cornbread until it was closer to dinnertime.

Tessa let out a sigh. She really missed the sense of purpose that came from working. Even more, she missed the security of knowing Greta could rely on her. She desperately hoped her future would include not only returning to her old reality . . . but also allowing Parker to be a part of the side of her that thrived on her work and her freedom.

She put a tea towel over the bowl as Parker walked into the kitchen.

"Hey. What are you up to?" he asked.

"I was just getting a head start on dinner." She leaned against the counter. "Chili and cornbread." She gestured toward the oven. "I started the cornbread, but I'll wait until closer to dinner to finish it."

"That sounds good." He glanced out the window, where clouds hung low in the sky.

She retrieved a can of kidney beans from the cabinet. "What time do you want to eat? I can make the chili now and then let it simmer until we're ready."

"That's a good idea. I was thinking about going for a walk if you're up for it," Parker said.

"I'd love to. I was hoping to get outside before it gets too cold."

"Judging from those clouds, I'm guessing we're going to see rain sometime tonight."

The urge to check the weather app on her phone surfaced. "I haven't had my phone for days, and it's still driving me nuts that I can't check things like the weather or the time."

"I know what you mean, and I've only been without my phone for a day." He moved closer. "Want some help with the chili?"

"Sure. You can open the cans for me." She handed him the beans and rummaged in the cabinet until she found the tomato sauce and diced tomatoes.

Once again, she was struck by how easy Parker was to be around. Working together, they prepared the simple meal, and once the chili was on to simmer, they both donned their shoes and coats.

A brisk wind whipped over them, and Tessa suspected today's walk would need to be on the shorter side to keep them from freezing.

They turned toward the lake. The clouds had dropped so low that they could no longer make out the landscape in the distance.

"I'm suddenly very glad that we went down to the hotel yesterday instead of waiting until today." Parker slid his arm around her waist. "I wouldn't want to be riding the four-wheeler in this."

"Me neither." They reached the dock and walked to the end of it. Here, on the edge of nature, she could pretend the rest of the world didn't exist and that the turmoil in her life was simply a bad dream. "Everything looks so peaceful."

"It is peaceful." Parker turned so he was facing her. "And you're going to find your own peace soon."

Tessa wasn't sure how he had read her

thoughts so clearly, but his innate ability to ascertain her moods was becoming more expected than not. "I know I've already told you this, but I'm really glad I met you."

Parker trailed his finger down her arm and leaned in. He brushed his lips against hers once, then twice. Goose bumps rippled over her skin, and Tessa couldn't resist letting the kiss linger.

Parker eventually eased back and smiled. "Believe me, the pleasure has been all mine."

Kimber stood behind the two directors' chairs, where Ian and the director currently sat as they discussed the upcoming scene. On the set in front of them, the stage crew switched out props and adjusted the lighting.

Lisa, one of the screenwriters, approached with papers in her hand. "Gabriel, here are those changes you asked for."

The director skimmed over the offered pages. "This looks good. Make sure you print out the new scripts and get them to Ian and Allison."

"I need to leave in a few minutes for a doctor appointment, but I'll have Daniel do it."

Kimber stepped forward. "I can come get

those for you." She gestured toward Ian. "Ian and Allison are both in this next scene. If you can print them, I'll deliver them for you."

"That would be great. Thanks."

"No problem." Kimber turned her attention to Ian. "I'll be right back."

Ian nodded and returned to his conversation with Gabriel.

As soon as they reached the hall and the door closed behind them, Lisa said, "So, you're Ian's new assistant?"

"One of them, anyway," Kimber said. "He has another one who handles his fan mail and such."

"Be glad you're not dealing with that side of things. There are a lot of crazies out there."

"So I'm learning." Kimber gestured in the general direction of the production offices. "My first day was supposed to be Wednesday. I came up the elevator to find Ian talking to the police."

"I still can't believe someone killed Juliet." Lisa shook her head. "It's unreal."

"It really is," Kimber said. "It doesn't seem like anyone would have a reason to kill her."

"I know, right?" Lisa shook her head. "I mean, she got along with everyone, even

Sheridan and Bob."

"I've met Sheridan, but who is Bob?"

"He works in the editing suite." Lisa lowered her voice. "He's amazing at what he does, but you don't want to be around him when he's working. He can get pretty intense."

"Good to know." Especially if Bob's intensity could lead to violence — or murder.

Lisa stopped beside a closed door and knocked once before opening it. "Hey, Daniel, this is Kimber, Ian's new assistant."

"Yeah." He nodded. "I think we met when Ian was introducing you around on Thursday."

"I think you're right." But Kimber hadn't been able to have a conversation with him beyond saying hello. "How are you liking working on this show?"

"It's always nice to be with one that's expected to run for a while." He swiveled his chair so he was more fully facing Kimber. "Didn't expect the real-life drama though. Poor Juliet."

"Any idea of who would do something like that to her?"

"Not a clue."

Lisa sat at her desk and clicked on a few keys on her laptop. "I heard the police were looking for someone, but I don't know who."

Kimber wished she didn't know either, and she prayed that the police would find a new suspect.

After chatting with the two screenwriters for a few more minutes, Kimber left their office with the updated script and headed back to the studio. When she entered, Allison had taken the seat beside Gabriel, and Ian was nowhere to be found.

Kimber approached Allison. "Here are your updated pages for Monday. Lisa asked me to give them to you."

"Thanks." She accepted the offering.

Kimber looked around the set, still not seeing Ian anywhere. "Have you seen Ian?"

Gabriel gestured toward the door. "He left right after we finished our last take."

"He's probably in his dressing room." Kimber took a step back. "Have a good weekend."

"You too," Gabriel said.

Allison gave her a little wave before picking up her conversation with the director again.

Kimber passed by the cameras and the few stage hands storing the various props for the weekend. She had considered staying longer to ask more questions of the few crew members remaining, but doing so would likely raise suspicions, especially on a Friday night. Plus, she couldn't deny that Ian's offer to give her a ride home would cut at least a half hour off her commute.

When she arrived at Ian's dressing room, it was empty. She proceeded to set the new script pages on Ian's desk and then packed up her notes. After a quick look in the hall, she pulled out her work cell phone and dialed Ian's number. No answer.

"That's odd." Her phone still in hand, she sat in her desk chair. The phone rang almost instantly, but it wasn't Ian. It was Brandon.

"Hey. Are you already off work?" she asked in lieu of a greeting.

"Yeah. I just got off the subway," Brandon said. "What about you? Are you home yet?"

"No, but Ian said he'd give me a ride. I should be home in a half hour or so."

"Great. I'll pick something up for dinner on my way."

"Sounds good. I'll see you soon," Kimber said, appreciating the simple fact that she could expect to eat her evening meals with Brandon without either of them needing to confirm their plans.

"Oh, one more thing. Any chance you can see if Rafi has a laptop I can borrow until I get mine back?"

"I'm way ahead of you. I already picked one up."

"You're the best. Thank you." Relieved that she wouldn't be without a computer for the weekend, she ended the call.

Several minutes passed before Ian finally walked through the door.

Kimber stood. "Where have you been?"

"I'll tell you later." Ian shrugged out of the suit jacket he'd worn in his last scene and hung it on the rack. "Are you ready to go?"

"Yeah. I think so."

"Let's go, then." They made their way outside to Ian's waiting car. Ian's driver opened the back door and waited for them to climb in before circling to the driver's side.

"Can you tell me now where you were?" Kimber asked.

"Let's talk when we get to your place," Ian said, his voice low. "Will Brandon already be home?"

"Yes. He called a few minutes ago, and he was already on his way."

"Good. He'll want to hear this too."

Chapter 27

Brandon opened the door to his apartment to find both Kimber and Ian on the other side. "Ian. I didn't expect to see you tonight." Especially since Ian had never been to his apartment before. In the past, every time he'd joined Kimber to visit Ian, it had been at one of Ian's homes, or they'd met in the city somewhere.

Ian tilted his head toward Kimber. "We have a few things to chat about that would be best done away from the studio."

"Come on in." Brandon stepped aside and waited for Kimber and Ian to cross the threshold before he closed the door. "Do you want to join us for dinner? I picked up some Chinese food."

"I'm sure Phoebe already has something planned for us for dinner." Ian shot a boyishly hopeful look at Kimber. "But if Kimber is hiding any of the pumpkin bars in your freezer, I'll take one."

Kimber shook her head. "Nice try."

Disappointment flickered briefly in Ian's expression before he shrugged. "Now that the door's closed, I really needed to talk to both of you about something."

"What?" Brandon gestured for everyone to sit in the living room.

Ian settled into the oversized armchair by the fireplace. "Don't get mad, but I had a friend take a look at the surveillance footage of the hall in the timeframe when Tessa went in and out of Juliet's office."

Brandon couldn't keep the obvious question from spilling out. "You did what?" Protecting evidence and their access to it was key to finding the truth. "Ian, you can't share confidential information with people."

"I knew you would say that, but we can trust Bob."

"Bob?" Kimber asked. "The guy who works in the editing suite?"

"Yeah. I've known him for years." Ian held up his hand. "And before you lecture me about how he might have been involved, Bob wasn't even in New York when Juliet was killed."

But alibis could be faked. "Where was he?" Brandon asked.

"He was in LA for his daughter's wedding last weekend. He didn't fly back in until

Wednesday night."

Brandon made a mental note to have Rafi confirm that detail.

"So why was it that you wanted Bob to look at the feed?" Kimber asked.

"When we first watched it, something seemed off," Ian said. "I wanted a second opinion, and I'm right."

"About?" Brandon prompted.

"The lighting is off." Ian leaned forward and rested his forearms on his knees. "I think someone edited the surveillance feed before giving it to the police."

Hope sparked inside Brandon and reflected in Kimber's eyes. Brandon shot to his feet and retrieved his laptop from the kitchen table. Quickly, he opened it and pulled up the surveillance feed. Handing the laptop to Ian, he said, "Show me."

Ian waited until both Brandon and Kimber moved to stand behind him so they could all see the screen. Then he hit the Play button.

"Look at the brightness of the hallway when Tessa is walking toward the office." Ian gestured to the edge of the image. "And there isn't any shadow."

"There usually isn't in a brightly lit room," Brandon said.

"Exactly." Ian paused until Tessa disappeared into the office. "Now check out what happens when Tessa comes back out into the hall." Ian skipped forward to the moment when Tessa emerged and returned the video to normal speed. Tessa and her shadow filled the screen.

"Why would she have a shadow now when she didn't before?" Kimber leaned in. "Could a lightbulb have gone out or something?"

"I don't think so," Ian said. "I checked with maintenance this morning, and they said they didn't have any record of replacing any lightbulbs this week. And I checked that hall. All the lights were on."

Brandon's mind raced until the impossible suddenly made sense. "A lot of offices automatically shift to conservation mode at night. Which means less light at night."

Kimber straightened, and her gaze met Brandon's, awareness shining in her eyes. "So the image of Tessa walking into the office isn't Tessa at all."

Ian swiveled in his chair. "That's my guess."

"Someone must have doctored the security feed." Brandon pressed both hands on the table, his thoughts swirling. "Ian, do you have any idea who would have had access?"

"Obviously, the security team would be

able to get the feed, but I have no idea who in there has the ability to edit it."

"In today's world, it wouldn't be hard for someone to figure it out," Brandon said.

"I don't know." Ian adjusted the image on the screen again. "The transition of the lighting difference is too subtle for someone to have just clipped two feeds together."

Ian let the video start again, running it from the time the woman entered the office to the time when Tessa emerged. Sure enough, the lighting changed so subtly in the time elapse that it was hardly noticeable.

"What are you thinking, Ian?" Brandon asked.

"I think whoever did this is a pro, someone who has experience in the editing booth."

Kimber straightened. "If you think it was one of the video editors, why did you talk to Bob? He could tell someone you were asking questions."

"We can trust Bob," Ian said again. "And like I told you, he wasn't in the city at the time of the murder, and he didn't get back until after the police already had the video feed."

"Do you think Bob could help us find out who altered the surveillance feed?" Kimber asked.

"I do." Ian pushed back from the table and stood. "If all goes well, before next week is over, we'll have some answers."

"I hope so," Kimber said. "I'm ready for Tessa to come back home."

"We all are." Ian moved to the door before he turned back around to face Brandon and Kimber. "I'm going to head home, but I think you two should consider going to Juliet's funeral tomorrow."

Attending a funeral for someone they'd never met . . . Brandon supposed seeing who attended could end up being useful at some point. If nothing else, it would help him see their suspects in person.

"Send us the details." Brandon slid his arm around Kimber. "We'll be there."

CHAPTER 28

Dressed in a simple black dress, Kimber stood between Ian and Brandon at the graveside service. The memorial service had concluded over an hour ago, but it was here in the cemetery that they could truly analyze the others who had come to pay their respects.

Juliet's family comforted one another beneath the awning that had been set up over the casket. The various cast and crew members had clustered together on the left side of the awning, with numerous other friends encircling the back and the other side. Almost directly across from Kimber, she spotted a man in his thirties who was oddly familiar.

She leaned close to Ian. "Do you recognize that guy? Black shirt, red tie?"

Ian took a step away from Kimber and ducked his head a bit, likely to get a better look. Then he returned to her side. "I think he's one of the security guards."

"Maybe he's the boyfriend." That meant he could be the real killer. Though tempted to suggest Brandon talk to the man, Kimber suspected she would appear less threatening, especially in this situation. "I'll try talking to him after the service."

Brandon leaned close and whispered, "Are you sure?"

She nodded.

Brandon took her hand and squeezed it. "Then Ian and I will split up and see if we can pick up on anyone else worth keeping tabs on." He leaned closer still. "But I'll be close by if you need me."

And they were in a public space. Surely, even if Kimber did corner the killer, he wouldn't try anything here. And though she preferred not to use them, she had gone through a good deal of training with the CIA to enhance her self-defense skills. Despite the training, tension rippled through her body, buzzing like an electric current beneath her skin.

The man conducting the graveside service stepped forward and welcomed those who had gathered to mourn. Over the next fifteen minutes, Kimber studied the others present, her gaze frequently returning to the man they believed to be Juliet's married boyfriend. More than once, Heath Quentin's eyes teared up, and he alternated between blinking rapidly and swiping at his damp eyes.

Whether he was guilty of causing Juliet's death or not, his grief appeared to be sincere.

A final prayer was offered, and Brandon leaned down to whisper in Kimber's ear. "Be careful."

She nodded and whispered back, "You too."

During the two seconds Kimber looked at Brandon, Heath Quentin disappeared from her sight. Urgency rushed through her, and she moved quickly in the direction of where she had seen him last. It took a few steps before she spotted Heath separating himself from the crowd and heading toward the line of parked cars.

Kimber sidestepped an older couple and angled across the grassy area at the edge of the gravesite. When she was within a few yards of her target, she called out, "Heath Quentin?"

The man turned, surprise illuminating his expression. "Do I know you?"

"We haven't met, but I worked with Juliet at the studio." Kimber stepped past him so she was between him and the cars. She then extended her hand. "I'm Kimber. I'm so sorry for your loss."

He furrowed his brow. "Thanks."

"I know things weren't great with you and Juliet at the end, but I can't imagine how hard this must be for you."

Heath took a step back, distancing himself from Kimber in the direction he had originally been walking. "I don't know what you mean."

"I know you were both keeping your relationship quiet, but Juliet shared a lot with me." Another stretch of the truth. Juliet had never said a word to Kimber, but the examination into her life had certainly spoken volumes so far.

He folded his arms across his chest. "She never mentioned you."

"Since she didn't know about your wife, it seems like she wasn't the only one segmenting the different parts of her life."

His eyes widened. "You know —"

"I know she saw the two of you together, and I know that's why she broke things off."

"Look, it's not what you think," Heath said hastily. "My wife and I were separated when Juliet and I started dating."

"Let me guess: You decided to give it another shot, but you weren't sure whether to tell Juliet about your marriage."

He blinked rapidly against the new tears that formed in his eyes. "Had I not gotten back together with Suzanne, I would have been with Juliet the night she was killed."

"I heard you did see her that night."

He sucked in a quick breath. "You don't think —" He shook his head, apparently unable to finish the sentence. "I would never hurt her. I loved her."

"What time did you last see her the night she died?"

"It was a bit after ten. Maybe quarter after." He stared off into the distance for a long moment, and fresh tears formed in his eyes. He swallowed hard before continuing. "From what the police said, she was probably killed shortly after I left."

"Did you see anyone else?"

"There was a woman walking down the hall when I got onto the elevator, but I don't know who she was."

Even though Kimber suspected the woman he'd seen was Tessa, she forced herself to ask the question. "What did she look like?"

"I didn't get a good look at her, but she was brunette, probably mid-twenties."

Just like Tessa.

"Did you hear or see anyone else?"

"No, but I was only on Juliet's floor for a

few minutes." He shook his head again, but this time, his tormented expression suggested he was fighting against a difficult memory. "I got to Juliet's office, we argued, and she insisted I leave." He sniffled. "That's the last time I saw her until I got the call that she'd been killed."

"One more question." Kimber straightened her shoulders and tipped her chin up before she asked, "Did your wife know about Juliet?"

His eyes widened, and shock flickered over his face. A moment passed as the implications sank in. He stepped forward, and his voice filled with fury and fear. "My wife didn't have anything to do with Juliet's death, and neither did I."

Though Heath hadn't answered Kimber's question with his words, his actions screamed his answer. His wife had most definitely been aware of his relationship with Juliet. Kimber took a step back and spoke with sympathy. "I really am sorry for your loss." She turned back toward the gravesite.

She hadn't detected any deception in Heath's account of his actions, but even if he were innocent, his wife was worthy of adding to their list of suspects.

Parker put another log in the fireplace and

replaced the screen as the flames licked the side of the fresh wood. Curled up on the couch, Tessa balanced his computer on her lap as she read through the latest pages his uncle had sent.

"It's crazy to think Juliet could have been killed by her boyfriend's wife, especially if she really didn't even know the man was married."

"Yeah, the poor woman. Talk about bad luck."

"It's hard to believe her husband's affair would drive her to murder his mistress." Tessa ran her finger over the mousepad. "Of course, I can't imagine anyone getting so angry over anything that they would kill another person."

"That makes two of us." Parker joined her on the couch and stretched his arm out to rest his hand on her shoulder. "If the wife has possessive tendencies, it could be that she saw killing Juliet as a way to make sure her husband stayed with her."

"That's twisted."

"Agreed."

Tessa closed the laptop and set it on the couch beside her before she snuggled into Parker's side. "Do you think Detective Murray will look into the new suspect?"

"I don't know." But if his uncle Ian's and

Kimber's concerns were valid, he doubted it. Regardless, he and Tessa were due for a break from the stress of Juliet Clark's murder and the impact the woman's death had had on Tessa. "You know, there's really not much anyone can do until Monday. How about we watch a movie or something to get our minds off all this?"

"I'd like that."

Relieved to take a break for a while and simply spend time with Tessa, Parker stood and crossed to retrieve the television remote from where it lay on the mantel. He made it halfway back to the couch before the rumble of a car engine sounded outside.

Parker froze, and his heartbeat quickened.

Tessa furrowed her brow. "What's wrong?"

Had she not heard the car pull up?

The motor cut off, and a few seconds passed before a car door slammed.

Tessa immediately bolted to her feet, and the blanket covering her legs slid to the floor. Her eyes widened, and fear reflected in the deep green. She quickly crossed to him and grabbed his arm. "What do we do?"

What should they do? If the police showed up and he lied about her being here, they'd both end up in jail. He prayed it was someone else.

He covered her hand with his and squeezed it. "For now, go into your room. I'll come get you when I know what's going on."

Tessa swallowed hard and nodded. Then she turned and hurried down the hall to her room.

Parker waited until her door closed before he moved to the window. He pulled the curtains aside just enough that he could peek outside. In the darkness, he could barely make out three figures moving toward the porch. One of them held a cell phone with the flashlight shining on the path. The other two carried suitcases toward the front porch.

Not the police. But who would be showing up here at the cabin? Micah hadn't mentioned anyone from the family planning a vacation here.

As they neared the door, the person in the back passed the other two and set the cases down. Parker moved away from the window and turned toward the entrance as the lock flipped and the knob turned.

The door swung open, and two women entered followed by a man. It took a moment for Parker to identify the new arrivals. Micah, the friend who had lent him this cabin, along with his girlfriend, Olivia, and

Olivia's sister Zoey. So much for a quiet weekend with Tessa.

"Hey, Parker." Micah kicked the door closed and set the suitcases down.

"What are you doing here?" Parker asked, fighting against the sense of invasion that pressed in on him.

"Didn't you get my message?" Micah asked.

Parker wasn't about to admit that he'd deliberately left his phone at the hotel down the street, especially not in front of Olivia and Zoey. "Sorry. My phone hasn't been working." At least not in a way he could use it at the moment. "What are you doing here?" he repeated.

"I hadn't heard from you for a while, and Olivia and I wanted to get away for a few days." Micah gestured to Zoey. "And we thought since you were here alone, we'd bring Zoey with us." The gleam in Micah's eye was impossible to miss. He was trying to set Parker and Zoey up — again.

Zoey took a step forward and put her hand on Parker's arm. "I hope you don't mind me joining you."

Parker took an automatic step back, breaking the contact between them. "No, I don't mind," he lied. "But I'm actually not here alone."

"What?" Micah asked. "I thought you were coming up here to do some writing."

"I am, but my girlfriend is here with me."

"Girlfriend?" Micah tossed his coat over the back of the couch. "When did this happen?"

"It's pretty recent." Parker wasn't even sure the word *girlfriend* applied to Tessa yet, but he was more than a little surprised at how much he wanted it to.

Zoey folded her arms across her chest. "So where is this girlfriend?"

"She's just in her room." Hiding. "We were about to watch a movie. Do you guys want to join us?"

Micah looked down at Olivia.

Olivia shot an apologetic glance at her sister before she nodded. "Yeah, sure."

"Let's get everyone settled in their rooms." Micah picked up the luggage again. "Then we'll join you." He took a step toward the east wing hallway. "Which rooms are you guys in anyway?"

"I'm in my usual room, and my girlfriend is in the one next to the office."

He nodded and gestured to the two women. "All right, this way."

The three gathered their belongings and headed to the hall that lay opposite the one Tessa had disappeared down a minute ago.

Not thrilled with the change in their situation, Parker strode toward Tessa's room. They needed a plan to make sure their unexpected guests didn't learn why he and Tessa were really here.

Chapter 29

Tessa paced her room, unable to sit still. She'd tried pressing her ear to the door to make out the voices from the living room, but other than being able to distinguish that there were both men and women speaking, she couldn't make out anything being said.

Footsteps sounded against the wooden floor of the hallway, and she stopped her pacing and whirled to face the door as someone knocked.

She didn't speak, fear gripping her throat. What if the person on the other side was a police officer?

Parker's voice carried to her. "It's me."

Relief flooded through her, and she hurried to open the door.

Parker slipped inside and closed the door behind him. "My friend whose family owns this cabin just showed up with his girlfriend and her sister."

The panic Tessa had experienced moments ago faded, morphing into a new sense of unease. "What if they tell someone I'm here?"

"Don't worry." Parker took both of her hands in his. "I doubt they would have anything to do with the police or the investigation."

She supposed that was true. Even though the woman's murder had likely made the news because of where it had occurred, Tessa had no idea if her own name and photo would be released or if anyone would associate her with that particular headline. She prayed they wouldn't. "How long are they staying?"

He squeezed her hands. "Just a few days."

"Is it bad that I'm already missing our time alone?"

"No." He rubbed his thumb over the back of her hand. "I feel the same way."

"How are we going to work on the scenes for Kimber and Ian with them around?"

"Micah knows I came here to write, and I told him you're my girlfriend, so it will make sense that we would want time alone." His gaze met hers, an unexpected intensity reflected in his eyes. "Would you mind being my girlfriend?"

Warmth filled Tessa at the prospect of exploring a deeper relationship with Parker, but she couldn't ignore that she was likely wanted by the police, and her future was anything but certain.

She wavered on whether she was even capable of stepping into a relationship right now, with her life in such turmoil. Opting for honesty, she said, "I would love to be your girlfriend, but I don't think that's such a good idea right now."

"Why not?"

She leaned closer and lowered her voice to a whisper. "Parker, if the police find me, I could be arrested. You don't want to risk ruining your chances of getting another play picked up."

"We both know you aren't a criminal."

"But that doesn't mean the police don't still think I am." Tessa pulled her hands free and took a step back. "If I'm arrested, it wouldn't be a good look for you if anyone found out you were my boyfriend."

"It's a risk worth taking." Parker reached out his hand and brushed her hair behind her ear. "Besides, the truth will come out eventually. The police will find the real killer, even if your sister and my uncle have to hand the evidence to them on a silver platter."

A sliver of hope worked through her and opened the door to her heart. "I want to believe that." And she wanted Parker in her life.

"Then believe it." He closed the distance between them and leaned in for a kiss.

When his lips met hers, a thrill whipped through her. Goose bumps rippled over her skin, and her stomach flipflopped as though she were riding a roller coaster, rounding an unexpected turn. It was the same as the first time he'd kissed her yet somehow different.

He wanted to be her boyfriend, and she couldn't deny that the prospect of making a commitment filled her with an excitement she couldn't remember experiencing before.

She eased back and lifted her gaze to his once more. "You're making it hard to say no to you."

He pressed his lips to hers for another brief kiss. "Then don't say no."

Doubts filled her, tempered by hope. "Are you sure you want this?"

"Yes." He caressed her cheek. "I'm sure."

Unable to deny the connection between them or her desire for it to continue, she lifted her hand and wrapped her fingers around his arm. "Okay."

He leaned back slightly and lifted his eyebrows. "Okay?"

Now she smiled. "Yes, I will be your

girlfriend."

Parker grinned and pulled her into a hug. "This is turning out to be a much better day than I expected."

"Even though your friends showed up?"

"Maybe I should thank them." He leaned back so he could see her clearly. "If they hadn't, we probably wouldn't have had the relationship talk quite this soon."

"That's true." She hadn't reached the point where she'd needed to have a relationship talk with most of the men she'd dated.

Parker released her and gestured toward the door. "You ready to go out and meet them?"

"No, but we might as well get it over with."

He gripped the doorknob but then turned back to face her. "One more thing: What's your middle name?"

"Lynn. Why?"

"Because a murder case associated with a television show is likely still in the news. If the police have already announced that they're looking for you, it'll be best if you use your middle name with my friends."

And just like that, reality was back. "If you think my name might be in the news, my photo probably is too."

Parker released the doorknob and faced

her more fully. He reached out and tucked a lock of hair behind her ear. "Do you always wear your hair down?"

"Yes, unless I'm at some fancy party. Then sometimes I wear it up. Why?"

"If you put your hair back in a ponytail and take off your makeup, you'll look a lot different." He gathered her hair in his hands and pulled it back away from her face. "I bet any photos the police have of you would show you looking completely put together."

She couldn't deny that. Even her driver's-license photo had her hair down and her makeup carefully intact. She turned to the dresser, where she'd left her makeup bag, and retrieved a hair tie and makeup wipe. After she removed her makeup and tied her hair back into a simple ponytail, she turned to the mirror. Her light dusting of freckles was now visible, and her lack of makeup made her look more like a teenager than a twenty-something-year-old.

She turned toward Parker. "What do you think? Do you think this will be enough?"

"I wish we had some prop glasses for you to wear, but this will have to do."

"Great idea." Tessa grabbed her purse and fished out a pair.

Parker lifted his eyebrows. "You carry prop glasses around in your purse?"

"Of course I do. I work with celebrities all day." She slipped the glasses into place. "I always carry a pair or two in case someone needs a quick disguise."

"You're amazing." Parker leaned in and kissed her cheek. "You ready?"

She wasn't, but she drew a deep breath and nodded.

"Good. And don't forget you aren't Tessa right now. You're Lynn."

"Right. Lynn it is."

Parker stepped into the hall and took Tessa's hand in his. Now that Tessa was officially his girlfriend, he couldn't be more delighted to have a future with this fascinating woman as well as a barrier between him and Zoey.

They walked down the hall to the sound of voices. Tessa slowed her steps as they approached the living room, and Parker glanced down at her. The apprehension shining in her eyes was unmistakable.

Hoping to put her at ease, he stopped and kissed her forehead. "It'll be fine," he whispered.

She pressed her lips together and seemed to gather her courage. Then she gave him a subtle nod.

"Come on." Parker led her into the living room, where Micah and Olivia sat on the couch and Zoey was comfortably settled on the love seat. "Hey, everyone. I want you to meet my girlfriend, Lynn." He proceeded to introduce everyone to Tessa. With no place available for him and Tessa to easily sit together, he led her to the oversized chair beside the fireplace and sat down. Then he stretched one arm along the back of the chair and tugged on Tessa's hand to encourage her to sit with him, despite the space being a bit cramped.

He couldn't help but smile when she sat and snuggled into his side.

Once they were settled, Micah asked, "Lynn, how did you get Parker to let you come up here with him? Usually when he's writing, he doesn't want anyone around."

"And yet you came up here anyway," Parker said pointedly.

Micah simply grinned. "I knew you needed a break. Besides, I wasn't talking to you."

Tessa adjusted her glasses and looked at Parker before she spoke. "I didn't know Parker bringing someone on his writing retreats was unusual."

"Oh yeah." Micah nodded emphatically. "Every time he gets focused on a project, he turns into a hermit."

Olivia tucked her feet up underneath her

on the couch. "I figure that's why he never dates anyone for long."

"Maybe I never lasted long with anyone because I hadn't met the right woman yet." Parker gave Tessa's shoulder a squeeze. "Lynn's different from anyone I've ever dated before."

Out of the corner of his eye, he caught the way Zoey glared at him. Apparently, she had been a willing participant in the plan to set the two of them up.

Hoping to ease the tension, he asked, "Zoey, what have you been up to lately?"

"I'm working for a law firm in midtown while I study for the bar exam."

He remembered now. Zoey had still been in law school the last time he'd seen her. "That's great." He placed his hand more firmly on Tessa's shoulder. "If you need to study, you'll have plenty of quiet up here."

Zoey flicked a glance at Tessa before responding. "I kind of hope to get a break from studying while I'm here."

"A break can be good too," Parker said amicably before turning his attention back to Micah. "You said you're staying for a few days. When do you plan to head back?"

"On Monday."

"We all have to be back to work on Tuesday," Olivia added.

Tessa tensed, and Parker rubbed his hand along her shoulder. He could only imagine how hard this must be for her, loving her job and not being able to work or even talk to her boss.

Micah tilted his head toward the front door. "By the way, where's your car?"

"It's in town. It was having some issues." Like being equipped with GPS that the police might try to track.

"Your car and your phone are having issues?" Micah shook his head. "Man, you've been having some bad luck lately."

Not nearly as much as Tessa had. And once they could clear her name, he would be able to look back on this whole situation as a shot of good luck for meeting Tessa. Since he could hardly admit to his thoughts, he changed the subject. "So, what movie do we want to watch?"

Tessa spoke up before anyone could respond. "I vote for a comedy."

"As long as it's not a chick flick, I'm fine with anything," Micah said.

"There's a new Madison Peters movie on Amazon Prime," Tessa suggested.

Parker nodded. "I could go for that."

Chapter 30

Brandon had hoped the weekend would give him and Kimber time to rest and recover from the crazy week of juggling their day jobs and the murder investigation. Unfortunately, that wasn't to be. For better or worse, Kimber's chat with Juliet's boyfriend had expanded their suspect list. Now, here they were, sitting in Kimber's living room, staring at their computer screens.

For better or worse. That phrase repeated in his mind, and he glanced at Kimber. She'd tucked her dark hair behind her ear, her focus entirely on the laptop Rafi had lent her to use until she got hers back from Murray.

She really was so beautiful, but more than that, her innate kindness and desire to help others had been what had captured his heart. And in these quiet moments together, he couldn't help but marvel at the way their lives had intertwined into what was quickly turning into a happily ever after. But before he could consider what would happen next in their relationship, they needed to eliminate the current stress Tessa's unusual predicament was causing.

Kimber lifted her hand and rubbed at her neck.

"Here." Needing a break, he set his laptop aside and shifted so he could massage her shoulders.

She turned so he could have easier access and hummed her approval. "That feels so good."

"It's supposed to." Brandon continued to rub at the tight muscles in her neck and shoulders. "Any luck yet on the surveillance?"

"From what I can see, Heath's story checks out," Kimber said, resignation in her voice. "He was on the sixteenth floor before the murder, but he went back downstairs to the lobby after that for about ten minutes. Then he went upstairs, but he started at the forty-third floor and used the stairs to work his way down."

"How far did he get before the call came in about Juliet's death?" Brandon asked.

"The thirty-eighth." She shook her head. "If he'd been closer, we could make the argument that he got to the crime scene by using blind spots or overriding camera feed, but he shows up in too many spots for all of these to have been altered before being sent to the police."

"So he's in the clear, but his wife isn't." Brandon trailed his thumbs along the top of Kimber's shoulders before pressing a kiss to the nape of her neck. "How's that?"

Kimber tilted her head from one side to the other. "Better. Thanks."

"No problem." He gestured to her laptop. "Want to help me dig into his wife?"

"Sure." She propped her legs up on the coffee table and rebalanced her laptop on her lap. "Where do you want me to start?"

"Can you work through her social media accounts?" Brandon asked. "I'll look through her phone and email logs."

"Sure." Kimber opened a new tab on her laptop. "What are the chances that Rafi would be able to get us access to her financials?"

"I have no idea, but it can't hurt to ask," Brandon said. "If he can get them, do you want to enlist Mark's help to look over them? You're already juggling too many jobs."

"Since we're looking at domestic banking records, that may not be a good idea."

"Why not? He's helped us before."

"I know, but he's my best friend, and he's had a crush on Tessa for forever," Kimber said. "I don't want to involve him unless absolutely necessary."

"Why not?" Brandon furrowed his brow. "He's a good guy, and I'm sure he'd want to do everything he can to help Tessa."

"I know, but based on the pages Parker has sent lately, I have a feeling my sister is off the market." Kimber tapped her fingers on her keyboard. "I'm not sure how Mark is going to take the news."

Brandon hadn't considered the dynamics of Tessa being in such close proximity to Ian's nephew this week, but such situations often created bonds that were both unusual and strong. "You need to at least consider the possibility of involving him. Regardless of Tessa's relationship status, Mark would want to help."

"You're right, but I can do anything he can do when it comes to the domestic side."

"True." Letting the conversation drop, Brandon scrolled through the wife's call log, taking time to note the names of those she'd communicated with over the past week. When he reached the night of the murder, her phone was noticeably quiet. "The wife didn't make any calls or texts from nine fifteen to eleven ten on the night of the murder."

Kimber looked up from her screen, hope illuminating her expression. "That's interesting."

"Very." Brandon tried to access the location log for the woman's cell phone, but it wasn't included in the information Rafi had shared with him. "Looks like the GPS data is missing. We'll have to wait until Monday to see if Rafi can pinpoint where her phone was that night."

"I'm not sure there's much more either of us can do until then." Kimber leaned forward and set her laptop on the coffee table. "Her social media accounts are all about her fitness routine and her dog."

Brandon sighed. "I guess it was wishful thinking that she'd put something incriminating online."

"Yeah, but it was worth checking." Kimber drew her legs up beneath her and turned to face him. "It's amazing how many people post something that leads to the police solving a crime."

"At this point, I'd settle for any clue that proves Tessa didn't kill Juliet."

"You and me both," Kimber said. She rolled her shoulders and gestured to her laptop. "I guess I should write up our findings so far in a new scene for Parker."

"Tell you what." Brandon pushed to a stand. "You do that, and I'll check with Rafi for updates."

"That sounds good." A smile played on Kimber's lips. "But it would be better if you also check in with Trudy to see if she's seen the police hanging around again."

Brandon cocked an eyebrow. "You're hoping she'll send cookies home with me, aren't you?"

Kimber's smile widened. "I'm pretty sure I smelled gingersnaps when I walked by her apartment."

"I love those." Brandon leaned down and brushed his lips over hers. The touch sent a familiar ripple along his skin, and he couldn't resist pulling her closer. Kimber leaned into him, and a sense of wonder filled him. How had he gotten so lucky to have this amazing woman in his life?

The kiss lingered until Kimber pulled back. She put her hand on his chest. "You need to stop distracting me. We have work to do."

"Oh, all right." Brandon gave her another quick kiss. "I'll race you."

"Writing a scene for a play is going to take longer than the ten minutes it'll take you to call Rafi and visit Trudy."

He kissed her again, this time lingering

when his lips met hers. "I have faith in you."

Colin tugged on his tie and wished for the hundredth time that his wife hadn't insisted he attend her friend's wedding reception. After working with dead bodies all week, the last thing he wanted was to socialize with a bunch of people who wanted nothing more than to believe the world he lived in didn't exist.

He and Kristin crossed through the hotel lobby toward the ballroom doors. Colin wiggled his tie again in the hope that it would stop strangling him.

"Stop messing with your tie." His wife grabbed his hand to prevent him from trying to loosen it further.

"How long do we have to stay at this thing?"

"That all depends on how long it lasts."

So she intended to stay to the bitter end. Great.

Kristin lowered her hand, his still clutched in hers. Then she reached up on her toes and kissed his cheek. "Come on. It'll be fun."

Fun was sitting at home, watching a ballgame.

Begrudgingly, Colin escorted Kristin through the double doors that led to the reception. Round tables covered in blue tablecloths filled both sides of the room, and a dance floor had been sectioned off near the long table at the far end of the room, where the bride and groom currently stood with the rest of the wedding party.

"We're at table seven." Kristin pointed at a table off to the right where a place card identified the table number.

One couple already sat there when Colin and Kristin reached it.

"Hey, Amber, Devonte." Kristin hugged the woman and nodded to the man. "This is my husband, Colin."

"It's nice to meet you." The pretty brunette shook his hand.

"Colin Murray, right?" Devonte asked.

"Yeah."

"I saw you in the news a couple weeks ago when everyone was talking about that lawsuit," Devonte said. "Must be rough."

And there it was — yet another reason Colin didn't want to be here. "It's never easy finding out mistakes were made."

"Did you ever figure out who the real killer was?" Devonte asked.

"We're still working on it." But even with reopening the investigation, all the evidence still pointed at Wyatt Harvey. Colin still couldn't figure out how the evidence could be so wrong. Even worse was the idea that the real killer was still roaming free.

Pressure built up in his chest as he considered the Clark murder case. It was eerily similar to the Harvey case. The evidence continued to point at a single suspect, but the motivation for the murder remained unclear. He hated it when that happened. Without understanding what would drive the killer to commit murder, it made the prosecutor's job increasingly difficult when it came to convincing a jury.

In the Clark case, they couldn't even prove that their prime suspect knew the victim. Not good.

"Did that conviction getting overturned mess up your position with the police department?" Devonte asked.

"No." Reciting the same story he'd shared dozens of times, Colin said, "The internal investigation proved that I didn't do anything wrong." But it hadn't revealed who might have misdirected the investigation. Eager to change the subject, Colin asked, "What do you do?"

"I work on Wall Street with Zane," he said, referring to the groom. "I think this honeymoon they have planned may be the longest vacation he's ever taken."

"That just seems wrong," Kristin said.

"What's the point of making money if you never get to enjoy it?"

Colin had no idea since he rarely had money to spare. "Where are they going on their honeymoon?"

"They're planning to head up to the Catskills. And I have to say, a week relaxing in the woods does have its appeal," Amber said.

The Catskills. That was where Parker Sawyer had gone after he'd last seen Tessa Seidel. He narrowed his eyes. Maybe it was time to take a road trip and have a nice in-person chat with the man. And while he was there, he could check out the area to see if he could find a nice little cabin where he and Kristin could hide away for a few days, away from the questions and blame. And away from the guilt of putting an innocent man behind bars.

Chapter 31

Tessa awoke to the sound of voices and jolted up in her bed. It took a moment before she remembered that she and Parker were no longer alone.

She blew out an unsteady breath and raked her fingers through her hair. Normally, she would love the chance to socialize and meet new people, but between the fear of being discovered and the way Zoey had glared at her for the better part of last night, she looked forward to Monday when Parker's friends would leave. The image of the three newcomers departing and the prospect of her and Parker being left alone here again rolled through her mind. Would she still need to stay hidden by then? Right now, she could barely imagine what it would be like to regain her freedom.

A knock sounded on her door, and she startled again. She really needed to get a grip on her emotions.

She pushed the covers aside, the morning chill rippling over her. She quickly pulled her hair back into a messy bun and slipped the prop glasses on before she crossed to the door and opened it.

Parker stood on the other side, his hair damp from his shower. "Hey, did I wake you?"

"No, I just got up." She kept her hand on the doorknob. "What time is it?"

"Eight." He tilted his head toward the living room. "Everyone else is planning to hit the trails this morning. Did you have any interest in going hiking?"

Tessa narrowed her eyes. Was he seriously asking if she wanted to go out in public?

Parker leaned closer. "The trails are pretty secluded, but it's fine if you'd rather avoid going. I just needed them to hear me ask you."

That made more sense. Speaking at a normal volume, she said, "Thanks for asking, but I don't think I'm up for hiking right now." As an afterthought, she added, "What about you? Are you going?"

"If you're staying home, I'll probably just hang out here with you and try to get some writing done." He winked at her. The simple gesture suggested his "writing time" would consist of reading through any new scenes from Kimber. "Olivia and Micah made breakfast. Want to come eat something?"

"Sure. Let me throw on a sweatshirt, and I'll come eat before I shower." She retrieved Parker's sweatshirt and pulled it over her head. Then she followed him down the hall toward the scent of eggs and sausage.

When they reached the kitchen doorway, he slowed and took her hand in his. The reason behind the gesture didn't catch up to her until they walked into the kitchen. Micah and Olivia sat together, and Zoey had taken the spot across from them, situating herself between the two remaining empty chairs. No matter where Parker chose to sit, he'd have to sit beside Zoey and wouldn't be able to sit with Tessa.

"So are you coming with us?" Zoey asked.

"Sorry, but I really need to get some more writing done, so Lynn and I are going to stay here."

It took a second for Tessa to remember that Parker's friends knew her by her middle name.

"I thought you usually take Sundays off," Micah said.

"I do." Parker collected two plates from the cabinet and handed one to Tessa. "But I want to read through what I have so far, and Lynn is helping me with some of the research."

"Research on what?" Olivia asked.

Tessa could hardly admit that Parker was tapping into her firsthand knowledge of being the first person to arrive after a murder. Not sure how to respond, she looked at Parker, willing him to come up with a fictional twist on the truth.

Parker looked down at Tessa for a second before answering. "The main character in my play is a personal assistant like Lynn."

"I wouldn't think you'd need much insight into what a personal assistant does for work."

"You know Parker." Tessa chose the seat between Zoey and Olivia. "He insists on making sure all the details are right."

Parker sat on the other side of Zoey and scooped some eggs onto his plate before passing the bowl to Tessa.

Awkwardly, Tessa reached past Zoey and took it from him.

Parker took a bite of his eggs. "Mmm. This is good."

Recognizing his ploy to change the subject, Tessa took a bite of her own. Though she preferred a bit more cheese and seasoning in her eggs, she nodded. "They are good. Thanks for making them."

"You're welcome," Olivia said. "I like to

cook, and we need energy food before hitting the trails."

Zoey adjusted her body so she was facing Parker more fully, her back to Tessa. "Are you sure you don't want to come, even for a little while? It's not often you're here when the leaves have all turned."

"I know, but I can't afford the distraction right now." Parker used his fork to transfer two links of sausage from the serving plate onto his own. "What time are you heading out?"

Tessa couldn't see who Parker had directed his question to, but Micah answered. "We'll get going as soon as we finish breakfast and get cleaned up."

"Olivia cooked," Tessa said. "We can take care of the dishes."

"Yeah, it's not a problem." Parker leaned forward so he could see Tessa. "Lynn, do you want some sausage?"

"No, thanks." She didn't really care for sausage, and she especially didn't want to deal with the awkwardness of trying to pass food around Zoey again when the woman was clearly trying to pretend Tessa didn't exist.

Micah finished his food and pushed back from the table. "I'm going to warm up the car. Come on out when you're finished eating."

"We'll only be a few minutes." Olivia took another bite of her toast.

Micah shrugged into his coat and headed for the door.

Zoey put her hand on Parker's arm. "Why don't you come and do one of the shorter hikes with us? That way you can still do some writing, but we'd be able to hang out for a few hours."

"Thanks, but like I said" — Parker stood even though Tessa suspected he wasn't finished eating yet — "Lynn and I have plans."

Parker stretched his legs out in front of him, enjoying the warmth of the fire in the fireplace and the sensation of Tessa snuggled up beside him. He drew her closer. "Is it too much to hope that Micah, Olivia, and Zoey will eat dinner in town and get back late tonight?"

"No, but I'm not sure we'll get that lucky." Tessa rested her head on his shoulder. "And if they don't bring food back with them, we may need to see if Micah can drive you to the store tomorrow to pick up some more. After breakfast this morning, we only have two eggs left."

"Yeah." Parker shook his head. "You'd think they would have brought their own groceries."

"Maybe they planned to pick some up after they settled in."

"Knowing Micah, he probably planned to order pizza and then deal with grocery shopping today." And since there had already been food in the cabin, Micah had likely dropped shopping off his to-do list.

A car engine sounded.

Tessa sighed. "So much for them eating out tonight."

"And us enjoying a couple more hours of peace and quiet."

"Just one more day until they leave." Tessa straightened. "It's so weird that I feel like we've been invaded when this is Micah's cabin."

"I've had the same thought." And even though he looked forward to the day when Tessa's name was cleared and she regained her freedom, he was going to miss spending so much time with her. And going back to his uncle's place in the Hamptons was too far from Tessa's apartment in New York. "You know what we should do tonight?"

"Hide in our rooms until your friends leave on Monday?"

Parker laughed. "No, although that's

tempting." He rubbed his hand over her shoulder. "I think you should help me find a new apartment."

The door opened before Tessa had the chance to respond, and Olivia and Zoey tromped in, their boots caked in mud.

Micah followed behind them and closed the door. "It's getting cold out there." With no regard to the mess he was tracking across the floor, he strode to the fireplace and stood in front of it.

"How was the hike?" Parker asked.

"Good," Micah said.

"You missed out on some gorgeous views," Olivia added.

Zoey took off her coat and hung it on the rack by the door. "What have you two been up to?"

"Working on my play." Parker rubbed Tessa's shoulder. He paused for a moment to remind himself to use her middle name. "Lynn has been a great help."

Micah unzipped his coat and took it off. "I can't believe you're letting someone help you with your play." He set his jacket on the hearth to dry. "You usually won't even let anyone see it, besides maybe your uncle Ian."

"Lynn has some unique insights." And while he couldn't explain why, he didn't mind having Tessa nearby when he was writing. "Have you all had dinner?"

"Not yet," Micah said.

Olivia joined him by the fire. "We thought we would come get warmed up and changed and then go out to eat."

"We're going to the Italian place down the road." Zoey focused on Parker. "You should come."

"Thanks, but I'm really not in the mood to go out." But pizza did sound good. "Any chance you want to bring something back for us?"

"You've been hiding out in this cabin for almost a week now. You need to get out and do something."

"Maybe tomorrow." He did need to go to the grocery store. Assuming Micah would agree to bringing them food, he asked Tessa, "What kind of pizza do you want?"

"Mushroom?"

"Sounds good." Parker turned his attention back to Micah. "I can call it in and pay over the phone so it'll be ready when you finish eating."

Zoey sat on the love seat and leaned forward. "If you're going to eat here, maybe we should just order all the pizza to go."

So much for more time alone with Tessa.

Fighting against his disappointment, Parker nodded. "That works too."

Chapter 32

Kimber rubbed at her eyes and leaned her head against the back of her office chair. Except for spending an hour helping Ian with his lines, her entire morning had been consumed with searching Suzanne Quentin's credit-card and banking activity. Or rather, the last hour had been. Convincing Rafi to use his connections to get a warrant for the woman's financials had taken nearly two hours, but he'd finally convinced a judge that a jealous wife was worthy of looking at when her husband's mistress had been the victim.

It was too bad they had yet to find anything on the security feed at the building, but with one of the lobby cameras malfunctioning, Kimber suspected the real murderer had used that blind spot to escape detection. If they could prove the security guard's wife was aware of that blind spot, they would be able to create a reasonable doubt that Tessa wasn't the only person who could have been on the sixteenth floor when the murder had occurred.

Ian walked into his dressing room, loosening his tie. "Any luck?"

"Not yet." Kimber let out a sigh and straightened in her chair. "Two more credit cards to look through."

"How many does she have?"

"Eight, and they're very active." Kimber tapped on her keyboard to bring up the next account. "How did your last scene go?"

"It was fine. We're on our lunch break now. Want me to get you something from craft services?"

Kimber swiveled in her chair to face him. "Shouldn't I be asking you that question?"

"Not today." Ian tossed his tie aside and took off his suit jacket. "I'll pick something up for both of us, and we can eat in here. I need help going over my lines for the next scenes. They changed them up again."

"I'm about ready for a break from this anyway." She lowered her voice. "Have you talked to Bob yet?"

"No." Ian shook his head. "I stopped by the editing suite, but he wasn't in yet."

Kimber narrowed her eyes. "Is it normal for him to come in so late?"

"He usually works a bit later than everyone else, but I'll give him a call to see when he plans to be here." Ian retrieved his phone from his desk and dialed. After a moment, he hung up and tried again. He hung up a second time. "He isn't answering. I'll send him a text and ask him to call me."

A sick sensation burned in Kimber's throat. The one person who knew about their suspicions wasn't where he was supposed to be. This wasn't good. "Try him again," Kimber said.

Ian dialed a third time, but Bob still didn't answer.

"It could be that he's on his way in and couldn't get to his phone," Ian said.

"If we don't hear from him in the next hour or so, maybe I can have Brandon or my FBI friend stop by to check on him."

Concern clouded Ian's face. "You don't think anything could have happened to him, do you?"

She did, but she didn't want to admit it. "It's always better to be safe than sorry."

Apparently mollified, Ian nodded. "I'll be back in a few minutes."

Ian headed out the door, and Kimber skimmed through the credit-card activity on Suzanne's American Express card — one of her American Express cards. Why someone needed three was beyond Kimber.

She reached the date of the murder, noting two charges that had occurred shortly before ten that night. One was at a pharmacy less than a quarter mile from the studio and the other at a restaurant two blocks away.

Kimber picked up her phone and dialed Rafi's number. "Hey, I think I might have something." She described the two charges. "Both of these happened between nine and ten on Monday night. If Suzanne picked up food and brought it to her husband, it's possible she stumbled onto her husband's affair and acted on it."

"Have you seen her on any of the security feeds?" Rafi asked.

"No, but it's possible she knows about the blind spot in the lobby." Kimber tried to piece the facts together in a way that could make sense. "And as crazy as it sounds, it's possible that her husband helped her either alter or delete other spots where she might have been seen."

"That's a stretch, especially if Ian is right about the editing job of the studio security feed being a professional job."

"I know, but it's possible." Grasping at straws, Kimber asked, "Can you reach out to the police to see if they'll follow up? It's doubtful Suzanne is even on their radar."

"I'll make a call, but I think you should keep looking for other suspects," Rafi said. "This still feels a bit far-fetched to me."

Kimber wished she knew where else to look. "I'll keep searching. Just let me know if the police come up with anything helpful."

"I will."

"Oh, and one more thing: Can you order a well-being check on Bob Kelley? He didn't report to work today, and he isn't answering his phone."

"How long has he been out of contact?"

"We saw him last on Friday, but we didn't try calling him until today," Kimber said.

"That would fall under the local police's jurisdiction, but if you want, I'll pull his address," Rafi said. "There's nothing to say that Brandon couldn't stop by to check on him."

It was better than nothing. "Thanks, Rafi."

"I'll text you the address."

She thanked him again and hung up the phone. A minute later, Ian walked in with a plate in each hand.

"Any luck?" he asked.

It took Kimber a moment to shift her focus from Bob's well-being to the financials she had been analyzing all morning. "Maybe." She waited until Ian closed the door behind him before she continued. "But when I talked to my friend at the FBI, he told me to keep looking. He doesn't think the wife could have made it past all the security cameras without being spotted somewhere."

Ian handed Kimber one of the plates. "Then I guess we keep looking."

Colin hung up the phone, irritated on principle that Agent Ebeid was once again directing his investigation. As if he hadn't already figured out that the boyfriend's wife would be a logical suspect. Okay, so maybe he hadn't realized Heath Quentin was married, but he would have . . . eventually.

He cast a glance at Derrick. He was the one looking into the other suspects. Why hadn't he picked up on that detail? "Did you know Heath Quentin was married?"

Derrick narrowed his eyes for a moment before he shook his head. "I don't think that came up when we interviewed him."

"We need to look into his wife to show we did our due diligence." Heaven knew the attorneys would ask about that when this case went to court. "The FBI already pulled her financials. Can you look them over and see if anything pops?"

"You know we have other cases, right?"

Derrick lifted a file from his desk. "I still have to finish the report on the Petroski case."

"Fine. I'll look at the financials."

"How long are we going to pretend Tessa Seidel isn't the killer?"

"This is the last lead we have, so if we can rule out the boyfriend's wife, I think we have to go public that we're looking for Seidel."

"I'm ready to have this case behind us." Derrick slapped the file he held back onto his desk and heaved out a sigh. "I'll check the financials if you'll track her movements."

"Deal." Colin hated looking at other people's spending habits. He put in the request for the warrant to track the GPS on the wife's car and electronics.

While he waited for the approval to come through, he did a quick check of the DMV records. Within moments, he was able to determine that neither Heath nor Suzanne owned a car.

Once the warrant came through, Colin traced Suzanne's movements based on her cell phone and her smart watch.

"It looks like Suzanne visited the building where the murder took place about an hour before Juliet Clark was killed," Colin said.

"Her credit-card activity isn't showing much, but there were a couple of charges in that area, probably right before she went there," Derrick said. "If you give me the time when she got to the building, I'll check the security feed."

"Thanks." Even though Colin was ready to lock this case down, maybe they *had* zeroed in on the wrong person. At least Suzanne had a motive, which was something he had yet to find for Seidel. Still, he also couldn't explain why Seidel had disappeared after the murder.

With that thought in mind, he accessed the phone logs for Seidel's sister, Kimber. Kimber's phone log was relatively straightforward. Phone calls to her boyfriend, several exchanges between her and Ian Sawyer, and a few other random calls sprinkled in to people at the studio. He half expected to find out she was the one behind the FBI's involvement, but her log didn't include any calls to the FBI or Special Agent Ebeid.

"I've got the feed for when she arrived and left the building," Derrick said. "Want to take a look?"

"Yeah." Colin rolled his chair over to Derrick's desk. As soon as he could see his screen, Derrick hit Play.

"She arrived at nine thirty-five, about five minutes after her credit card was used at a restaurant down the street."

On the screen, the dark-haired woman entered the lobby, a plastic bag in her hand. She approached the security desk and passed the bag to the security guard Colin now knew was the victim's boyfriend.

The guard spoke to his partner at the desk, and then both Heath and his wife walked to the side of the lobby. They spoke for a moment before Suzanne became agitated and gestured sharply toward the elevator.

"Looks like there's trouble in paradise," Colin muttered.

"That's obvious," Derrick said. "He was cheating on her."

"And from the looks of this conversation, she knew it."

Heath put both hands on his wife's arms, clearly trying to calm her down while he spoke. After a moment, Suzanne nodded. Then she turned toward the doors and walked outside.

"Looks like she wasn't even in the building when the murder took place," Derrick said.

"Which brings us right back to Tessa Seidel." Colin needed to find a motive that would make sense. Then they would be able to truly lock this case down. "Any hits on Tessa's credit cards or bank accounts?"

"Nothing."

"Someone has to be helping her." It was the only thing that made sense.

"I agree. But who?"

"I don't know, but we're going to figure it out." Colin rolled his chair back to his desk and pondered the question. Tessa's sister or parents were the most logical culprits, but from what Colin had seen, her parents hadn't been in contact with either daughter since the day before the murder, and Kimber hadn't had any communication since the day after.

That detail circled through his brain. Seidel had disappeared, and while her sister seemed concerned, she was far calmer than he would have expected for a person who couldn't get in touch with a close family member in trouble. Something was definitely wrong here. And one way or another, he was going to find out what.

Chapter 33

Tessa had hoped Parker's friends would spend the day out of the cabin again rather than hanging around, but the steady rainfall outside had prevented the visitors from going apple picking like they'd planned. For the entire morning, Olivia and Zoey had been in the kitchen, first fixing breakfast and then baking cookies.

Lunch had been a free-for-all, resulting in nearly all their bread, lunch meat, and cheese getting eaten. Even the sausages Parker liked had been devoured.

Now, sitting at the kitchen table while everyone chatted after their midday meal, Tessa debated how to bring up the very real fact that they needed groceries. Not wanting to address the topic directly, she spoke to Micah. "Since this is your last night before you head back to the city, what do you guys want to eat for dinner tonight?"

"Food," Micah answered without hesitation.

Olivia laughed. "In case you didn't notice, Micah isn't very picky."

Directing her comment at Micah, Tessa said, "If you and Parker don't mind picking some things up at the grocery store, I could make some baked ziti."

"Oh, that sounds good," Olivia said.

"That does sound good. But I don't really want to go back into town." Micah cut off a bite of his sausage and speared it with his fork. "Parker, you can just borrow my car if you want."

"Yeah. That sounds great. Thanks." Parker turned his attention to Tessa. "Make me a list, and I'll go after lunch."

"Perfect. I think I have the stuff to start on the sauce while you're gone." Tessa had never really witnessed someone's eyes lighting up, but the moment she spoke, Zoey's entire countenance changed, and her expression brightened.

"I'll come with you to the store. I want to pick up a few things for our drive back tomorrow."

"We can add what you want to our list," Parker offered.

"I won't know what I want until I look through the aisles."

Parker cast an apologetic look at Tessa, apparently resigned to spending time alone with Zoey. “Okay, then. We’ll go as soon as Lynn gives me her list.”

Micah took a sip of his water. “I didn’t ask you, but how much longer are you planning on staying?”

“I’m not sure yet.” Parker stretched his arm out and settled it on the back of Tessa’s chair. “If Lynn can manage the time away from work, I’m hoping we can both stay until I finish my play.”

Micah’s eyes widened. “I thought you started writing it last week.”

“I did.”

“Correct me if I’m wrong, but didn’t your last play take you almost a year to write?” Micah shook his head. “Surely you won’t want to stay here that long.”

“The last one took that long because I was still learning the craft, and I kept changing things,” Parker said. “At the rate this play is going, I could have it finished within a couple weeks.”

“Wow. That’s crazy.”

Parker glanced down at Tessa. “Fingers crossed I’ll be able to figure out the ending soon.”

Tessa sure hoped so. And she prayed the ending included the police arresting the real killer. She put her hand on Parker's knee. "I'll get started on that shopping list."

Parker stood. "I'll help you."

Zoey smiled. "And I'll get my coat."

The last thing Parker wanted was to spend time alone with Zoey, but taking Tessa out in public wasn't worth the risk, and Micah and Olivia had already insisted on staying at the cabin.

With Tessa currently in the kitchen making her shopping list, Parker retreated to his room to grab his wallet. He checked the top of the dresser, but only his car keys lay on the otherwise empty surface.

Surprised that his wallet wasn't with his keys, he checked the pocket of his coat. Empty.

He'd done his laundry since he and Tessa had left his car at the hotel, so he was certain he hadn't left his wallet in the pocket of his jeans.

He grabbed his coat and walked into the kitchen. Micah and Olivia still sat at the table, finishing their lunch. Parker looked past them and focused on Tessa. "Hey, Lynn. Have you seen my wallet?"

"I don't think so." She finished writing something on the paper on the counter and looked up. “Could you have left it in your car?”

He thought for a moment. He’d definitely had his wallet when he’d checked into the hotel room. The hotel. He must have left his wallet in the hotel room.

“I’ll have to stop by and see if it’s there.” Though he hated to ask Tessa for money, he forced the words out. “Do you have any cash in case I can’t find it?”

“I’ll go see what I have in my wallet.” She handed her pen and paper to Parker. “Can you check this over to see if I missed anything?”

“Sure.” Parker took the pen and paper, noting the extensive list Tessa had written. He really hoped he could find his wallet so he could buy everything they needed.

“Hey, Parker, I can give you some cash.” Micah stood and pulled his wallet from his pocket. “You and Lynn saved us from having to go grocery shopping when we got here.” Micah slid two one-hundred-dollar bills from his wallet and handed them to Parker along with his car keys.

“Thanks.” Parker folded the hundreds and tucked them into his pocket.

Zoey walked in, her shoes on and her coat hanging over her arm. “Are you ready?”

“Just about.”

Tessa entered holding several twenties. “Sorry. This is all I have.”

“Hopefully, I won’t need it.” Parker took them from her and put on his jacket. “I’ll be back in a little while.” He caught the look of unease in Tessa’s eyes, though he wasn’t sure if it was for his upcoming outing with Zoey or the idea of her being left alone with Micah and Olivia. Hoping to put her at ease, Parker leaned forward and kissed her. “If you think of anything else you need, just have Micah text Zoey.”

“Okay.” She took his hand and squeezed it before she released him.

Parker turned toward the front door, expecting Zoey to follow. She didn’t disappoint.

They both climbed into Micah’s car, and immediately, Zoey swiveled in her seat and put her hand on his arm. “I was wondering if we would ever get some time alone.”

“I have a girlfriend. It isn’t appropriate for us to spend time alone,” Parker said. “This is just us going shopping.” He pointed at her seat belt. “Buckle up.”

She fastened her seat belt and, thankfully, kept her hands to herself as he started the car. “You aren’t serious about Lynn, are you?”

“I am.” Parker said the words to make it

clear that he wasn't interested in Zoey, but the moment the words passed his lips, he recognized the truth in them. He was serious about Tessa. In fact, he couldn't imagine wanting to be with anyone else.

How had this happened? He'd known her for barely a week. How could he be serious about her?

"I can't believe you have a serious girlfriend, and you never even told Micah."

"I didn't expect to fall for her so fast." That might be the understatement of the century. Parker started the car and headed for the hotel. "I have to make a quick stop to see if I left my wallet in my car."

They drove in silence until he reached the hotel parking lot and he'd pulled up beside his car. Suspecting his wallet really was in his hotel room, he said, "I also need to run into the hotel really quick." He put the car in park but left the car running. "I'll be back in a minute."

"I can come with you." Zoey started to unbuckle.

"There's no need. I won't be long." Parker climbed out of the car. He did a quick check of his car to make sure he hadn't left his wallet in the cupholder. Seeing it was empty, he made his way into the hotel and approached the man at the reception desk.

"Hi. I think I locked myself out of my room. I'm in 203."

"Name?" the man asked.

"Parker Sawyer."

The clerk went through the process of pulling up Parker's scanned driver's license to verify his identity. He then created a new key. "Here you go."

"Thanks." Parker hurried to the stairwell and jogged up to the second floor, where he let himself into his room and found that his wallet was indeed lying on the desk, right next to his cell phone.

Taking advantage of having access to his phone, he sent quick text messages to his mom and his sisters to make sure they knew he was still alive. He then called Ian.

The phone rang three times, and then a woman's voice came over the line. "Hello?"

"Who is this?" Parker asked.

"It's Kimber." She rushed on before he could respond. "Is everything okay?"

"Yeah, I'm just heading out to the grocery store and wanted to check in with Uncle Ian. I wanted to know if he had any new suggestions for me on my play."

"I think he should have a few for you tonight, but he wanted to check some details first."

"Good to know," Parker said. "Let him

know I called and that I'll email him later."

"I will." Kimber's voice grew husky. "And, Parker, thanks for everything."

"You're welcome."

Brandon gripped the oversized envelope in his hand and waited by Ian's dressing room door until Kimber finished her call. It had taken some effort, but when the cover for Kimber's new book had been approved today, he'd convinced Amelia to let him hand-deliver a printout of it to Kimber on his lunch hour.

He glanced at his watch. Maybe one of these days, he'd actually be able to take a lunch hour before two.

When he was certain Kimber was off the phone, he stepped inside. "Was that who I think it was?"

Kimber nodded and gestured for him to close the door. As soon as it latched, she said, "Parker didn't say much, but they seem to be doing okay."

"That's good." Brandon sat on the small sofa across from her.

"How has your day been?" she asked.

"The new assistant seems to be holding up okay. And since I saw her walk in with the right coffee order for Amelia, she must have believed me that my survival guide was really to help her succeed."

"Thank goodness. It's about time someone else took over the assistant duties for Amelia."

"I agree completely." And he couldn't wait to spend more of his time at his day job doing editing instead of running errands. Although the errands did make a good cover for his CIA work when he needed to buy a few extra minutes for himself. Or in today's case, to see his girlfriend. He held up the envelope that contained the book cover. "I have something for you."

Her eyebrows drew together. "What is it?"

He passed it to her. "Open it and see."

Kimber took the envelope. When she pulled out the glossy printout of her cover, she gasped. "Oh my gosh! This is amazing." She stared at the cover for a moment, then looked up. "When did you get this?"

"The cover art was just approved this morning," Brandon said. "I convinced Amelia to let me bring this by to show you on my lunch hour."

"Thank you." She held it out again and stared.

Delighted by her excitement, Brandon said, "Can you believe that a year from now, that book will be on the shelves?"

"It's hard to imagine." Kimber's mood

sobered. "Now if we can make sure Tessa will be free to celebrate my book release next October, everything will be great."

Brandon didn't want to think about how a wrongful conviction of her sister would impact Kimber. The idea of any innocent person going to prison was unthinkable. "Any progress on our suspect list?"

"I just finished going through the security feed. Suzanne Quentin was here that night, but she clearly left the building before the window of time for the murder." Kimber leaned back in her chair. "I even checked the local ATM cameras and the subway cameras. She was home alone at the time of the murder, and she can prove it."

So they were back to the possibility of the killer being someone here at the studio. Brandon still hated the idea of Kimber being close to whoever had framed Tessa.

"Any clue as to what happened to the planner and laptop from Juliet's desk?" he asked.

"Still nothing, and no idea what was on it that would be worth killing for."

"The fact that they were taken does suggest that her death was related to something here at the studio."

"Probably." Kimber picked up her phone. "There is one more thing: Any chance you can take a detour on your way back to work?"

"I thought that's what I was doing by coming here."

"Okay, another detour." She pressed the screen on her phone, and an instant later, Brandon's phone chimed with an incoming text message. "I just sent you the address of the video editor Ian was working with. He didn't show up at work today, and he isn't answering his phone."

"And you want me to check on him."

"Would you?" She gestured in the general direction of the studio. "Ian and I are going to be late tonight so they can catch up on a couple scenes they missed from last week."

"I'll head over there now."

"Thank you." She stood and leaned in for a kiss. The touch of her lips sent the familiar heat rocketing through him. When she pulled back, she rubbed at his lip to wipe away any traces of lipstick. "You're the best."

Unable to resist, Brandon cupped his hand behind her neck to hold her in place and leaned in for another kiss. "You just keep thinking that."

"Don't worry." She smiled. "I will."

Chapter 34

Zoey was all smiles when she walked in the door until she spotted Tessa sitting on the couch. Then Zoey narrowed her eyes as though she were hurling a warning shot across the bow of an enemy ship.

Parker followed Zoey inside, his hands laden with bags of groceries, his focus on Zoey.

For a fleeting moment, Tessa entertained the possibility that Zoey's time alone with Parker had convinced him that he'd made the wrong choice in standing by Tessa. After all, Zoey was beautiful and clearly interested in a relationship with him. Plus, she didn't have the additional baggage of a potential arrest for murder hanging over her head.

Tessa stood as Parker approached, his expression unreadable, and her insecurities nearly convinced her that he would be leaving with his friends.

Then he stopped in front of her and kissed

her cheek. "Can you take these? I have a bunch more in the car."

"Sure." She relieved him of the bags he held and carried them into the kitchen, where she set everything on the counter and began putting the food away.

Parker returned a moment later.

"Is that all of it?" Tessa asked.

"No, I have another load or two."

"Do you want me to help?"

He shook his head. "It's starting to rain out there. I don't want you to get all wet."

"I don't want you getting all wet either."

He put his hand on her back. "Don't worry. I'll be fine."

He made three more trips to the car before he finally set the last of his purchases on the kitchen table. "I already put the laundry detergent and toilet paper in the laundry room."

Tessa took a step closer to him and lowered her voice. "I really hope all these groceries don't mean that you expect us to stay here indefinitely."

"Best to be prepared." He turned to face her and took both of her hands in his. He leaned close and whispered, "Plus, we have no idea how much they'll eat before they leave tomorrow." He tilted his head toward the living room.

"That's true." Just one more night until she and Parker would be left alone again. "How was shopping with Zoey?"

Parker rolled his eyes. "She insisted on going up and down every single aisle."

"It was obvious you got way more than what was on my list."

"Like I said, best to be prepared." He pulled a package from one of the bags. "Speaking of which, I picked up some pulled pork, hamburger buns, and potato salad. I thought it would be nice to have something easy for tomorrow night, especially since you're cooking tonight."

"That sounds great. Thank you."

He put the pork in the fridge and peeked through the doorway into the living room. Then he closed the distance between them again. "When I stopped by the hotel to get my wallet, I tried calling my uncle, but your sister picked up."

"Anything new?"

"Not that I could tell, but I suspect we'll have new pages by the end of the day, if we don't already."

"Maybe you should go check while I put the rest of these groceries away."

"I'll help you first." He leaned close again. "With my luck, Zoey will try to follow me to my room. And I don't want that."

Neither did Tessa. "Okay, fine. Let's get everything put away, and then we can check your email together."

Parker leaned in for a lingering kiss. "Good plan."

Brandon hadn't planned on a trip to the Bronx, but here he was, an hour past his lunch break, standing at Bob's apartment door. Thankfully, Candace seemed to have figured out the basics as Amelia's assistant, so Amelia wasn't as likely to notice he was missing — at least not for a while.

When no one answered the door, Brandon knocked a second time. Still nothing. He pressed his ear to the door, but he couldn't sense any movement from inside.

The building didn't include such amenities as a doorman, and the security cameras on this floor appeared to be by the stairwells and the elevator.

Brandon knocked yet again. "Bob?"

Still nothing.

Brandon debated whether he should assume the man simply wasn't home or if he should be proactive and let himself in. He pulled his phone from his pocket and called Kimber.

As soon as she answered, she asked, "Did you find Bob?"

"No. I'm at his place, but he isn't answering."

"I have a bad feeling about this."

Brandon stared at the door. "Me too."

"How are your lockpicking skills?"

"I don't know, but we're about to find out," Brandon said. "Just promise to bail me out if I get arrested."

"You know I will," Kimber said, but instead of humor in her tone, he sensed only her tension.

"I'll call you as soon as I get inside."

"Thanks, Brandon."

Brandon hung up and retrieved his lockpick kit and a pair of crime-scene gloves from his pocket. He supposed he should be grateful that his time working overseas had trained him to always carry them.

The lock in the doorknob took a few seconds to open, but the deadbolt required a bit more effort. After a minute, he straightened, checked the hallway to make sure he was still alone, and then went back to work. Forty-five seconds later, he finally managed to gain access to Bob's apartment.

After slipping his lockpick kit back into his pocket, he knocked one more time, waiting a few seconds before letting himself in.

The overhead light illuminated the simply furnished living room and spilled into the adjoining kitchen. From his first breath inside, Brandon inhaled the scent of death that permeated the air.

His stomach curled as he slipped inside and closed the door with his gloved hand.

The unpleasant smell and his sudden unease were enough to push him to retrieve the Glock holstered at his waist.

He walked just slightly farther into the living area before he spotted the prone figure on the floor beside the sofa. Despite the lifeless eyes staring up at him, Brandon leaned down and checked for a pulse. Nothing.

He took a brief moment to mourn the loss of life before reality hit, that the death of Bob Kelley was likely connected to Juliet Clark's murder.

Clicking into work mode, Brandon lifted his weapon and quietly padded across the carpet toward the hall. He cleared the bathroom to his left and the bedroom and closet to his right. After another check of the living room and kitchen, he holstered his weapon and retrieved his phone. Though he knew Kimber was anxiously waiting for news, he dialed Rafi's number.

"What's up?" Rafi asked.

"We have a problem," Brandon said. "I came by to check on the video editor who didn't show up to work today. He's dead."

The casual tone of Rafi's voice disappeared. "Where are you?"

"His apartment."

"I'll call the police," Rafi said, his voice clipped. "Make sure you don't touch anything."

"I'm already wearing gloves."

"Good," Rafi said. "And make sure you stay there until the police get there. I don't want to risk them tagging you as a suspect."

Like Tessa. "Understood. What's my cover story?"

"Use your FBI credentials and say you were conducting a wellness check."

"Got it. Thanks, Rafi." Brandon ended the call and took another look at the crime scene. No sign of a struggle beyond the victim and what appeared to be a single gunshot to the chest.

Beyond the worn furniture in the small living space, a television hung on the wall with an HDMI cord dangling from it. The kitchen held a few dishes in the sink, all of which appeared to have been from whatever meal Bob had last prepared for himself.

Another pass through Bob's bedroom didn't hold any clues, and it wasn't until Brandon circled back to the living room once more that the hanging HDMI cord prompted a new realization. His search hadn't revealed a computer of any kind. Surely Bob would own one.

A knock on the door was followed by the shout, "Police! Open up."

"The door's open," Brandon called out.

He pulled his FBI credentials from his inside suit jacket pocket and held them up.

Two police officers entered, both of them with their weapons in hand.

Brandon didn't move. "Brandon Hale. FBI."

The officer who entered first continued forward to inspect Brandon's badge. Then he holstered his weapon and turned to his partner. "Call the coroner."

CHAPTER 35

Colin typed in the newest information gleaned from his investigation. The evidence was undeniable. Heath had clearly been cheating on his wife with Juliet. The man's wife, Suzanne, had obviously found out about it. Yet despite having a clear motive to want Juliet out of the picture, both Suzanne and Heath had airtight alibis for the time of the murder.

Derrick's phone rang, and he answered it. "Randall." A few seconds passed before Derrick stood abruptly. When he opened his desk drawer and pulled out his pistol, Colin followed his lead. Something was up, and it looked like they were about to have a reason to get away from the office and their endless paperwork. "Got it," Derrick said into the phone. "We'll be right there." He hung up. "We've got another murder. The victim worked on the same TV show as Juliet Clark."

"Who is it?"

"Robert Kelley. He was a video editor. When he didn't show up for work today, one of the employees sent her boyfriend to check on him. A couple of uniforms have already secured the scene."

"Then let's go."

"Before we do, maybe it's time to release a statement to the public about Tessa Seidel." Derrick gestured to Colin's computer. "We have no idea where she is, and now that this has escalated into two murders, don't you think it's time to get some help in finding her?"

It had been almost a week since the first murder. And as much as he wanted to have a clear motive for Seidel as their killer before they publicly pinned the murder on her, Colin knew the video evidence was clear. She was the logical suspect. "Fine. I'll release the statement and her photo." Colin sat back down at his desk. "And I'm going to put another tail on her sister. Kimber knows something. Maybe a new set of eyes on her will give us another angle to finding Tessa."

"Sounds good. I'll get the car and meet you out front," Derrick said.

Colin sent in the surveillance request first. Then he pulled up the press statement he'd written days ago. Derrick was right. Obvious motive or not, the evidence had not changed. Maybe once they located their elusive suspect, she would shed some light on why she had killed not once but twice now.

Kimber hung up the phone with Brandon, her chest tight with emotion. He'd confirmed her worst fears, and now she was faced with the prospect of telling Ian that the man who had planned to help them was dead.

Before she had time to process this new information herself, Ian walked into his dressing room, his suit jacket draped over his arm. He closed his door. "I tried to find Bob again after my last scene, but he still isn't in yet. I'm getting worried."

For good reason. Not ready to admit her new findings, Kimber asked, "How many more scenes do you have today?"

"I just need to do the closeups for the last one, and then I'll be done." He held out his suit jacket. "This got something on it. Do we have a double?"

"Yes. It's on the rack." And the fact that Ian needed to concentrate on work was the perfect excuse to avoid telling him about Bob. She stood and retrieved the suit jacket that was identical to the one Ian held, sans the smudge on the sleeve. "I'll come with you to the studio."

"No research you need to work on?"

"Not at the moment." At least none that she could do without analyzing the other members of the cast and crew. She traded jackets with Ian. "I'll run this down to wardrobe first, and then I'll see you in there."

"Sounds good." Ian slipped on his jacket and checked himself in the mirror, tugging at the sleeves a bit. "Oh, and do me a favor and swing by the editing suite. I want to know if Bob ever showed up."

Kimber nodded, even though she already knew she could skip that assignment. She was all too aware of Bob's current whereabouts.

With the soiled jacket in hand, she followed Ian into the hall and pulled the door closed behind her, then made her way to wardrobe, but the door was closed when she arrived. She tried the doorknob. Locked. Just like when Tessa had attempted to drop off the clothes the night of the murder.

Kimber checked her watch. It was already half past five, which meant Elena likely got off at five unless someone requested that she stay late.

Interesting. Tessa had mentioned that she'd come by after hours on the night of the murder. It wasn't like her to make a delivery without confirming someone would be available to receive it. So, had her sister assumed someone would be here, or had someone messed up? Elena had clearly not been expecting the delivery that night, but maybe someone else had planned to be here. Maybe it was even Juliet who had been expected to sign for the clothes.

Kimber turned toward the studio. She checked to make sure the recording light wasn't on and slipped inside as the director called out, "Places!"

Kimber stayed at the back of the room while the cameras zoomed in on Ian, who recited his lines over and over again. When the director was finally satisfied, Ian left the set and approached her. He leaned close and whispered, "Any news from Bob?"

"Not exactly." But she wasn't about to have this conversation here. "Are you ready to go?"

"Yes. Can you call my driver and tell him to meet us downstairs? It'll take me a few minutes to change clothes."

"I'll let him know." Kimber made the call, choosing to remain in the set area while Ian went to change his clothes. She scanned the few people still present. Eli, the last cameraman to leave the night of the murder. Gabriel, who was currently speaking with Sheridan and Lisa. Any one of these people could have been involved in Juliet's murder. So why couldn't she pinpoint which one had both motive and opportunity? And who among them didn't have an alibi for the time of Bob's murder?

Of course, to answer that last question, she would need to know exactly when Bob's murder had occurred. And for that, she'd have to wait for the autopsy report. She really hated waiting.

Parker closed the door and leaned against it. Alone. Finally. He peeked out the window to make sure all three of his friends got into Micah's car.

Behind him, a board creaked, and he turned. Tessa stood at the entrance to the hall. "Are they gone?"

"They're getting in the car now."

The engine started, and Tessa padded across the room in her sock-clad feet. She put her hand on his back and peered around him to see for herself that their unexpected guests were indeed departing.

The warmth of her touch seeped through the fabric of his shirt, and he turned to face her. “What should we do to celebrate our newfound freedom?”

She took off the prop glasses that had been a permanent fixture on her face for the last few days. “You do still have a play to finish.”

“I haven’t seen any new emails from Uncle Ian, so I think we can wait on that for a bit.” He put both hands on her arms to hold her in place as he leaned close. His lips brushed against hers once, then twice.

The familiar ripple of pleasure rushed through him, and he released her arms, now lifting his hands to frame her face.

He stared at her for a long moment, his gaze holding hers as their breath mingled. A yearning built inside him, and he couldn’t help but close the distance between them again.

His lips met hers, and this time, he let himself savor every detail — the scent of Tessa’s raspberry shampoo, the softness of her cheek beneath his touch, the way her fingers curled into his shirt as though she needed to hold on to keep her balance.

The brilliance of the kiss exploded in his head, overshadowed by the sheer magnitude of his growing feelings. Everything about Tessa drew him into this unprecedented depth of emotions, from her kindness to her strength and even her vulnerability. She had captured his heart, and he could no longer imagine feeling whole without her.

That thought startled him, and he drew back, his lips still tingling from the kiss.

She lifted a hand to his cheek. "Is it weird to think that I missed you the last few days, even though we've been staying here together this whole time?"

"No. I felt the same way." He combed his fingers through her hair. "I missed it being just us."

"Me too. It will be nice not to have another woman vying for your attention."

The little hint of discomfort in her voice made him smile. "Don't tell me you were jealous."

"I wasn't thrilled when Zoey was the person going to the store with you instead of me."

"I wish it could have been you with me." And it would be once Tessa's innocence was proved. "But for now, Zoey is gone, and she won't be bothering either of us again."

Tessa let out a relieved sigh. "Thank goodness."

Chapter 36

The police were following Kimber again. She didn't have to be a genius to catch sight of the man outside the studio or the unmarked sedan now following three cars behind them. Or maybe it wasn't intelligence that was needed to spot their tail so much as the awareness that had come from her enhanced intelligence training.

From her spot in the back seat beside Ian, she leaned forward and spoke to the driver. "David, can you take us directly to Ian's place?"

"Yes, ma'am."

Ian shifted in his seat as though trying to see her better. "Why don't you want to get dropped off first?"

"There are a few things we need to talk about before I head home." And once again, she was in the position of needing to tell Ian information too sensitive to discuss in front of his driver.

Ian opened his mouth to speak and then closed it again. After a moment, he asked, "Should I let Phoebe know you'll be joining us for dinner?"

"You don't have to feed us, but I did ask Brandon to meet me at your place."

"Then you should stay and share a meal." Ian pulled out his phone and sent a text to his wife.

Kimber wasn't sure any of them would be interested in food tonight after Ian learned of Bob's death. She took a quick peek over her shoulder, confirming that they were indeed still being followed.

"Is something wrong?" Ian asked.

"I think the police are getting a bit desperate," Kimber said, avoiding the truth that there was most certainly something wrong. "They have someone following me again."

"They're going to think you're always at my place at this rate," Ian said. "You came and saw me the last time they did this."

"There's nothing illegal about Brandon and me visiting you and Phoebe."

"Very true." Despite his words, Ian turned so he could look out the back window.

David glanced at them in the rearview mirror. "Sir, I'm sorry, but there's a road closure ahead. I'll have to detour."

"That's fine," Ian said.

More time to think about how to tell Ian about Bob. Needing a distraction from the conversation to come, Kimber asked, "Do you want to go over your lines for tomorrow on our way to your apartment?"

"Sure."

Kimber pulled a copy of the script from her bag and handed it to him. "Look it over, and let me know when you're ready for me."

For the rest of the half-hour ride, Kimber helped Ian prepare for tomorrow morning. When they finally arrived at his building, Brandon waited in the lobby.

The moment Kimber saw him, her emotions threatened. Brandon must have sensed she was struggling because he closed the distance between them and pulled her into a hug.

He whispered in her ear, "Sorry this hasn't been the day we were hoping for."

She swallowed hard. "Me too."

Brandon pulled away and looked past her. "Is someone following you again?"

She nodded. "It looks that way."

Ian had already reached the doors leading to the elevators. "Are you two coming up?"

"Yes." Kimber took Brandon's hand, needing the comfort that connection would provide.

They made their way upstairs together,

and Ian unlocked his front door. As soon as he led them inside, tomato sauce, melted mozzarella, and garlic toast scented the air.

Ian pulled the door closed behind them. "What aren't you telling me?"

"Maybe we should sit down." Brandon gestured toward the living room.

Phoebe stepped out of the kitchen, a bread basket in her hand. "Dinner's ready."

"Change of plans." Ian held out his right hand to guide them into the dining room, where four places were set. A pan of lasagna and a garden salad occupied the center of the table.

Everyone sat, and Phoebe set the bread basket on the table. She then took it upon herself to serve everyone a piece of lasagna before passing around the salad. "Was traffic bad? You're later than usual."

"There was a road closure." Ian took a piece of bread from the basket and passed it to Kimber. "I don't think I can stand the suspense anymore. Did you find out something about Bob?" he asked.

Kimber struggled to find the words. Thankfully, she didn't have to.

Brandon put his hand on hers and spoke first. "Kimber asked me to go check on Bob today." He paused. "I'm sorry, Ian. Bob was killed sometime over the weekend."

Ian had picked up his water glass, but he set it back down with a thunk. "Bob's dead? But —"

"Oh no." Phoebe put her hand on Ian's arm.

"I'm so sorry, Ian." Kimber's chest tightened. "I didn't want to tell you while we were at the studio. I was afraid the news would make it too hard for you to work, and no one else there knows about Bob's death yet."

"Someone knows." Ian clenched his jaw.

"That's true," Brandon said. "Whoever killed Bob definitely knows about it."

Colin took his time as he passed through Robert Kelley's apartment. No sign of forced entry. No sign of a struggle. Either the victim knew his killer, or he hadn't had time to defend himself.

The coroner was already examining the body, but before Colin dealt with the details of the man who had died, he needed to get a better sense of how the man had lived.

The apartment could have belonged to anyone in the city who rarely spent time at home. The photos hanging on the wall suggested the victim had a college-age daughter. No sign of a wife though. Divorced maybe?

He continued into the single bedroom. The desk in the corner held two monitors, the cords dangling from where they were mounted, but the man's computer wasn't anywhere in sight.

Colin checked the single desk drawer to reveal the expected contents: pens, paper clips, a couple of notepads, and a flash drive still in the packaging.

He continued his search — dresser drawers, closet, under the bed.

Derrick stepped into the bedroom doorway as Colin straightened back to a stand. "Anything interesting?"

"No computer, but other than that, nothing suspicious." Colin jutted his chin in the direction of the living room. "What did the ME say?"

"His best guess so far is the victim died between midnight and 4:00 a.m. on Sunday." Derrick leaned on the door jamb. "I already checked with building security. Looks like the surveillance system was going through an update that night. They haven't been able to pull any footage up for that time frame."

"You can't be serious." Colin shook his head.

"I'm afraid so.

"This can't be a coincidence." The timing

was way too convenient. "Any chance our killer could have forced the system update?"

"That's my guess. And there's something else." Derrick held up a plastic bag that held a hair tie, strands of brown hair tangled in it. "I found this under the couch."

Finally, a solid lead. "Make sure you hand it off to forensics. Maybe we'll get lucky and be able to pull DNA off the hair."

"That's the hope." Derrick straightened and took a step back. "I sent the two uniforms to talk to the neighbors in case anyone heard or saw anything."

The scene they walked into flashed in Colin's memory. The two police officers had been present with the coroner, but he hadn't noticed anyone else. "What about the person who found the body? Did you already interview him?" Colin asked.

"No. He left after he gave his statement, but the police officer who interviewed him said he was a fed. Apparently, he has some connection to someone at the studio. That's why he was called to check on the victim."

"FBI?"

"Yeah. I already have the statement and his contact info." Derrick held up his phone. "The guy's name is Brandon Hale. Isn't that the name of Kimber Seidel's boyfriend?"

"Yeah." Colin furrowed his brow and

replayed his interactions with Hale. "But Kimber's boyfriend is the guy from her publisher. He didn't identify himself as FBI at the studio, so it's probably just someone with the same name." Colin left the bedroom and followed Derrick down the hall to where the coroner was preparing the body for transport. "Anything else you can tell us about the victim?"

"The stab wound was perfectly placed, right between the ribs and straight to the heart," Derrick said. "It was so precise it looked like a gunshot wound at first glance."

Colin fisted his hands. "Just like Juliet Clark."

"Yes, detective." The ME nodded. "If I were a betting man, I'd say we're dealing with the same killer."

"Could a woman have done this?"

"Yes, but man or woman, whoever your killer is, he or she likely had some combat training."

Derrick rocked back on his heels. "Tessa Seidel studied martial arts for years."

"Martial arts doesn't usually include teaching people how to murder with a knife."

"Maybe. Maybe not." Derrick held up the evidence bag again. "Once forensics pulls the DNA for us, we should know for sure."

And finally, they would have an irrefutable case against the real killer.

Chapter 37

Tears trickled down Tessa's cheeks as she read the new scenes Ian had emailed Parker. Another person dead. Another family mourning.

In the kitchen chair beside her, Parker stretched his arm out and wrapped it around her shoulders. "It's going to be okay." He pressed a kiss against her temple. "I know it's terrible to think this way, but if the killer is the same as the person who murdered Juliet, that's good for you."

"How is someone getting killed good for me?"

"You have a clear alibi for this murder." Parker pulled her closer. "Several, in fact. Micah, Olivia, and Zoey can also testify that you were here all weekend."

That was true, but it didn't negate the fact that Ian had lost another colleague. Yet Tessa couldn't ignore the spark of hope that ignited inside her. "Do you think the police will believe me now?"

"I don't know." Parker rubbed her shoulder. "I'm sure Kimber and Ian will tell us when it's safe for you to return to the city."

"Part of me wants to go back, but I can't deny that I'm scared."

"Selfishly, I wouldn't mind you staying a bit longer." Parker trailed a finger along her neck. "At the rate we're going, I could have the rough draft of my play done in another week or two."

Tessa loved the idea of spending extra time with Parker, but she'd much prefer enjoying that time without worrying whether the police were looking for her or if the killer was working in proximity to Kimber and Ian. Just the thought of the danger they could be facing caused her stomach to churn. "Do you think you could write a nice ending, one that gives us and everyone we care about a happily ever after?"

"I think that can be arranged." He leaned in for a long kiss, and Tessa let herself fall into the fictional world she and Parker had just spoken about. Now if the real world would fall in line with her dreams of a future with this incredible man, she really could capture the life she hoped for.

Parker drew back and slid his hand forward to cradle her chin. "If this play gets produced, I want you front row center on opening night."

How was it that he could sound more confident about her being proved innocent than about his play making it to the stage?

"Not *if*." Tessa lifted her hand to cover his. "When."

Parker leaned in for another kiss. Goose bumps rippled across her skin, and Tessa let herself focus solely on this man holding her. Her heart thudded in her chest, and love swelled within her.

Her hand tightened on his, and her emotions caught up to her. Love. Could it be that she had fallen in love with Parker in such a short time? Shocked at the possibility, she started to pull away, but Parker held her in place and drew the kiss out.

When he finally pulled back, he leaned forward until his forehead touched hers. "If I tell you something, do you promise not to freak out?"

Tessa dropped her hands into her lap. Was it possible that he'd learned something during his trip to the store? Maybe her photo was in the newspaper, or he'd seen something online when he'd stopped at the hotel to check his phone. "Are the police trying to arrest me?"

"I don't know," Parker said, a flash of fear

appearing in his eyes. "I wasn't thinking about that."

"Then what else could you tell me that would freak me out?"

Now he took her hand in his. "I think I'm falling for you."

Despite her earlier thoughts, Tessa leaned back. "You've only known me a week." And her future still wasn't hers.

"I know it doesn't make sense. But I've never felt like this about anyone."

Tessa stared for a long moment, torn between stepping into an uncertain future together and trying to protect both of them from the possibility that the justice system could separate them.

Parker kept his eyes on her, as though willing her to share her feelings. "If you don't feel the same way —"

Unable to deny her emotions, she shook her head. "I do feel the same way, but it scares me."

"Why?"

"Because I still don't know if my future is mine."

"It will be." Parker lifted her hand and kissed her fingers. "Somehow, we'll make sure everything works out."

Brandon and Kimber walked toward the

nearest subway station with the intent of stopping by Tessa's apartment for one of their regular visits. Kimber had stopped by at least once every day since Tessa had gone into hiding just in case the police were watching.

He should have been relieved that the latest murder case would prove Tessa innocent. Unfortunately, the police following him and Kimber had increased the unease since finding Bob Kelley dead, and it didn't help Brandon's concerns for his girlfriend's sister either.

Kimber leaned close. "Do we lose them or let them follow us?"

They could evade the police, but it would only draw more attention to them and heighten Detective Murray's suspicions. Plus, having the cops follow them to Tessa's would only reinforce the thought that Kimber was also looking for her sister.

Brandon took Kimber's hand in his. "We don't have anything to hide." Nothing that would hold up in court anyway. The exchange of pages between Ian and Parker may mirror the investigation of Juliet's murder, but the police would be hard-pressed to prove Brandon and Kimber had access to the police file that provided the extra details they were privy to.

Barely speaking, he and Kimber made their way to the train. The undercover police officers kept their distance, though one followed them into the same train car. The other disappeared into the crowd, but Brandon suspected he entered the car behind them.

With no seats available, Brandon gripped the grab bar nearest him. Kimber placed one hand right below his and used the other to hold on to his waist right above his gun.

Brandon's phone rang, and he pulled it from his pocket. Rafi. Brandon angled the phone toward Kimber so she would know who it was before he hit the Talk button. She leaned close in an obvious attempt to hear both sides of the conversation.

"Any news?" Brandon asked.

"I'm not sure if you'll consider this good news or bad, but I do have news. Detectives Murray and Randall have been assigned to the Robert Kelley murder," Rafi said.

All too aware that he was in a crowded subway train, Brandon chose his words carefully. "I figured they'd assign the same ones since the two cases are likely related."

"From what I've been able to pull so far, it looks like the police are linking the two cases due to the common employer," Rafi said. "They found a woman's hair tie at the scene of the crime, and Murray has already put in a rush order on the DNA results."

"A hair tie?" Interesting. Kimber must have thought so, too, because she pulled away from Brandon and cast him a speculative look.

"So they're looking for a woman?" she whispered.

Brandon repeated the question for Rafi.

"They are," Rafi said, confirming Kimber's suspicion. "Please tell me Kimber's sister has an alibi for last weekend."

"She does." Thank goodness Ian's nephew had been willing to stay with her for the past week. "Anything else you can tell us?"

"Not yet, but I'll call you when I get the updated police report," Rafi said. "The DNA results should be in on Wednesday or Thursday."

Kimber tightened her grip on Brandon's waist.

Brandon gave her a reassuring squeeze before he spoke into his phone again. "Thanks for the update." He hung up the phone and whispered, "Did you catch all that?"

Kimber nodded. "Sounds like we're in for another waiting game."

"I'm afraid so."

Chapter 38

Kimber rolled over in bed a half hour before her alarm was set to go off. Six in the morning, and she couldn't sleep. She really hated waiting for the police to do their job, and the clue about the hair tie had been brewing in her thoughts since she'd learned about it last night. A woman. The person who murdered Bob was a woman. If they were right about the killer being a member of the cast or crew, that put Lisa or Sheridan at the top of the suspect list. And then there was also Elena. She could very well have circled back into the studio after leaving hours earlier.

Kimber's cell phone rang, and she narrowed her eyes. She'd asked the agency to forward her regular calls to this cell phone until she got her personal cell phone back, but still, who would be calling at this hour? Even Brandon never called before seven.

She unplugged her phone from the charger and checked the screen. Tessa's boss?

Kimber hit the Talk button. "Greta? Is everything okay?"

"I'm sorry to call so early, but I'm about to fly out to LA for a few days and wanted to know if you have any news about Tessa?"

"Not really." Only suspicions. "Thank you for being so patient with her being off this past week."

"It hasn't been easy, but I feel responsible for all this," Greta said. "Had I not told Sheridan I'd get those costumes to her the night of the murder, Tessa never would have been in this mess."

"Wait." Kimber climbed out of bed. "Sheridan is the one who asked for the costumes to be delivered that night?"

"Yes. I asked Sheridan if Tessa could bring them in early the next morning, but she said the costume manager had to do the inventory and prep everything that night."

"I talked to the costume manager," Kimber said. "She said no one told her Tessa was dropping the clothes off that night."

"Sounds like there were some communication problems, then." Over the phone, Kimber heard a boarding call. Greta waited for it to finish before she spoke again. "My flight is about to board, but please call me if you learn anything new. And if there's anything I can do to help Tessa, just say the word."

"I will. And travel safe." Kimber ended the call and sat back down on her bed. Sheridan and Elena. Both women, and based on what Greta had just told her, one of them was lying.

Determined to find out who, Kimber pulled up her favorites list on her phone. As much as she had hoped to avoid involving her best friend at the CIA, desperate times called for desperate measures, and Mark was the person who could help her get the information she needed the fastest.

He answered on the third ring. "Why are you calling me at six ten in the morning?"

"Because I need a favor, and I wanted to catch you before you go to work."

"Whose bank accounts do you want me to access today?" Mark asked. "And are you getting me a warrant so I don't get fired?"

"Rafi already has the warrant, but the FBI and the police are taking forever on the financials." Or rather, they hadn't found anything, and Kimber wanted to see the numbers herself.

"You don't trust them," Mark said, guessing at her motivation without any effort. "Are you going to tell me what this case is about?"

Kimber gave Mark a quick rundown of the situation Tessa had landed in.

"You should have told me when this first happened," Mark said. "I could have helped sooner."

"I know, but this is a domestic case, which isn't what you usually handle," Kimber reminded him. "Unfortunately, I think the police may be looking in the wrong places for a money trail." Kimber grabbed her notepad off her bedside table. "I want to know if either of my top suspects has any overseas accounts. The local police and FBI wouldn't necessarily dig that far, especially without a primary suspect beyond Tessa."

"I'll do some digging and get back to you."

"Thanks. The sooner the better."

"Is this your way of telling me to go to work early?" Mark asked.

"You know it."

"I'd say I miss you, but I'm rethinking that."

"You don't have to tell me you miss me. I already know," Kimber said. "But call me as soon as you have anything."

"I will." Mark ended the call, and Kimber grabbed her laptop off her bedside table. Time to look over the financial reports Rafi had given her. Somewhere within those pages, there had to be a clue about who had really killed Juliet Clark.

Tessa was going stir crazy. She had thought the departure of Parker's friends would bring relief, but she now recognized that their presence had created a distraction, one she hadn't realized she'd needed.

Parker had stayed up late last night, working on his play, and he'd yet to emerge from his room this morning, even though it was after eleven. There was one way to fix that. Tessa opened the refrigerator and pulled out the bacon. The scent would surely get his attention. Now to decide if she was in the mood for eggs or french toast to go with it. She chose french toast. She needed some comfort food.

Within minutes of her putting the bacon in the oven, a door opened down the hall, and footsteps sounded. Parker appeared in the kitchen doorway, his hair disheveled and a two-day beard shadowing his face. "Morning."

"It won't be morning for much longer." Spatula in hand, she gestured to the clock on the wall.

"I didn't realize I'd slept so late." He crossed to her and kissed her cheek.

"How late did you stay up?"

"I didn't even look at the clock when I crashed."

Tessa checked the half-cooked french toast and flipped them over. "Did you get much done on your play?"

"Not really. I was reading through everything we've already written and cleaning it up a bit." Parker leaned against the counter beside her. "You know one thing that keeps bothering me?"

"What's that?"

"Why did the killer take Juliet's laptop and planner?"

The oven timer went off, and Tessa pulled the bacon out of the oven. "Obviously, there was something on them that the killer was worried about. Something he or she wanted to hide."

"Yes, but how did he or she know that?"

Tessa layered two paper towels on a plate and used the spatula to transfer the bacon onto it as she pondered the question. "The killer must have known Juliet pretty well, but we already suspected that."

"We suspected the killer knew her, but it had to be someone she works closely with if they knew to take both the laptop and the appointment book."

"Who would fall into that category?" Tessa asked. "Kimber and Ian seemed pretty sure the other PAs were innocent."

"Maybe they need to look a bit closer." Parker snatched a piece of bacon off the plate and took a bite.

Tessa thought through the few times she'd visited Ian at the studio. "The production assistants work with just about everyone. Your question doesn't really narrow the suspect list."

"Maybe not." He sighed. "I really thought we'd have more to go on by now."

"I know." She transferred the french toast onto a plate and handed it to Parker. "But I'm starting to think the killer might have really committed the perfect crime."

"Trust me." Parker slipped his hands around her waist. "The one thing I've learned in all my research is that there is no such thing as a perfect crime."

Chapter 39

Colin checked for the DNA results, not surprised that they weren't in yet. It had been barely twenty-four hours, and even though he'd requested a rapid result, he had no doubt there were dozens of other similar requests competing for the lab's time. With the arrest warrant already issued for Seidel, updating it to include a second victim would be easy enough. Yet, once again, he couldn't find any ties between their suspect and the victim.

He turned in his chair to face Derrick, who was currently standing by his desk, a cup of coffee in his hand. "What do you think the chances are that Seidel could be a contract killer?" Colin asked.

Derrick shook his head. "I don't know. That's a stretch."

The idea took root and grew. "Think about it. She's young. She travels. No one would ever suspect her."

"For good reason." Derrick sat in his chair and leaned back. "I didn't find any sign of the kind of money an assassin should have."

"Check again. Maybe she has an offshore account." And if that were the case, they needed to know more than simply the person who had committed these two murders. They needed to identify the person who wanted Juliet Clark and Robert Kelley dead. Oddly, despite the extra work that detail might entail, the possibility of Seidel being a pro gave him comfort in the whole motive issue he'd been struggling with.

"Do you want me to look into possible motives for the other people at the studio?" Derrick asked.

"Are you up for it?" Colin asked. "I can take that on if you want."

"It's fine. I'll look for motive." Derrick turned toward his computer. "You focus on trying to find out where our killer is hiding."

The same task Colin had been working on for a week now. And the fact that he hadn't succeeded reinforced the idea that she could be a professional killer. It was even possible that she had taken on a new identity, which would explain why he'd been unable to locate her.

Colin checked for credit-card activity

again, not surprised when nothing flagged. His search of transportation records also didn't yield anything of use.

Starting back at the beginning, he reviewed everything he had on Seidel. When he read through the transcription of her phone conversation with her sister, he paused when he reached the spot about Tessa turning in a witness statement the night of the murder.

Colin pushed back from his desk and headed for the elevator. Maybe a quick trip to the front desk would give him time to clear his head and see things from a new perspective. Not that he expected to find anything. Derrick had already gone through the security feed for the lobby and hadn't seen any sign of Seidel.

Colin reached the ground floor and approached the front desk. Stanley, an older cop with a few years until retirement, looked up and waved a greeting. "Hey, Detective. What brings you down here?"

"I'm trying to track down a lead." Colin leaned his elbow on the counter. "By any chance, do you have a witness statement for the Juliet Clark murder? It would have been turned in last Tuesday night."

"Let me check." He retrieved a folder and flipped through a few papers. "There's one here that reports a possible murder. The woman left before anyone interviewed her, though, and we don't have a case file number for it." Stanley held out the handwritten witness statement.

Colin took it from him and read the name: Tessa Seidel. Colin skimmed over it, the details describing much of what had been on the phone recording between the Seidel sisters. He narrowed his eyes. If Tessa had turned in a statement, why hadn't Derrick seen any sign of her on the security feed?

"Is that what you were looking for?" Stanley asked.

"Yeah, thanks." Colin headed back upstairs. With this new piece of information, he and Derrick had a lot to consider. He was almost to his desk when his phone rang. "Murray."

"Hi, this is Zoey Campbell. I'm calling about Tessa Seidel," a woman said. "I saw on the news that you're looking for her."

Colin shot to his feet. "You know where she is?"

"I think so," the woman said. "She said her name was Lynn, but when I saw the photo, I'm pretty sure it was her."

A lead. Finally! "Where did you see her?"

"At a cabin in the Catskills."

The Catskills. That was the last known

location of Parker Sawyer, which meant he had likely helped Tessa leave the Hamptons. And if that was the case, the young Mr. Sawyer was guilty of making a false statement.

"Can you tell me where you saw her exactly?"

The woman gave him the address. "I went with my friend Parker to the grocery store, too, and we stopped by a hotel nearby."

That was likely where they believed Parker Sawyer was staying.

"Did you see Parker at the cabin too?"

"Yeah, but I don't think he knows who Tessa really is," Zoey said. "He always called her Lynn, and he said his phone was broken. His car was having issues, too, so he might not have seen the news."

Parker didn't need to see the news. Based on Colin's phone interview with the man, he was well aware of who Tessa Seidel was and why the police wanted to speak to her.

Colin took down Zoey's contact information and thanked her. As soon as he hung up, he turned to Derrick. "You up for a road trip?"

"Yeah. Where are we going?"

"To the Catskills. I've got a lead on Seidel."

"So do I. The DNA results just came in."

Derrick stood and grabbed his coat. "The hair tie belonged to her."

Finally, they had her. Colin pulled his weapon from the side drawer of his desk and holstered it. "Let's go."

Brandon opened his office door, and Rafi rushed in, barely stepping inside before closing the door behind him. His mere presence at Brandon's workplace was enough to send red flags flying. Rafi opened his mouth as though to speak, but when he caught sight of Phoebe, he promptly closed it again. Gesturing toward the door, Rafi said, "I need to speak with you. Privately."

"If this is about Tessa's case, you can talk in front of Phoebe. She's Ian Sawyer's wife, and she's been helping me analyze the case."

Rafi hesitated a second before he grabbed the back of the chair beside Phoebe's. "I found something, and it's not good."

"What?" Brandon asked.

Phoebe turned in her chair and looked up at Rafi. "Please tell me you found the person really responsible for the murder."

"No, but I may have found an accomplice after the fact." Rafi lowered into the chair and leaned forward. "The DNA results came back on the hair tie found at Robert

Kelley's apartment. It matched Tessa."

"That can't be right." Brandon gripped the edge of his chair. "Tessa never met the guy, and we know she wasn't in New York the night of his murder."

"That's what Kimber said when I called to tell her, and it got me thinking." Rafi rubbed both hands along his thighs. "I went through the two cases for wrongful conviction and compared them to the Juliet Clark and Robert Kelley cases to see if there might be anything that pointed to mishandling or manipulation of the evidence."

"And?"

"When I checked the logs for the questionable evidence, every time, it was originally processed by the same person."

Phoebe's eyes widened. "You think the police are deliberately manipulating the evidence to get a conviction?"

"It appears that way."

She shook her head. "That's terrible."

Brandon had suspected that might be the case, but hearing the words spoken chilled his blood. "Was the officer responsible Detective Murray? If so, we should be able to have him removed from the case."

"Colin was the lead detective on the cases, but the person who collected the evidence in question was Derrick Randall. Looks like the two are partners."

"We met him when we were looking over the crime scene."

Phoebe held up a hand. "So you're saying that even though everyone is making Detective Murray out to be a bad cop, it could actually be his partner who's dirty?"

"The chain of evidence makes that a distinct possibility," Rafi said.

"It's just like the pilot of Ian's current show," Phoebe said.

Now Rafi focused on the woman beside him. "What do you mean?"

"In the opening episode, Ian's character investigated a cop who had been accused of falsifying evidence, but in the end, it was someone else. In that case, it was a member of the forensics team."

Brandon stood abruptly. If the cast and crew had witnessed such a story play out, it was entirely possible that the killer had used that knowledge to pay off someone in the police department.

"Are you thinking what I'm thinking?" Rafi asked, also rising to his feet.

"If you're thinking that our killer has some tie to Derrick Randall, then yes."

"It could be Lisa, Nicole, or Sheridan," Phoebe said, referring to one of the screenwriters, a production assistant, and the producer. "They're all women, so any of them could have been the person seen going into the PA's office."

Rafi retrieved his phone from his pocket. "I'll dig into the possibility that one of them has a connection to Randall, but all of their alibis appear solid."

Brandon placed both hands on his desk and leaned forward. "If we're to believe the killer is a woman, we're out of suspects."

"Unless the altered security feed is leading us to believe it's a woman to throw us off." Rafi held up his phone. "The evidence points that way, but evidence can be misleading."

The pieces of the puzzle fell into place. "If one of the investigating officers was hired to manipulate evidence, one of these women could have made sure to have a solid alibi for both of the murders to keep her off the suspect list."

Phoebe looked from Brandon to Rafi. "You said this Detective Randall was likely the one manipulating the evidence?"

"That's right."

"Could he be the killer?" Now Phoebe pushed to her feet. "I mean, who better to hire to get rid of someone than the cop who was setting up Tessa?"

"She's right." Brandon straightened and

pulled up his notes on his laptop. "From what I've seen, both Murray and Randall have been on the weekday shift this month. The coroner's report clearly indicates Bob was killed late Saturday night or early Sunday morning."

"Let's see if the detective has an alibi for the time of Kelley's murder." Rafi dialed his phone.

After a moment, a muffled voice carried into the room, but Brandon couldn't make out the words.

"Yes, I need to speak to Captain Jeffries." A pause. "Yes, I'll hold." Rafi shifted the phone from one ear to the other. "Captain, I need you to question Detective Randall on his whereabouts for Saturday night. If you can do it without it sounding like an interrogation, all the better."

More mumbled words, and this time Rafi clearly didn't like what he heard. He lifted his chin and asked, "Where is he?" A brief pause. "When did they leave?" Rafi grabbed a pen off Brandon's desk and slid a notepad closer. "Give me both of their phone numbers and the vehicle information."

With Rafi leaning closer, Brandon could now make out the captain's words. "What's this about?"

"We believe Detective Randall may be

involved in manipulating evidence in the Juliet Clark and Robert Kelley cases."

"That's absurd."

"Whether you believe it or not, I expect your full cooperation. Now, give me their phone numbers and the vehicle information."

The captain complied, and Brandon sat at his desk, immediately pulling up the program that would allow him to track the GPS signals on the two detectives' phones. He'd barely put in Randall's number when Rafi hung up.

"Brandon, we've got to go." Rafi reached for the door handle. "Randall and Murray are on their way to the Catskills. They know where Tessa is."

"Oh no." Phoebe's gasped words mirrored the panic rushing through Brandon.

"Phoebe, call Kimber and tell her what's going on," Brandon said.

Without waiting for her reply, Brandon rushed past Phoebe and followed Rafi out the door.

Chapter 40

Kimber stared at the figures in front of her, needing to make sure she was reading them right. After reviewing them for the third time, she could no longer deny the facts. Nearly a million dollars had been embezzled from the show's budget, and the only person who could have processed all the misappropriated payments was Sheridan.

Across the room, Ian set his script on his desk. "I know that look. What's troubling you?"

Kimber stood and crossed to Ian's dressing-room door, peeking into the hall to ensure it was empty before she pulled it closed. She grabbed the back of her chair and rolled it closer to Ian's desk. "It looks like Sheridan has been embezzling from the show."

Ian's eyes widened and illuminated with understanding. "You think Juliet found out and Sheridan killed her?"

“It would fit.” Kimber sat down and leaned forward. “Her build is similar enough to my sister’s that she could have been the woman we saw actually walking into the production office before Juliet was killed.”

“Since the woman entering Juliet’s office wore the same coat as the one Tessa had on, my guess is that Sheridan looked at the surveillance feed first and then edited over the real surveillance feed after the fact to make it look like Tessa was the only person there,” Ian said.

Kimber suspected that was exactly what had happened. “Would Sheridan have had the ability to edit the security feed herself, or would she have needed help?”

“Oh, she could do it,” Ian said with certainty. “She started as a video editor before she moved into production.”

“Bob must have said or done something to tip her off that he was suspicious of the security files that were handed over to the police.”

“And Bob was killed before he could confirm our suspicions.” Ian sighed.

“I’m sorry.” Kimber put her hand on his arm and gave it a comforting squeeze. “You couldn’t have known that it would put Bob in danger.”

“I should have though.” Ian shook his

head. "You and Brandon tried to warn me of the danger, and I thought I was above it."

"It's not your fault, Ian. We should be blaming whoever killed Bob."

Ian fell silent. Finally, he gestured to her laptop. "With what you found, will that be enough to prove Tessa is innocent?"

"It will create doubt, at least." She let out a sigh of her own. If only they could find proof that Tessa had been set up rather than snippets of evidence that simply made it possible that she was innocent.

"You should be excited about this," Ian said. "Why aren't you?"

"Because Sheridan has twenty people who can vouch for the fact that she was in Boston the night Bob was killed."

"But Tessa has an alibi for that night too," Ian said. "The police just don't know it yet."

"That's true, but how did Tessa's hair tie end up at Bob's apartment?" Kimber asked. "I still can't figure that one out."

"Maybe one fell out of her purse when she was here at the studio the night of the murder," Ian suggested. "It's possible the killer found it and used it to try to frame her."

That would make sense, except that Tessa hadn't used a hair tie in weeks, not since before she'd started using the new purse Kimber had given her for her birthday. "I don't think so. The only place someone could have gotten that hair tie was from her apartment."

"I don't suppose there's a security camera that would let us see if someone broke into her apartment, is there?"

"Not right by her door." And Kimber had stopped by her sister's apartment multiple times to make it look like she was checking to see if Tessa was home yet. She would have noticed if her sister's door had been forced open.

Ian's phone rang. "It's Phoebe." He answered. "Hey, honey. What's up?" A few seconds passed before he said, "Hold on. Kimber's right here. I'm going to put you on speaker."

As soon as Ian hit the Speaker button, Kimber spoke. "Phoebe? Are you still with Brandon?"

"No. He and Agent Ebeid just left Brandon's office," Phoebe said, her words coming in a rush. "They're on their way to find Tessa."

"What?" Kimber gripped the arms of her chair. "Why?"

"They think one of the police officers might be involved with Bob's death."

Phoebe proceeded to spell out the possibility that Detective Randall might have been paid off to frame Tessa.

"The police visited Tessa's apartment after she didn't show up for her interview," Kimber said. "One of them could have taken the hair tie during the search."

"Which reinforces the idea that there might have been two killers working together," Phoebe said.

"I have a friend digging into the financials for possible overseas accounts for our top suspects," Kimber said. "I'll call him and see if he's found anything that might suggest a payoff to Randall."

"What about Sheridan?" Ian asked. "We have to tell the FBI about her."

"You're right." Kimber moved to her laptop. "But first, I need to send Parker a warning. And then we'll look for the evidence that will prove Sheridan not only had motive but is also really a killer."

Parker circled the cabin, his gaze sweeping over the open space between him and the lake and into the nearby trees. He couldn't say why he felt the need to make sure he and Tessa were really alone, but ever since breakfast, he'd been uneasy.

It made no sense. His friends' departure

should have given him some much-needed peace, but this was the third time today that he'd been prompted to check outside under the guise of going for a walk to clear his head. Now here he was, with the sun lowering on the horizon, and he was alone when he should be enjoying the view with Tessa. He suspected his girlfriend must also be distracted, or she would have insisted on coming with him on this latest walk outside.

His girlfriend. The mere thought that two weeks ago Tessa had been nothing more than a faceless name who had occasionally called her sister during Kimber's writing retreat with him and Aunt Phoebe blew his mind. She was so much more now. Given the opportunity, he could see himself building his future with her. She could be his everything.

Parker reached the front entrance and stepped inside. Not surprisingly, Tessa waited right inside the door. The mere sight of her was like the calm amid a storm.

She put her hand on his arm. "Everything okay?"

"Yeah." He locked the door behind him and shrugged out of his jacket. "There's nothing out there."

"That's a relief." She moved to the living room window and peeked through the curtains. "I don't know why I keep expecting someone to be outside."

Tessa's words heightened his own uneasiness.

"Maybe we should think about relocating." Parker checked the lock on the door again to make sure it was secure. "If we're both feeling like something's wrong, maybe there's a reason for that."

"It's already getting dark." Tessa turned to him. "I'm not sure we'd want to take the four-wheeler out this time of night."

"I can always drive down myself to pick up my car. Then I can come back here to pick up you and all our stuff." Parker made the suggestion, but the thought of leaving her alone, even for a half hour, heightened the tension already brewing inside him.

"I know I'm being silly, but I don't want to stay here alone."

Parker crossed to her and drew her into his arms. "You're not being silly." He debated their options. It made sense to wait until tomorrow to move. That would give him time to think through their options, but he couldn't shake the urgency pulsing through him. He drew closer and kissed Tessa. "How about we both go pack? As soon as we're done, we can head down to pick up my car."

Tessa didn't argue. She nodded and stepped back. "Should I pack the groceries too?"

"Don't worry about that for now." The phone rang. "That's probably Micah. He's one of the few people who would think to call the landline to get in touch with me."

"Go ahead and answer." Tessa started down the hall. "I'll start packing."

Parker strode after her and turned into the office. He snatched the receiver off the base. "Hello?"

Micah's voice carried over the line. "Are you alone?"

Startled by the odd question, Parker answered automatically. "Yeah. Why?"

"Parker, it's all over the news," Micah said quickly. "Your girlfriend Lynn is really Tessa Seidel, and the police have a warrant out for her arrest. They say she killed someone."

Parker tightened his grip on the phone. It was official. Tessa really was a fugitive, and he could no longer deny that he was aware of it. He swallowed hard and forced out a response. "There must be some mistake."

"I wish there were, but her photo is everywhere online," Micah said. "You need to get away from her."

"No matter what you saw online, there's no way she killed anyone," Parker insisted.

"I promise you that."

"Believe whatever you want, but you don't want to get mixed up in this."

Knowing he wouldn't be able to explain the details of Tessa's situation, he opted to cut the conversation short. "Micah, thanks for letting me know about all this. I'll give you a call when I get back to the city."

"Watch your back."

"Don't worry about me." Parker ended the call and turned.

Tessa stood in the office doorway, her face ashen. Tears swam in her eyes. "The police are still looking for me?"

Though he wanted to deny it, Parker nodded. "Micah said the police issued an arrest warrant." Parker put his hands on her shoulders. "Tessa, I'm sorry."

Tears spilled over, and she blinked against them.

"Come here." He pulled her into his arms. "It's going to be okay." He said the words, hoping and praying they were true, but even he was having a hard time believing them. No longer was Tessa the only person facing jail time. If he continued to protect her, he could find himself in front of a judge too.

Tessa's body trembled, and her fingers curled into the back of his shirt. The instinct to protect her flooded through him, fighting against the knowledge of what the law required of him. He needed to keep Tessa safe, but if he ended up behind bars, he would be of no use to her.

He pulled back and stared into her teary eyes. His heart broke for her, and there was no denying that no matter what he did now, his actions could cost him the woman who was quickly capturing his heart.

Chapter 41

Tessa only had to look into Parker's eyes to read his thoughts. He wanted to help her, but doing so would get him arrested one way or another. And she cared for him too much to let him jeopardize his future.

She knew what she had to do. Gathering her strength, she blinked back her tears and drew a deep breath. "I need to turn myself in."

"Tessa —"

She cut off his protest with a kiss. "You know I'm right." Stepping free of his embrace, she gestured toward the phone. "Now that we know about the arrest warrant, you'll be breaking the law if you keep hiding with me, whether it's here or somewhere else."

"But if you turn yourself in, you'll end up behind bars."

Her heart seized. She couldn't imagine it, didn't want to imagine it. "I know."

"There has to be another way." Parker closed the distance between them again. "You can take my car, and I can tell the police that I know you were here but that you left."

Tessa tried to picture it, going on the run by herself. Beyond the loneliness and fear that would certainly follow, she couldn't be sure the police wouldn't punish Parker if he admitted that he'd been with her all this time. "The only way to be sure the police won't go after you is if I give myself up." She took his hands. "I love that you want to protect me, but we have to trust the legal system for now."

Parker put his hands on her shoulders. "I don't like this."

"I don't either, but we're out of options." She sighed. "No matter how you write the ending to your play, the police are about to become a big part of the story."

"So will I." He already was. He squeezed her hands. "I'll be ready to post bail as soon as it's set."

"If they'll even grant it." She'd seen the cop shows. "The prosecutor will claim I'm a flight risk."

"You just have to convince them that you feared for your life," Parker said. "It's true."

But would anyone believe her? "We need

to finish packing."

"You don't really want to go back tonight, do you?" Parker asked.

"No, but I still can't shake the feeling that if we stay here, something will go wrong." Probably the police showing up and arresting both of them.

Parker straightened, but his gaze locked with hers. He lifted his hand to her cheek, caressing the soft underside of her jaw with his thumb. "Are you really sure about this?"

Her stomach knotted, but she forced herself to nod. "I'm sure."

Kimber leaned against the back wall of the studio as the second-to-last scene for the day played out for the fourth time. Different angles, minor adjustments of the lighting and the camera angles. And in the center of it all, Ian acted like this was just another day rather than the one when his producer would likely end up in handcuffs. Kimber had to give it to the man. His talent ran far deeper than most people could possibly understand.

Discreetly, she checked the time on her phone and willed it to ring. Not that she would hear it since her phone was on silent, but the vibration would alert her if a call was coming in.

Still nothing. All day, she'd been waiting for Mark's call, but she hadn't heard a word, nor had she received any emails or messages that would indicate that he'd found anything.

From where Gabriel stood beside the camera, he yelled, "Cut."

The scene ended once again.

"Okay, everyone," Gabriel continued, "let's move on to the last scene so we can wrap up for the day."

Several of the cast members headed for their dressing rooms, with only Ian and Allison staying behind.

Ian approached Kimber. "This scene should be a quick one. You can wait in my dressing room if you want."

She didn't miss the subtle gleam in his eye. He was saying the words for the crew so they wouldn't know that he was giving her permission to go check in with Mark. Not that Ian knew Mark worked for the agency. Most likely, Ian suspected she was pulling in a favor from someone at the FBI.

Kimber took a step toward the door. "Just let me know if you need anything."

"I will." Ian moved back to the set, where his costar waited for him. As the two began rehearsing their lines, Kimber left the studio and headed back to Ian's dressing room.

Unable to wait any longer, she dialed Mark's office number and closed Ian's dressing-room door behind her. The phone rang twice before Mark answered.

"This is Mark."

"Hey, it's me," Kimber said, deliberately avoiding giving her name since they were on an unsecured line. "Please tell me you have something."

"Oh yeah. I just finished encrypting it so I can email it to you," he said. "It'll be in your inbox in just a minute."

Kimber fought the urge to ask for details. "How much am I going to owe you for this?"

"Big-time."

Kimber couldn't help but smile. "I was hoping you would say that."

"If you don't see my email in the next five minutes, give me a call."

"Will do." Kimber hit the End button and opened her laptop. Instantly, the new email from Mark popped up in her inbox. She ran the attachment through the encryption program and opened the file.

She skimmed over the financial transactions listed, and her eyes widened. Mark had traced the embezzled funds to an offshore account that belonged to Sheridan, and he'd also identified two large payments to a second overseas account. And this one belonged to none other than New York Detective Derrick Randall.

Colin gripped the wheel as he finally reached the exit that would take them to the cabin. In the seat beside him, Derrick tapped on his cell phone. Colin rolled his shoulders to work out the stiffness that had settled there. Too long behind the wheel, especially since he and Derrick had been forced to take a different vehicle than their usual. Of all the days for the motor pool to decide their car was due for an oil change.

He resisted the urge to adjust his seat. No matter how much he fiddled with it, he couldn't get comfortable, but he couldn't say whether it was the car causing his tension or the urgency rushing through him because they'd finally found Seidel.

"I just checked. Parker Sawyer's cell phone and car are still at the hotel."

"Why would he leave his car and cell phone at the hotel if he's staying at the cabin with Tessa?" Parker had seemed honest enough when Colin had spoken to him on the phone, but maybe his initial suspicions had been correct. "Unless he's trying to throw us off."

"He's got to be helping her," Derrick said,

his thoughts clearly aligning with Colin's. "Who knows. Maybe he's even involved with the murder too." Derrick straightened in his seat, and fresh excitement filled his voice. "Maybe he's the connection between Seidel and the victims."

Colin supposed it was possible that Ian Sawyer's nephew was acquainted with Juliet Clark and Robert Kelley. "I still don't see how Seidel fits into all this."

"Maybe Parker put her up to the murder." Derrick tapped his fingers on his thigh. "The tipster did say that he's dating Tessa."

"This is a lot of elaborate speculation." Colin made the next turn. "I'd really like a solid motive."

"Who knows what motivates the people in the entertainment industry?"

Derrick had a point. Movie stars often joined the ranks of those with money or power who believed they were above the law. Then again, there were plenty without wealth who also fell into that category.

Colin's cell phone rang from the cupholder where he'd set it when he'd first climbed into the car.

"Want me to check who it is?" Derrick asked, already reaching for Colin's phone.

"Yeah, thanks." They never bothered to pair their phones to the Bluetooth in the loaner cars, but maybe he should have. He shook that thought away. It wasn't worth it for one day.

Derrick plucked it out of the cupholder. "It's the captain." He hit the Talk button, but rather than put it on speaker, he lifted the phone to his ear. "Hey, Captain. What's up?" Derrick paused and looked at Colin. "He's driving right now, but I can give him a message. Is anything wrong?"

Curious as to the reason for the captain's call, Colin gestured to his phone. "Put it on speaker."

Derrick looked over at him but didn't comply. He simply held up his finger and fell silent again. Colin strained to make out the captain's words but couldn't. After a moment, Derrick said, "Okay, I'll tell him."

"Tell me what?" Colin asked. "And why didn't you put it on speaker?"

"I didn't want to interrupt him or miss anything he said." Derrick put the phone back in the cupholder. "Apparently, he got another call from the FBI. Agent Ebeid wants you to check in after we have the suspects in custody."

Colin had hoped the captain had new information to share, not just an administrative matter to tell them about. "I'm surprised he even bothered to call."

“He’s probably just tired of having the FBI breathing down his neck.”

“Maybe so.” Regardless of the captain’s reasons, once Colin and Derrick took Seidel into custody, they would all be free of Agent Ebeid and his constant interference.

Chapter 42

Brandon fought for calm as he sat in the passenger seat of Rafi's car. They were still forty minutes away from the cabin where Parker had taken Tessa to hide out, a half hour behind the two detectives who were set on arresting the woman who would hopefully soon be his sister-in-law.

"Even if Tessa is arrested, it's not the end of the world," Rafi said. "We can intercept them at the police station when they question her."

"I know, but when they find Parker with her, he's bound to face charges too." Brandon fisted his hands. "And knowing Randall could be one of our killers makes me nervous."

Rafi didn't respond to that, but the way his grip tightened on the wheel made Brandon suspect Rafi also had reservations about Parker's and Tessa's well-being.

Brandon's phone rang with the ringtone

he'd assigned to Kimber. He hit the Talk button and put it on speaker. "Hey. Anything new?"

"Yes, and you need to hurry."

"What's wrong?"

"My friend helped me locate offshore accounts for both Sheridan and Randall," Kimber said hurriedly. "Brandon, there are two payments between them. They both line up with the dates of when the victims were killed."

Which meant a key figure in both murders was heading straight for Tessa. Brandon exchanged a horrified look with Rafi. If Randall went in and somehow made it look like Tessa was a threat, he could kill her and claim self-defense.

Rafi shook his head. "You don't think —"

"I've already tried calling Detective Murray," Kimber answered before Brandon had the chance to. "My calls are going straight to voicemail. It's like his phone is turned off."

"Or out of the service area," Rafi said.

"I'm more worried that Randall knows we're on to him," Kimber said. "If he does, Tessa isn't the only person in danger. Parker and Detective Murray are at risk too."

"We'll call the locals to see if they have a unit close enough to take Tessa and Parker into custody before Randall and Murray get there," Rafi said. "But in the meantime, call the police station and let the captain know about the new evidence you found. I want Sheridan behind bars now."

"I'll call the police right now," Kimber said. "But let me know as soon as you find my sister."

"We will," Brandon said. He ended the call and looked up the closest police station only to discover it was a half hour away from the cabin.

"This isn't looking good. The police station isn't even close to the cabin."

"Inform them of the situation anyway," Rafi said.

"Fine, but only if you drive faster."

Colin fought the urge to slam his fist against the wheel. Three times he'd let his GPS guide him to the address his source had given him, and every time, he'd ended up at a vacant lot.

"You sure you took down the address correctly?" Derrick asked yet again.

"Yes." Colin shook his head. "Let's head to the hotel. We can check out the room Parker Sawyer is supposed to be staying in, and maybe someone there can give us directions to the cabin."

"Sounds good."

"And while we're at it, hand me my phone. I want to call the station and have someone check the address in the file for me." Colin held out his hand. "With any luck, maybe the captain will have new information for us too."

"I doubt there's any new information to find." Derrick retrieved his own phone from his pocket. "Besides, I can pull up your notes from here." He tapped on his screen and then checked the address on the car's navigation screen. "You've got the address right. How about we head to the hotel, and I'll call to see if we have any updates."

Even though it was odd that Derrick ignored his request, Colin nodded. With the sun already hanging low in the sky, they didn't have much time before it would be dark, and they didn't need any more obstacles to finding their intended destination. He plugged the hotel address into the nav system and made a U-turn to head back to the main part of town.

Derrick made his call. "Hey, I wanted to see if there are any updates on the Clark case." He paused for a brief moment. "We haven't been able to find the cabin where Seidel is hiding out yet, but we're headed to the hotel where Parker Sawyer is checked in. Someone there might be able to give us directions."

Another pause, this one much longer. "Understood. I'll let Colin know."

Derrick hung up. Almost instantly, his phone chimed with an alert, the same one that Colin received every time he received money in his Venmo account.

"Anything new?"

"Yeah, a lot actually." Derrick pocketed his phone. "Looks like the theory that Seidel is a paid assassin was right after all. The new financial information came in on her overseas accounts."

"Seriously?" Even though they had to consider the possibility, nothing in Seidel's background and family life had hinted at such a career.

"Yeah. And there's an Interpol notice out on her. There's a warning out on her to assume she's armed and dangerous."

"Then that's what we'll assume." Colin tightened his grip on the wheel. So much for this being a simple case of taking a suspect into custody.

Kimber set down her phone as the door opened behind her. Ian had been right. That scene hadn't taken long. She turned, but it wasn't Ian standing behind her.

Sheridan stepped inside and closed the door.

"Sheridan. What are you doing here?" Kimber asked the question, hoping she sounded casual as she reached for her purse and the gun secured inside it.

"Oh, no you don't." Sheridan lunged forward and knocked Kimber's purse to the floor.

"What are you doing?" Kimber started to reach for the fallen purse, but Sheridan kicked it under the desk, out of reach.

"Do you think I'm stupid?" Sheridan reached into her pocket and produced a knife with a sharp, narrow blade.

Kimber instinctively took a step back and held her hands out in an attempt to appear nonthreatening. Ian could walk in at any time, and she didn't want to know what Sheridan would do if that happened.

Kimber's mind raced as she debated between her two options: She could pretend she had no idea that Sheridan was guilty of murder, or she could face the truth head-on.

With the knife gleaming under the overhead lights, Kimber chose the second option. "Why did you kill Juliet, Sheridan?" she asked. "Was it because she found out you were embezzling?"

Sheridan's eyes narrowed. "I see you have it all figured out."

"All except how you think you're going to get away with it." Even though Kimber had yet to make the call to the police, she fell back on logic. "The FBI already knows you were involved. I suspect the arrest warrant will be issued before you can even leave the building."

Anger and a hint of panic flashed in Sheridan's eyes. "You're lying."

Kimber took another step back. "You know I'm not." Her gaze lowered briefly to the knife. "You wouldn't have pulled a weapon on me if you hadn't overheard me talking to them on the phone."

"I'm not stupid. You were talking to your boyfriend."

"Yes, I was." Kimber kept her voice calm and even. "I guess I never mentioned that he works with the FBI."

Venom filled Sheridan's voice, and she lifted the knife higher. "You're lying."

"I'm not. You saw him yourself when he and his partner came to look over the crime scene before they released it back to the studio."

Sheridan's face paled. "Are you going to tell me you're a cop too?"

"No." Admitting to having both martial-arts and weapons training would not help her current situation. Best to keep this woman off guard. Changing the subject, Kimber asked, "Why did you embezzle the money in the first place? I have to imagine you get paid well working here."

"I only get a fraction of what people like Ian rake in." Sheridan spat the words at her.

"It isn't fair, is it?" Negotiation 101. Try to make a connection. And Kimber needed time to find a way to defend herself and disarm Sheridan before Ian walked in.

"It really is too bad that you decided to stick your nose in my business." Sheridan took a step forward, leading with the knife.

Kimber mentally played through the contents of the desk behind her. Her laptop, a notepad, pens, paperclips, a letter opener. The letter opener. Not an ideal weapon, but with her gun out of reach, it would have to do.

Anticipating Sheridan's attack, Kimber waited until the other woman thrust the knife forward to act. Kimber jumped back, the blade narrowly missing her stomach.

The lack of contact caused Sheridan to stumble forward, and Kimber barely managed to avoid the blade again.

Sheridan grabbed the side of the clothing rack beside Kimber's desk and whirled back to face Kimber.

Without hesitation, Kimber grabbed the letter opener and brandished it in front of her.

"A letter opener?" Sheridan sneered. "You really think that's going to do you any good?"

Kimber didn't bother to answer; instead, she took a moment to analyze her opponent. With the steady way Sheridan gripped the weapon in her hand, Kimber suspected this woman had been Juliet's killer.

"You really were clever, hiring out Bob's murder to make sure you had an alibi." Kimber took a step to her left, not surprised when Sheridan countered her movement. "You make sure you have an alibi for the second murder. Randall had one for the first."

Sheridan's eyes widened for a split second, a clear show of her surprise.

"My question is if you enlisted Randall's help before you killed Juliet or if you paid him off after the fact." The timing of the first payment suggested it was the latter.

Sheridan clenched her teeth and lunged forward again, knife first.

Kimber parried with the letter opener, but the blade of the knife cut through the softer metal, mangling the end of the simple office tool.

Sheridan swiped the knife at Kimber again, but this time, Kimber let her martial-arts and weapons training take over. She ducked beneath the blade, dodging the attack and stepping past her attacker. Then she whirled back toward Sheridan and grabbed the woman by the wrist, forcing the hand holding the knife into the air and out of the danger zone.

Sheridan yelped as Kimber used her strength and the element of surprise to push her against the wall. Kimber slammed Sheridan's hand against the wall once, then twice, but Sheridan's grip on the knife handle remained firm.

"Give it up," Kimber said, her breathing coming in short bursts. "The police are on their way."

Sheridan lifted her free hand to try to break loose, but Kimber grabbed her before Sheridan could manage it.

Sheridan grunted again. "I'm going to kill you."

Kimber tried to calm her breathing before she spoke. "Your intentions are obvious, but I don't intend to play victim today." Kimber brought her knee up hard, connecting with Sheridan's thigh.

Sheridan cried out in pain.

Kimber slammed Sheridan's wrist against the wall twice more, and finally, the knife fell to the floor.

Kimber moved to strike again with her knee, but Sheridan caught her off guard when she used a burst of strength to push back against Kimber.

Kimber stumbled back a step, both of her hands still gripping Sheridan's wrists. Kimber stepped on the knife but didn't dare lean down to grab it, for fear of leaving herself vulnerable. Instead, she shifted her foot and kicked the knife, sending it skittering across the floor.

The door handle rattled. Ian! If he opened the door, it would hit Kimber and take away what little advantage she had at the moment.

Despite the fatigue of the fight, Kimber shouted, "Ian! No!"

But it was too late. The door opened at regular speed and knocked into Kimber.

Off balance, Kimber lost her hold on Sheridan and released her wrists.

"What —" That was as far as Ian got before Sheridan dove for the floor and came up with the knife in her hand again.

Kimber regained her balance. "Ian, run! Call the police."

"But —"

Kimber stepped between Ian and Sheridan. "Go."

This time, Ian listened and darted into the hall.

Sheridan laughed derisively. "I thought you said the police were already on their way."

"It doesn't matter if they were or not." Kimber put a hand on the metal bar of the clothes rack beside her. "The FBI and police know who you are and what you did. It's over."

"No." Sheridan shook her head as though her denial would change the facts. "I'm not going to jail. I'll just disappear and start over somewhere else." She lifted the knife, but Kimber didn't give her time to attack again. Kimber rolled the clothing rack between them and shoved it to send it toppling.

Sheridan cried out, her arms lifting but getting tangled in the array of suit jackets, shirts, and pants.

Kimber left her to her struggle and rushed to where her purse had landed under her desk. She grabbed her pistol and whirled as Sheridan came to her feet again.

Kimber faced off against her attacker, Sheridan now donning a white dress shirt draped over her shoulder. Sheridan lifted the knife again, and Kimber brought her gun into view.

Kimber forced steel into her voice and took aim. "I may not be FBI, but I'm not afraid to pull the trigger."

Indecision played over Sheridan's face.

Kimber took a step deeper into the room, her gun remaining steady. "Move and I'll drop you in one shot."

Rapid footsteps approached, and one of the security guards appeared in the doorway, a taser in his hand. A quick glance was all it took to identify the man as Heath Quentin.

He looked from Sheridan to Kimber and back again. Now focused solely on Sheridan, he spoke with anguish in his voice. "You killed Juliet?"

Sheridan clenched her teeth, and the muscle in her jaw twitched.

"Drop the knife, Sheridan," Kimber demanded. "Now."

Heath didn't give Sheridan a chance to comply. He squeezed the trigger and sent the two leads from the taser directly into Sheridan's chest.

Sheridan gasped, and her body jolted from the sudden electric current. Then the knife dropped to the floor, and her body followed.

Chapter 43

Tessa climbed onto the back of the four-wheeler and wrapped her arms around Parker's waist.

He patted her hand before he turned the key and started the engine. "You ready?"

"Yeah," she said, not because it was true but because it was the expected response.

Parker started forward, the chill in the air increasing as he picked up speed and navigated his way down the path through the trees.

It had been less than a week since she and Parker had made this drive between the cabin and the hotel, but the last time, she had still been able to cling to the hope that the real killer would be identified. Now she was drowning in a sea of hopelessness and dread.

By this time tomorrow, she would likely be sitting in jail with real killers. Panic clawed at her throat, and fresh tears stung her eyes.

Parker drove over a protruding tree root, and the vehicle jolted. Tessa tightened her grip on Parker's waist and pressed her cheek against his back.

His strength had given her so much comfort over the past week, and she couldn't deny the joy that had come from the possibilities that hummed between them. If only her current circumstances hadn't robbed them of the future they might have created.

Even if she were eventually cleared of the charges, Tessa had worked in the entertainment industry long enough to know what an impact such a scandal could have on Parker's career if he were linked to her.

The drive took less time than she'd hoped, and far too soon, the main road came into view. This time, instead of leaving the four-wheeler hidden in the trees, Parker continued on the shoulder of the road until he reached the hotel.

He pulled into the parking lot next to his car and cut the engine. Tessa released Parker and climbed off. He followed.

"I'm going to go grab my phone from my room and check out." Parker dug his car keys from his pocket.

A truck rumbled into the parking lot, and

a dog barked nearby. The uncomfortable sensation of being out in the open rattled her. She was going to turn herself in, but she wanted to do it on her terms, not because someone saw her and called the cops.

The front doors to the hotel opened, and a couple walked out. The man motioned to their luggage and said something to the woman before leaving her behind and striding toward a cluster of parked cars. In the side lot, a family loaded an oversized van, and at the opposite corner, a man wearing some sort of security-guard uniform smoked a cigarette.

People everywhere. People who might recognize her and call the police.

As though sensing her unease, Parker put his hand on her shoulder. "If you want, go ahead and head back to the cabin. I'll meet you up there."

Tessa nodded. Even though everything inside her demanded she stay with Parker, for her own sanity and — looking around at all the people again — for her own safety, she needed to get out of sight. Plus, it made sense that she should start loading up while Parker took care of his tasks.

Tessa hit the Unlock button on the key fob. "I'll see you in a few minutes."

She reached for the door handle, but Parker beat her to it. He pulled the door open and placed his hand on her waist. As soon as she looked up at him, he lowered his lips to hers.

The kiss tasted of desperation and goodbye, but that didn't stop her pulse from picking up speed. Goose bumps rose on her skin that had nothing to do with the cold, and Tessa couldn't help but fall into the kiss.

She lifted her hands to Parker's neck, and he drew her closer.

The dog barked again, but Tessa barely noticed, her focus consumed by the man currently holding her close.

Her heart swelled, the familiar warmth rushing through her. When the kiss ended, her feelings tumbled out in her words. "I wish this time with you could last forever."

His eyes widened briefly, his gaze now fixed on hers. Parker lifted his hand to her hair, his fingers tangling in her brown locks. "Don't assume that it can't."

But it couldn't. She was about to be arrested for murder, and she would lose her freedom for who knew how long.

Parker kissed her again before he released her. "I won't be far behind you."

Tessa climbed in and adjusted the seat. Parker would be with her soon, but within hours, they could very well be saying their last goodbyes.

Brandon hung up the phone with the local police, his frustration multiplying. "The police said there's something wrong with how the address of the cabin is pinned on GPS. They haven't been able to find it."

Rafi shook his head. "Don't they know how to use a map?"

"They pulled the property records and have the correct location now, but apparently, there are two streets with almost the same name, and they're a good twenty minutes apart," Brandon said. "The GPS originally sent them to a vacant lot, but they're on their way now."

"How far out are we?" Rafi asked.

"Let me check." Brandon plugged in the new GPS coordinates. "Twelve minutes. Looks like we'll beat the locals."

"That's a good thing," Rafi said. "Let's hope Randall had the location wrong too."

Brandon's phone rang. Kimber again. He hit the Talk button. "Hey, what's up?"

Kimber's rapid breathing preceded her words. "I think Sheridan put out a hit on Tessa."

Brandon straightened. "What?"

"The payments I found — a new one just

posted, and it was right after Sheridan received a call from a burner phone."

"If we're right about Randall being involved, it could be him."

"Which means we no longer have to worry about Tessa being taken into custody." Her voice broke off.

"You think Randall will try to kill her."

"Yes, and he might even try to kill Detective Murray." Urgency filled her words. "Brandon. You and Rafi have to stop him."

"We will. I promise."

Parker swiped his key card to unlock his hotel room door. He grabbed his phone off the desk from where he'd left it the last time he'd been here and dialed his uncle's number. It rang twice as he unplugged the charger and tucked the cord into his jacket pocket.

The phone rang.

"Parker, thank the heavens." Ian's relief carried through the phone. "The police are on the way to the cabin. Please tell me you aren't there right now."

The words and the fact that Ian made no effort to disguise his message behind Parker's play showed how urgent the situation was. "I'm not. I stopped by the hotel to pick up my phone, but Tessa's on her way back there to load up. She wants to turn herself in."

"Parker, you need to warn her," Ian said urgently. "We found the person behind Juliet's and Bob's deaths, but we think one of the detectives heading your way is also involved."

Parker headed for the door. "Is it Colin Murray?"

"No. We're pretty sure it's his partner, Derrick Randall."

Parker's plans to check out of the hotel took a back seat to his need to ensure Tessa's safety. "Uncle Ian, I'll call you back."

Parker hung up and rushed out of his room. He sprinted down the stairs and out the side door he'd entered just minutes ago. He took two steps before he spotted two men wearing business suits coming out the main entrance. They both walked with purpose, and though Parker had never seen either of them in person before, the taller of the two was the same man he'd seen in the news weeks ago — Colin Murray.

Not sure if the men were looking for him or Tessa here at the hotel, Parker waited until the detectives climbed into their car and pulled out of the parking lot before he walked quickly to the four-wheeler.

He sent a quick text to Ian. *The detectives were at the hotel. They just left.*

After pocketing his phone, he climbed onto the four-wheeler and started the engine. Then he headed for the path that would take him to Tessa and prayed he would get there before any danger could find her.

Chapter 44

With the porch light on to counteract the fading light, Tessa loaded her suitcase into the trunk of Parker's car, her emotions in turmoil. She should go pack the groceries from the refrigerator so they wouldn't leave anything to spoil, but the thought of being locked up was enough to draw her outside. Surely it wouldn't hurt for her to take one last walk out onto the dock while she waited for Parker to return.

She closed the trunk and wandered toward the dock, her gaze on the last lingering streaks of sunlight on the horizon. She made it as far as the firepit before an engine sounded in the distance. Was Parker already back?

She turned toward the path leading into the woods, expecting to see the glow of headlights from the four-wheeler, but the woods remained dark and still.

The engine grew louder, joined by the

sound of wheels against the gravel driveway. Another car?

For a second, Tessa guessed Micah or someone in his family had arrived. But that didn't make any sense. Micah had just left yesterday, and he'd mentioned his parents were currently in Europe. So who else would be coming here . . .

Unless it was someone looking for her.

Her heart pounded, and she rushed to the back of the house to ensure she remained out of sight.

The vehicle continued forward until it came to a stop, likely beside Parker's car. Tessa peeked around the side of the cabin, using the bushes at the corner of the house to shield her from view.

In front of her, two men climbed out of the plain sedan, leaving their car doors open as though using them as shields. Then suddenly, both men emerged into full view, each with a pistol in hand.

Tessa gasped and lifted her hand to her mouth to cover the sound. Were these men the police? Or were they the ones who killed Juliet and the video editor? And regardless of who they were, how had they found her?

The taller of the two men lifted his free hand and flashed some sort of hand signal before pointing in her direction. Had they seen her? Or was he just trying to get the other man to check out the back door?

The police. They definitely looked like law enforcement.

She ducked back out of sight. She planned to turn herself in. Should she walk out with her hands up and surrender now?

No. The word echoed through her mind as though it had been shouted through a megaphone. She needed to turn herself in on her terms, and the way to do that was to get to the police station in New York, preferably with her sister by her side. These men might be police officers, but whoever they were, Tessa had no interest in facing any man holding a gun.

She scanned her surroundings. The dock was too exposed, and there was nowhere to hide on the deck. With one option left, she darted toward the nearby trees. The thought that they would hear her footsteps didn't occur to her until a shout sounded behind her.

"Police! Freeze!" The words were barely out of the man's mouth when a gunshot sounded.

Her heart leaped into her throat, and she darted behind a thick pine. A split second later, another shot echoed, and bark flew into the air. This man was shooting at her!

She was unarmed and running away. What kind of person tried to shoot an innocent woman in the back? Even if he thought she was guilty, she'd seen enough movies to know that wasn't how the police were trained.

Another shot fired followed by the man's voice again. "Found her. Clear the house. I'll take Seidel."

Tessa took a gasping breath. The man looked like a cop, and he sounded like a cop. So why was he shooting at her?

The need to surrender on her own terms was overshadowed by her desire to live to see tomorrow. Desperate, she shouted, "Don't shoot! I'm unarmed!"

"Then come out with your hands up," the man shouted back.

He was sounding like a cop again, but fear crippled her and left her frozen.

In the back of her mind, she heard the rumble of another approaching engine, but she was too focused on the man with the gun to comprehend the direction it was coming from or the actual cause of the sound.

"Come on out, or I'm coming in after you," the policeman called out.

Tessa drew a deep breath, pressed her hand against the tree trunk, and prayed she would never hear a gun fired in her direction ever again.

Parker drove into the clearing by the cabin and fought against the panic rushing through him. If his suspicions were right, Tessa was in danger and the man aiming his gun wasn't just a police officer. He was also a killer.

Even in the fading light, Parker could make out the man's features enough to see his beard and identify him as Derrick Randall and not Colin Murray. With his gun raised and gripped in both hands, Randall took a step to one side as though trying to get a better angle on where Tessa was currently hiding.

"Don't shoot!" Tessa's raised voice carried over the motor. "I'm coming out."

"No!" Parker shouted.

He didn't know if it was his voice or the sound of the engine that drew Randall's attention to Parker, but either way, the man turned and swung his gun in his direction.

Acting on instinct, Parker stood up on the four-wheeler, swung his leg over the seat, and dove for the ground, leaving the ATV between him and the dirty cop. Parker's shoulder jarred on impact, and pain burst down his arm.

The four-wheeler stuttered to a stop, and footsteps carried to him. It would be a matter of seconds before Parker was in Randall's sights again. He quickly scrambled to his feet and raced toward the woods.

"Parker!" Tessa cried out.

"Stay back, Tessa! That man's a killer."

Two shots fired in quick succession. Something stung Parker's upper arm, probably bark flying off the tree that he darted behind.

"Don't make this any harder than it has to be," the cop said. "Come out with your hands up."

Parker couldn't see where Tessa had taken cover in the trees, but he estimated she was still a good twenty yards from where he currently stood. "Tessa, don't do it! This man is a paid murderer. He killed Bob."

CHAPTER 45

Tessa couldn't believe it. A cop who was also a murderer? But then, he had shot at her even though she wasn't armed or threatening him in any way. Could this be true? And how did Parker know about it?

Regardless of where he'd ascertained this knowledge, Tessa was much more inclined to trust the man she'd spent the last week with than the man who had shot at her moments ago. And where was Parker now? She hadn't seen him since he'd jumped off the four-wheeler and used it to create a barrier between him and the man with the gun.

Questions burned inside her, but the answers didn't matter now. What mattered was staying alive. But how? She and Parker didn't have any weapons. And even if they did, neither of them was trained to deal with situations like this. Even as that thought formed, the memories of her martial-arts classes with Kimber surfaced. She might not be familiar with how to shoot a gun, but she wasn't completely without skills.

Stealth. That was the answer right now. She needed to use the increasing darkness to disappear into the woods. She would find Parker. Then together they could follow the path down to the hotel and call for help.

Colin had cleared the main living area when an approaching engine had drawn his attention back outside. Judging from the suitcase by the door, he and Derrick had arrived just in time. The suspect had been preparing to leave, and if Colin was right, the engine outside had been from her accomplice trying to help her escape. The engine was silent now, which meant Derrick must have somehow intervened.

One cop with two suspects. Never good odds.

Abandoning his search, Colin sprinted for the back door that led to the deck. He was determined. By the end of the night, Seidel wouldn't be the only one behind bars. Parker Sawyer would be joining her for making a false statement and obstructing justice.

Colin stepped outside in the same instant Derrick fired toward the trees.

Colin pressed himself against the back of the cabin so he wouldn't become the suspects' new target.

Derrick stood at the edge of a stone patio and squeezed the trigger again, but no return fire came.

Gun in hand, Colin continued forward, pausing when he reached the stairs leading to the ground. "Status?" he asked Derrick.

"Two suspects, both armed," Derrick said, his voice low. Derrick dropped behind the stone barbecue as though remembering belatedly that someone might shoot back at him.

"Both of them?" Colin hadn't expected that. Nothing in the cabin showed signs of any weapons, not even a hunting rifle. And the background on Parker Sawyer hadn't given any indication that he had any experience with guns, much less that he would become violent.

"The man tried to run me over with his four-wheeler, but he took off into the trees before I could catch him."

Colin checked the position of the vehicle. It was a good ten yards away from where Derrick currently stood by the firepit, his pistol aimed at the trees.

Something wasn't adding up. If someone had tried to run him over, wouldn't the four-wheeler be closer to where Derrick had taken cover? And why had he been standing out in the open if both suspects were armed?

A man shouted from the woods. "We're unarmed."

"Then come out with your hands up," Derrick shouted back.

"No way. You're trying to kill us."

Derrick responded with a calm but firm voice. "We're the police."

"Yeah, but Derrick Randall killed Bob Kelley," the man said in an equally firm voice. "He planted evidence at the crime scene, and now he's trying to kill Tessa so he can frame her."

"You're crazy!" Derrick yelled out.

"Not as crazy as the cop who hires himself out as a contract killer," the man shouted back.

The events of the day flashed into Colin's mind. Tessa Seidel's police report that proved she had indeed visited the police station the night of the murder, even though Derrick had said surveillance showed the opposite. The way Derrick had answered his phone but hadn't put the captain's call on speaker. The position of the four-wheeler. Derrick's lack of cover when Colin had first rushed outside. And then there was Seidel's hair tie, the single piece of evidence that connected her to the crime scene, a piece of evidence Derrick had produced.

Colin's mind whirled with possibilities. Twice he had shouldered the blame when an innocent man had gone to prison. Could it be that Derrick had been involved?

Colin focused on his partner, the man who'd had his back for so many years. "Derrick?"

"He's trying to throw the blame on someone else." Derrick kept his eyes on the woods and squeezed off another shot. "These two will do anything to avoid an arrest."

It was almost fully dark now, the lights from the house spilling through the windows and into the yard. If the suspects wanted to disappear, they likely could, yet the man, presumably Parker Sawyer, was still there.

Though he didn't want to face it, Colin considered that Derrick might very well be the most dangerous person here right now. He pressed his hand against his bulletproof vest to remind himself that his vital organs were protected. Then he scanned the woods for movement before he faced his partner.

"How did he know your name?" Colin asked.

"His uncle must have fed it to him." Derrick didn't even look at Colin. "You know how these movie-star types are. They're connected."

Ian Sawyer had met Derrick, but Colin had been the lead detective throughout. If Ian was going to feed his nephew a name, Ian would have shared Colin's, especially since the wrongful-conviction suit had been in the news so recently.

Suspicion flooded through Colin in a flash, from the Kelley case all the way back to the first wrongful-conviction lawsuit. Derrick had worked with him on both of the cases that had been overturned. His partner had helped him arrest both of the innocent men who had ended up behind bars and lost years of their freedom.

His partner or the suspects? Who should he trust?

"The FBI is on the way," Parker said with surety. "It's over."

Though Colin could hardly wrap his mind around the possibility of Derrick being a killer, Colin couldn't help but admit that the facts lined up with what the man in the woods was saying. Colin checked the woods again before he took a leap of faith and stepped into open view of the suspects. No response. And no gunfire.

Colin's chest tightened as he did the unthinkable. He turned his weapon toward Derrick. "Derrick, drop your weapon."

Derrick turned toward him and lowered his weapon slightly. “Whoa, Colin. What are you doing?”

“I’m playing it safe.” Colin jutted his chin toward the woods. “If you aren’t involved, then I’ll apologize later.”

“Are you crazy? We’ve been looking for Tessa Seidel for a week, and now we’ve found her. Why are you believing her boyfriend out there?” Derrick turned and took a step sideways so he was now standing between Colin and the spot where Derrick had been aiming his gun a moment ago. “We’ve been partners for years. You know me.”

“I do know you, and a few things haven’t been adding up lately. Seidel turned in a police report the night of the murder, but you said you couldn’t find any sign of her on the surveillance feed. You found the hair tie that connected Seidel to the Kelley murder, and then you didn’t put the captain on speaker earlier.”

“What? That’s what has you freaked out?” Derrick took another step back. “I wasn’t thinking. I just answered.” He tilted his head toward the woods. “They’re just trying to play mind games on us.”

“They are?” Colin asked. “Or you are? You’re the one standing with your back to the suspects who you said were armed."

A flash of awareness and guilt sparked in Derrick's eyes.

The shock of seeing the evidence that Derrick had indeed been involved in something dirty paralyzed Colin for a fraction of a second. Then his training kicked in. He took aim, but Derrick was already in motion.

Derrick dove for the far side of the building, firing twice at Colin as he went.

Colin ducked to the left, but his efforts weren't enough. The first bullet tore through his thigh, and the second hit him square in the chest.

Despite the bulletproof vest, pain radiated from his ribs, overshadowing the stinging sensation in his leg. Fearing Derrick would get off another shot, Colin fought to stay upright and fired at the ground to keep Derrick pinned behind the built-in grill. Then he hobbled to the edge of the cabin and took cover from the man who had once been the person he trusted most with his life.

Chapter 46

Parker peeked around the closest tree in the same moment the injured detective lowered to the ground. He was definitely wounded, and now it was a question of whether Randall would try to finish off his partner or come after him and Tessa. The man ducking behind the grill looked like he was going to eliminate the only other person who truly had a gun, but when Murray fired toward the grill, Randall dropped back down and appeared to reconsider.

Randall scanned the woods again, likely trying to figure out where Parker and Tessa were hiding. If Parker knew where Tessa was hiding, they could both get out of here, but he couldn't leave without her. He hadn't seen her since his arrival, nor had he heard her for the past several minutes. He prayed she wasn't injured or worse.

"Give it up, Derrick," Murray said to Randall. "The FBI are on their way."

"You don't know that," Randall countered.

Parker used the darkness and the thick copse of trees to move in what he thought was Tessa's direction. He made it a few yards before he sensed movement by the cabin again. He turned toward it as Randall shot out of his hiding place by the grill and jumped behind the four-wheeler, his head low. Almost instantly, the motor started, and Randall used one hand to steer the vehicle, keeping it between him and his partner. Unfortunately, he was also heading right for an opening in the trees that lay right between him and where he'd last seen Tessa.

Tessa froze as the four-wheeler approached the spot right next to where she currently stood. If she were lucky, the detective would use this opportunity to try to get away. When the man cut the engine and pocketed the key to the four-wheeler, she had to face the truth that luck was not on her side today.

She had made it to the small clearing but had yet to risk running through it in an effort to get to Parker and the path that led to the hotel. Now she wished she would have tried. Maybe then they would be able to get past the detective with the gun and leave the police officers to themselves. Even as she had that thought, a sliver of guilt cut through her. One of them was injured, and if Parker's information was correct, it was the good cop currently bleeding on the ground.

In the darkness, Tessa didn't miss the way the man named Derrick gripped his pistol with both hands, the barrel pointed slightly downward but ready to fire at any moment. He reminded her of a hunter, and she was the hunted.

She fought for calm, controlling her breathing in an effort to remain silent.

The sound of an approaching engine carried to her. Maybe if it passed by, she could sneak away without being heard.

Derrick strode deliberately along the edge of the clearing, but he stopped twice, looking and listening. Then he turned and stared right at her.

He lifted his gun, and Tessa yelped in surprise. She jumped back and circled the nearest tree, anxious to put a barrier between them. But the tree trunk wasn't wide enough to protect her, so she ran.

Zigzagging through the trees, she raced forward. A gunshot fired, spitting more bark into the air. A cry escaped her, but she didn't slow down despite the darkness.

Maybe she should have. She made it ten or fifteen yards before she tripped on a tree branch the thickness of a baseball bat but almost twice as long. She fell to the ground and turned as the killer came into view. Just a few steps and he would pass the last few saplings between them and have a clear shot.

Desperate, she pressed her hands and feet against the ground and pushed herself backward. One hand landed on the branch, and she gripped it. Shifting onto her knees, she wielded the makeshift weapon.

Now nearly on top of her, the detective took aim.

"No!" Parker's shout echoed, his voice loud enough to indicate he was dangerously close.

Tessa swung the branch with all her strength, the end of it impacting the detective's right knee.

The thwack of wood against bone echoed in the same instant the detective fired. The bullet drilled into the dirt a mere inch from Tessa's arm.

Brandon heard the shot as he climbed out of Rafi's car, and he took off running toward the sound. Only his training prevented him from shouting Tessa's name.

He couldn't be too late. Kimber would never forgive him if he let her sister die.

Rafi raced after him, and they made it as far as the front porch before he saw a man lying on the ground on the far side of the porch, near the corner of the cabin, his phone in his hand. They reached his side, quickly identifying the injured man as Detective Murray.

"Status?" Brandon asked.

"It's my partner." Murray gasped before he continued. "He's in the woods. I think there are two others out there, too, and Derrick is trying to kill them."

Brandon gritted his teeth. "He's trying, but he won't succeed."

"I've already called for backup, but you need to go now." Murray lifted his chin toward the woods. "You have to stop him."

Rafi lifted his hand and signaled that he would go right. Brandon nodded and started left. Time to find the shooter and get Tessa and Parker to safety.

Parker sprinted forward as Tessa hit Randall again, but this time Randall dropped one hand from his gun and grabbed the end of the branch before it could make contact. He jerked the branch toward him and ripped it out of Tessa's hands.

Tessa stumbled and fell forward. Her breath whooshed out, and she gasped for air.

Another three steps and Parker would reach them, but then what? He and Tessa might have the detective outnumbered, but the detective still had his gun.

Randall lifted his pistol again, but this time, there was nothing to prevent him from hitting his target. And his target was Tessa.

Coming at the detective from the side, Parker dove forward and wrapped his arms around Randall's shoulders. The gun went off as the force of Parker's body against the would-be killer's knocked them both off-balance.

Parker stumbled forward, barely able to remain on his feet.

Randall fell to one knee, and his weapon dropped to the ground.

Parker bent down in the hope of grabbing it, but the detective was too fast. He grabbed the grip of the gun and swung the pistol toward Parker.

"Watch out!" Tessa yelled.

But there was nothing Parker could do but stare down the barrel of the gun that was about to end his life.

The sound of a weapon firing blasted through the air, but the expected pain from the bullet didn't happen.

Instead, Randall's body jerked, and an instant later, two men rushed toward them.

Within seconds, one of them secured the detective's arms behind his back and slapped handcuffs on his wrists.

Before Parker could process what had happened, Tessa was at his side, and her arms were around him.

"Are you both okay?" a man asked. It took a moment for Parker to recognize that the man was speaking to him and Tessa.

Parker looked down at his chest. No blood. No pain. "I think so." He pulled Tessa tight and asked, "Tessa, are you hurt?"

She shook her head, her embrace not loosening in the slightest. "Brandon, what are you doing here?"

"Looking for you." The man — Brandon — glanced over his shoulder before focusing on Tessa again. His awareness and the gun in his hand suggested he was law enforcement.

Trusting that his familiarity with Tessa meant he was on their side, Parker nodded toward the cabin. "There's a man who was shot over by the cabin."

"We know." Brandon put his hand on Parker's shoulder. "Come on. Let's get you both inside until our backup gets here."

Tessa pulled away from Parker and turned to Brandon. "Are they still going to arrest me?"

"No." Brandon shook his head. "We know who the killers are now, and we can prove it."

Chapter 47

Kimber stepped off the elevator and headed to her apartment. With the chaos Sheridan's arrest had created for Ian's show, she had stayed on to work for Ian for an extra two weeks, but today, she had officially resigned from her personal-assistant position. For the last task of her temporary job, she had delivered the last of Phoebe's pumpkin bars to Ian and Phoebe's apartment. The woman had made a new tray each week, and every week, Kimber had guarded the baked goods as though they were precious jewels.

She smiled at the way Ian had tried to intercept the delivery before his wife could confiscate it. Although with the way Parker had been eyeing the pumpkin bars, Kimber suspected Ian knew that he'd be competing with his nephew for the goodies in the condo until Parker moved into his own place.

Parker had been staying in Ian and

Phoebe's guest room in their New York apartment since returning to the city with Tessa. Kimber had never expected to find a positive to her sister's getting mixed up in a murder investigation, but after spending a few meals with the new couple, Kimber had to admit, she'd never seen Tessa happier or more in love.

Kimber understood the sensation well. She remembered those early days with Brandon when every minute together was a gift despite the challenges they were facing at the time. And her love for him had deepened with every passing day, but never so much as when she had learned of the way Brandon had helped save her sister. He had treated Tessa like she was his own family, and she couldn't imagine anything more endearing than that.

Brandon's door opened down the hall, and he walked out toward her. "I was hoping that was you."

"Are you hacking into the building's security cameras again to see when I get home?"

He grinned and took her hand. "Maybe."

She leaned close and whispered, "I'm not sure that the agency taught you that skill so you could spy on your girlfriend."

"Maybe not, but there also aren't rules

against it." He shrugged. "Keeping you safe is kind of my job."

He had a point. Technically, they were partners, even though their undercover roles often took them in different directions.

"By the way, I stopped by the hospital today," Kimber said. "Detective Murray should be released tomorrow."

"That's good news." Brandon gestured inside. "Can you come in for a minute?"

"Sure." Kimber stepped into the dimly lit room and immediately smelled the roses. Her eyes widened when she spotted the bouquet on Brandon's kitchen counter, with two taper candles flickering in the muted light. "What's all this?"

"This is my way of telling you that I can't wait any longer."

"You can't wait any longer for what?"

She turned to face him as he produced a small jewelry box from his pocket and lowered to one knee. "I can't wait to make a life with you, to share a home and start a family."

The shock of his gesture rendered her speechless, and Kimber lifted both hands to her lips.

"Kimber Seidel, will you marry me?"

A few weeks ago, she'd believed this would be too soon, but her heart answered for her, and the word *yes* tumbled from her lips.

Brandon's face lit up, and then suddenly, the beautiful diamond was on her finger, and she was in her fiancé's arms.

Tessa dropped her purse on her kitchen table and texted Parker to let him know she was home. For the past two weeks, they had fallen into a comfortable routine. As soon as Tessa finished work for the day, Parker met her at her apartment, and they spent their evenings together. As often as not, they ventured out to be with friends or attend the latest party or play, but she had to admit that the nights they stayed in were among her favorites. And best of all, they could finally be together without worrying that the police would show up and arrest her.

The whole murder scene and her small part in it still seemed like more of a nightmare than reality, but over the past several days, the truth had come out. An independent audit had confirmed that Sheridan had indeed been embezzling funds from the show. Based on her testimony, it appeared she had hired Derrick Randall first to help cover up the murder of Juliet Clark and then had proceeded to use her video-editing skills to erase his presence from the security feed and frame Tessa. She'd then hired Derrick as a contract killer to take care of Bob before he could prove she was behind it.

Only ten minutes had passed before a knock sounded at Tessa's door. "That was fast." She peeked through the peephole to confirm that it was Parker standing in the hall.

She opened the door and greeted him with a kiss. "How did you get here so fast?"

"I was around the corner, looking at an apartment."

"And?"

He stepped around her and closed the door behind him. "I already put in an application. It's less than two blocks away."

"That's great." Her boyfriend was not only making New York his home, but he would also be so close that they would be able to see each other even when one of their schedules got crazy.

"It is great, and I have more good news." Parker took her hand and led her to the sofa. He waited until they were both seated before he continued. "I finished the play."

"Parker, that's fantastic." Tessa threw her arms around him. "Congratulations."

"Thanks." He held on to her for a moment before easing back so he could see her face. "I can't believe how fast it fell together once we were able to talk to Ian, Kimber, and Brandon directly."

"I bet, although communicating through your play really was a brilliant idea." Tessa laced her fingers through his. "I can't imagine how all this would have turned out had you not helped me."

"I can't imagine my life now without you in it." Parker leaned forward for a lingering kiss that brought goose bumps to Tessa's skin. When he pulled back, he lifted his hand to her cheek. "And I know your work gets crazy during awards season, but I need you to talk to Greta about taking a week off this September."

"Why?"

"Because my first play will be opening on the West End in London as part of its second run, and I want you to come with me for opening night."

"I would love to, but I'll be even more excited to see your new one on stage." She thought about it for a moment. "Although it might be a bit weird to see all our drama acted out on Broadway."

"You're assuming it will make it onto Broadway."

"Of course it'll make it." She kissed him again. "You're brilliant and talented."

"I don't know about that, but I would love to see it make it big." He ran his finger along her jaw. "After all, it's dedicated to you."

"It is?"

Parker nodded. "I want everyone to know how important you are to me." He stared down at her with an intensity that she hadn't seen before. "You know, I could totally see myself falling in love with you."

Warmth spread through her, and her future unfolded before her. "You already are in love with me, but you aren't ready to say it." She smiled. "But don't worry, I can wait to tell you I love you, too, for another week or two. After that, all bets are off."

"Good to know." Parker laughed. "But just so you know, my uncle is taking credit for introducing us."

"One thing is for sure," Tessa said. "No one will ever be able to top the story of how we first met."

Parker leaned close and pressed his lips to hers. "Of that, there is no doubt."

ACKNOWLEDGMENTS

As with so many of my books, I want to thank my fabulous editor, Samantha Millburn, for shepherding this novel from the idea stage to the final product. You are amazing! I also want to thank Lara Abramson for your help in all the stages of the editing process.

Thank you as well to my critique partners, who have helped guide this story through the early stages: Ashley Gebert, Connor Olsen, Daniel Quilter, Eliza Sanders, Janette Rallison, Jennifer Griffith, and Tiana Smith.

My appreciation also goes to Amy Parker and her marketing team — Troy Butcher, Haley Haskins, Tasha Bradford, and Lehi Quiroz — and Brianna Cornell in sales. Thanks also to Chris Schoebinger and the rest of the team at Shadow Mountain, who do so much to support my books and open the doors for success.

As always, thank you to my family for

sharing me with my crazy career and travel schedule, especially my husband, Jon. Thank you to the CIA's Publication Classification Review Board for the work you do and for your continued diligence.

Finally, thank you again to the wonderful readers who have shared my fictional worlds with me. I treasure you more than you know.

ABOUT THE AUTHOR

Traci Hunter Abramson, a former Central Intelligence Agency officer, was born in Arizona, where she lived until moving to Venezuela for a study-abroad program. After graduating from Brigham Young University, she worked for the CIA for six years until she resigned to raise her family.

Traci is a popular writing instructor and keynote speaker. She has written more than forty-five best-selling novels, several of which have won awards. Traci was also honored with an Outstanding Achievement Award for her contribution to the writing community in 2025. She loves hearing from her readers.

You can contact her through the following channels:

Website: www.traciabramson.com
Facebook page:
facebook.com/tracihabramson

Facebook group: Traci's Friends
Bookbub:
bookbub.com/authors/traci-hunter-abramson
X: @traciabramson

The employees of Thorndike Press hope you have enjoyed this Large Print book. All our Thorndike Large Print titles are designed for easy reading, and all our books are made to last. Other Thorndike Press Large Print books are available at your library, through selected bookstores, or directly from us.

For information about titles, please call:
(800) 223-1244

or visit our website at:
gale.com/thorndike